EVERYTHING TO LOSE

A NOVEL

SHANNON WORK

This is a work of fiction. Names, characters, businesses, organizations, places, events and incidents are either products of the author's imagination or are used fictitiously. Any resemblance to actual persons, living or dead, or actual events is entirely coincidental.

ISBN: 978-1-7354353-3-6 (paperback)
ISBN: 978-1-7354353-5-0 (large print paperback)
ISBN: 978-1-7354353-4-3 (eBook)

www.shannonwork.com

"Cast off the works of darkness..."
—*Romans 13:12 KJV*

CHAPTER 1

Friday, June 15

THERE WAS A man in the forest.

Victoria Banks stood at the window of her bedroom, staring out into the darkness, a sheen of perspiration on her face. She took in and released several deep breaths, willing her heart to slow. But he was still out there, somewhere in the shadows, waiting for her to fall back asleep so he could chase her again.

It was the dream, the one that had plagued her since the night the men took her mother away twenty-four years ago. She knew the dream well.

But tonight the dream had been different. The man had just been starting to chase her when she heard a chime somewhere in the darkness and the forest had grown quiet around her. She stirred awake, struggling to catch her breath and wondering why the dream that had been the same hundreds of times before was different tonight. She had never heard the chime before, and it haunted her.

Victoria turned from the window, her bare feet sinking into the plush rug laid over the wood floor as she walked across the room. Elliot's side of the bed was still made, and she was disappointed he wasn't there. She had left him in the study hours earlier, still bent over his work.

They had been married for five years, and although she never told him about the dream, she had grown accustomed to waking from it and finding him lying beside her. It was a small comfort.

Victoria checked the time on her phone and saw that it was nearly midnight, then laid the phone back down on the bedside table.

In the bathroom, she fumbled in the dark for the faucet and splashed her face with cold water, trying to wash away the last vestiges of the dream. She toweled the water off as she stared into the mirror at her reflection. Shadowed by lamplight from the bedroom, Victoria thought she resembled a monster.

She stared a while longer, then carefully folded the hand towel, returning it to its spot next to the sink and turning away.

In the bedroom, she sat down on the bed and slid her legs back under the covers. As she leaned over to turn off the lamp, her cell phone rang, startling her. Who would call at this hour?

She glanced at the caller ID.

"Miles, what is it?" She didn't bother to mask the worry in her voice. "Is everything okay?"

Miles Preston was Elliot's oldest friend and a

regular guest at their house in Vail. But rarely did Miles telephone Victoria directly, and never at this time of night.

"I'm sure everything's fine," Miles reassured her. "It's just that I've been trying to reach Elliot for several hours, but he's not answering his phone. He's such a night owl, and I've never had trouble getting him to answer before. I know I'm being silly—"

"You're not being silly." Victoria smiled. She knew Elliot was still up, working, but she found Miles's concern endearing. She was often envious of their friendship, wishing she had an old schoolmate to share childhood memories with. Elliot, like Miles, was an only child; it was one reason she thought they had bonded years ago.

"I have news on the media's response to the merger," Miles said. "Elliot wanted me to call him as soon as I got it—no matter what time—and when I couldn't get ahold of him, well…"

"You know Elliot better than anyone," Victoria replied. "He's probably at his desk up to his elbows in production reports and seismic forecasts and let his phone battery die again. I'll find him and get him to call you back."

"You're the best, Victoria. Thank you. I hated to bother you at this time of night."

"It's really no problem. I'll have him call you in a second."

Victoria stuck her feet into shearling slippers, pulled on her cashmere robe, and set off for the study.

The house was enormous, and she knew it would take a minute for her to get there. She hadn't wanted such a large house, but Elliot had insisted. *Only the very best for my beautiful bride,* he'd said at the time. But Victoria knew he also secretly wanted a home to display his museum-worthy collection of Native American art and artifacts. The collection had been stored in several climate-controlled storage units for years.

Eventually relenting on the size of the house, Victoria had worked closely with the architects out of Denver and had overseen the construction of one of the largest houses in Vail. A beautiful mountain contemporary estate that had been featured in *Architectural Digest* in the year it was built, it was fourteen thousand square feet of concrete, steel, and glass that held its own in the majesty of its Rocky Mountain setting. Victoria thought it was ridiculously large for just the two of them, but she secretly loved every square inch of it.

But its size could also be an inconvenience. The master bedroom was at one end of the house, and Elliot's study at the other. In between was a long

curving corridor, the walls sheathed in waxed concrete and rising to a vaulted ceiling capped with steel
beams.

On either side of the hallway, large rooms opened
up to offer unobstructed views. To the south was
Vail Mountain and the surrounding Rockies, and to
the north were other mansions set on large tree-covered lots, though none of the houses were quite as
imposing as the Banks residence.

Victoria stopped in the kitchen and filled a crystal glass with water. Back in the corridor, she walked
through the large entry foyer and continued toward
Elliot's study. At the end of the hall, she noticed the
large double doors to the study were closed. This
was unusual. Elliot rarely closed the doors unless he
was taking a business call he knew would get heated,
attempting to shield Victoria from any unpleasant-
ness. She loved him for it and never told him she
could hear his conversations anyway, his raised voice
echoing in the large room and down the concrete
hallway to the other parts of the house.

Holding the glass of water in one hand, Victoria
slipped her cell phone into a pocket of her robe to
open one of the large teak doors.

"Elliot?"

When the door swung open, she froze at the
threshold, her breath caught in her throat.

Shock waves of nausea and disbelief surged through her.

The water glass slipped from her grasp and shattered into hundreds of pieces on the limestone floor at her feet.

CHAPTER 2

As THE POLICE had instructed, Victoria sat on the leather couch in the family room off the kitchen, out of their way. She was once again staring out a window toward Vail Mountain and felt numb as she watched the lights twinkle in the distance. She had no idea how much time had passed.

Elliot was gone. It didn't seem possible.

After she'd found him covered in blood, lying facedown on the floor of the study, she had collapsed, put her arms around him, and cried out his name. She'd begged him to get up, but there was too much blood. She knew he was dead.

She fumbled for the cell phone in the pocket of her robe, still pleading with him to get up, and with quaking fingers, had dialed 911.

When the police arrived several minutes later, they found her at his side, smoothing the back of his wrinkled, blood-soaked shirt.

A female officer helped her up and escorted her into the family room, Victoria walking slowly and unsteadily. She thought she might collapse again at any moment from the overwhelming weight of it all.

"What happened?" she asked the officer, her voice quivering. "Who would do this to him?"

The woman offered condolences, then told Victoria they didn't know anything yet but assured her they would find out.

It was then Victoria noticed the blood on the front of her robe and on her hands. She felt tears well up in her eyes as she held her shaking hands up to the officer. "I need to clean up."

"I'm sorry, ma'am. You have to remain here until forensics finishes their preliminary investigation or Detective Conner tells us otherwise." Her tone was remorseful yet stern.

So Victoria sat alone and in shock. At some point a detective sat down and asked her a few questions. He was terse and got right to the point. Had anyone been to the house to see Elliot that night? Did Elliot have any enemies? How had she gotten blood on her robe and her hands? He asked something about the tomahawk that hung on the wall of the study. Victoria struggled to answer what she could but was sure she had been no help.

She remembered Miles and pulled the phone from her robe. With shaking fingers, she dialed his number and told him that Elliot was dead. He volleyed her with questions, but like with the police, she didn't have any answers. Miles told her he would leave Denver immediately and would be there in less than two hours.

Elliot and Miles had grown up together—playing against each other in Little League sports, then on the same teams in high school. The two had gone their separate ways after graduation but had never lost contact. After college, Elliot started Banks Oil & Gas. Miles went to law school, eventually joining one of the largest law firms in Denver.

Banks Oil & Gas had its own legal department, but Elliot hired Miles whenever he needed personal legal work or advice outside of the business. Even in her current state of confusion, Victoria realized she would need Miles's help now.

She had no idea how long she sat there, staring through the glass into a dark world threatening to swallow her again. She wanted to escape but knew there was nowhere to go.

She barely noticed the people that came in and out of the house. Someone was taking pictures—she could see the reflection of the distant strobe light on the concrete walls of the corridor. She heard people talking but was unable to focus on what they said. It was all a blur, like she was stuck in another nightmare. Occasionally she would turn and catch one of the officers watching her.

She wasn't sure what time it was when Miles finally

got there. She could hear him in the foyer talking, then arguing with someone near the front door. In a few seconds he was at her side.

He took her hands in his, and she looked at him, her eyes swimming.

"Oh, Victoria, I'm so sorry."

Victoria dropped her head into his chest and sobbed. He sat holding her, not saying a word until she was ready.

"Who would do this?" Victoria asked finally, pulling away and looking up at him. "Why Elliot?"

"I don't know." He shook his head. "I don't know."

It was then she noticed he had tears of his own, and she was overcome with the realization that not only had she lost her husband, but Miles had lost his best friend.

They sat in silence for a while. Then Victoria looked down and saw the dried blood on her hands and her robe.

"I need to clean up, but they wouldn't let me." Her voice still quivered.

"Stay here a minute."

She watched as Miles spoke to the detective who had questioned her earlier. They were in the corridor just outside the kitchen, too far away for her to hear what he was saying. When Miles was finished talking, the detective said something and nodded. Miles then made a phone call, speaking with someone for a few minutes before he walked back to her.

"Detective Conner said you've answered enough questions for tonight but requested that you be at the station Sunday morning."

More questions. Victoria nodded wearily.

"He said you can change clothes now. Someone will accompany you to the bedroom. They need the clothes you're wearing as evidence." He must have seen the look of horror on her face. He sat down next to her and laid a hand gently on her arm. "Victoria, pack an overnight bag with clothes and whatever you'll need for a few days. The detective said they'll be processing the scene tomorrow and he'd let us know when we can come back. I just booked you a room at the Four Seasons."

At first Victoria was confused. Then she realized her home was a crime scene, just like the clothes she was wearing were evidence. Of course they wouldn't let her stay.

She started to nod but stopped, fighting the urge to cry again. "Can we stay until they take Elliot away? I don't want to leave him."

"Of course we can. But you have to listen to me, and there's no way to put this delicately. The police are going to find out who did this to Elliot, but in situations like this, the spouse is always their first suspect."

"They think *I* did this?"

Miles shook his head. "No," he reassured her. "It's a formality. The spouse is always a suspect until they rule you out—and they *will* rule you out. But you'll be at the top of their list until then."

She stared at him, frustrated. "But I didn't kill him."

"I know you didn't." He shook her arm gently. "But we need to take this seriously. The more we can do to help the police, the faster they'll realize you had nothing to do with it, and then they'll look for the person who did."

Victoria thought about it a moment. "You're right. I guess I'm not thinking clearly yet."

"Of course you're not. And nobody is going to fault you for that."

"Will you go with me Sunday? To the police station?"

"I'm already planning on it. I booked a room at the Four Seasons for me as well. I'll stay in Vail as long as you need me."

Victoria thanked him weakly, then stared at him, still trying to process everything that had happened. "I need to call Charles and Katie. They need to know."

"I'll call them while you're getting dressed and packing."

Victoria thought she should be the one to call them. Charles Stratton was the chief financial officer of Banks Oil & Gas, and his wife, Katie, was her best friend. But they would have questions for her, and Victoria knew she wasn't ready to answer them. "Thank you, Miles."

When Victoria stood up, the female officer was immediately at her side, standing erect, ready to escort her to the bedroom.

Miles glanced first at the officer, then quickly back at Victoria. There was a strained look on his face, the muscles in his neck tensed.

It was then Victoria knew.

Miles had assured her that being questioned by the police was only a formality, but she saw the truth in his eyes.

Elliot was dead, and the police thought she had killed him.

CHAPTER 3

CHARLES STRATTON RARELY went to bed before midnight. Nights were his sanctuary. He could finally delve into the intricacies of running a publicly traded oil and gas company without interruptions from phone calls, meetings, and emails. Charles was second in charge at Banks Oil & Gas, and during the day, the demand for his time was relentless.

He finally crawled into bed beside his wife, Katie, somewhere around one thirty and had just fallen asleep when he woke to his cell phone buzzing. He rolled onto his side and fumbled for it on the nightstand.

"Who on earth is calling you at this time of night?" Katie grumbled, turning her back to him and pulling a pillow over her head.

Charles cleared his throat and answered. He was silent a moment. "How did it happen?" he asked, propping himself on an elbow. He listened longer. "The police don't have any more information? No idea who did it?" He sat up, reached over, and turned on the bedside lamp. "Where's Victoria now?"

Katie pulled the pillow from her head and rolled over, listening. She had obviously caught bits and pieces of the conversation and sensed something was amiss. When Charles mentioned Victoria, one of her closest friends, Katie was suddenly wide-awake.

Charles looked at her and shook his head. He dragged his free hand down his face and massaged the bridge of his nose, screwing his eyes closed. "Okay. Thank you for calling, Miles. I'll alert the board first thing in the morning."

When he hung up, Katie was frowning at him. "What's wrong?"

"Elliot is dead."

Katie took in a sharp breath. "*Dead?* What happened?"

Charles could see in the lamplight that his wife's face had gone pale. There was no way to put it delicately. "He was murdered tonight at the house in Vail."

"*Murdered?*" She brought her hand to her throat and stared at him in disbelief.

"That was Miles Preston. He's at the house now—with Victoria. The police are there—"

"Do they know what happened? Who did it?"

Charles shook his head. "Miles didn't say."

"How did it happen?"

Charles looked at his wife and again decided there was no point in softening the blow. He would tell her the truth; she was going to find out anyway. "He was hit in the head."

"Oh my God, Charles. With what?"

"I don't know."

"But Victoria? She's okay?"

"She's fine," Charles reassured her. "Miles is checking her into the Four Seasons."

Katie threw off the covers and got out of bed. "I need to go to her."

"There's nothing you can do for her tonight."

"But she'll need somebody."

"Miles is with her."

"Miles is Elliot's friend," she said. "Not Victoria's."

Charles tried not to let his irritation show, but the last thing he needed was his wife getting caught up in any negative publicity, and it was only a matter of time before news of Elliot's murder reached the tabloids. He spoke in a calm voice. "There's nothing you can do tonight, Katie. Leave it alone. Miles said the police were questioning her on Sunday, and he'll be with her until then. You need to stay away from Victoria right now."

"Why?" She frowned at him again.

"She'll be a suspect." Charles saw her eyes widen at the possibility. "I have a lot to straighten out with the board now that the CEO position is vacant. This isn't going to be good for the merger."

"The merger?" Katie's voice dripped with

contempt. "How can you think about a thing like that right now? Elliot was just killed."

Charles tossed the covers aside and got out of bed. He was a formidable-looking man and used his intimidating presence to his benefit when he thought it would help get him what he wanted. And right now he wanted his wife to steer clear of Victoria Banks. He was on the verge of getting everything he'd ever dreamed of, and despite how tragic Elliot's murder was, he wasn't going to let it set him back.

He glared across the bed at her. "I've worked too hard to get this far, Katie. You're not going to screw it up now over sentimentality. You can see Victoria later, when the police clear her as a suspect."

Katie stared back across the bed. "Charles, you can't really think she could have done it."

"It's too early to think *anything* yet." He didn't believe Victoria was capable of murder, but he wanted to keep Katie away from what was going to be a public relations nightmare.

She stuck her hands on her hips. "You've got to be kidding me. I can't believe you think there's even the slightest chance Victoria could have murdered Elliot."

Katie was being defensive of her friend. Charles should have expected it. He remembered how excited Katie had been when Elliot proposed to Victoria years earlier. He never understood it, Katie being as loquacious and outgoing as Victoria was distant and withdrawn, but the two had become fast friends.

But he also knew how much Katie loved her designer clothes, her jewelry, and her shiny new Cadillac Escalade, parked in their spacious three-car garage. It might take some work, but Charles would get through to her.

He took in a deep breath, walked over to her, and laid his hands on her shoulders. "I don't think Victoria did it, okay?"

Katie studied him for a few seconds, then gave him a tentative nod.

Charles continued. "It's just that I've worked too hard—*we've* worked too hard—for all this." He swept an arm around the spacious bedroom. "It's just for a few days, Katie. Call her if you want, but don't go see her, not yet. We have to be careful about any negative publicity before we get the merger closed. Elliot's death is going to cause enough problems. The last thing we need is a photograph of you with a possible murder suspect."

"Charles—"

She was going to protest, but he pulled her in close and ran a hand over her hair, then tilted her chin up.

"I know this is hard on you. But let's think about the long term." When she didn't reply, he added, "There will be a little something special in it for you at the end."

She pushed him back, feigning a pout. "Something sparkly?"

"If you want it to be." Charles pulled her in close again. He would buy Katie whatever she wanted if it would help him execute the plans he had put into motion months earlier.

CHAPTER 4

THE CORPORATE HEADQUARTERS of Banks Oil & Gas was located on the top three floors of the Heritage Plaza building in downtown Denver. Chief Council Derek Lowe was always the last one to leave at night, but with the upcoming merger with Centennial State Energy, he had been working even later than usual.

It was one forty-five in the morning, and the parking garage was empty except for Derek's sleek convertible Porsche. But not just any Porsche, Derek noted with satisfaction—a new 911 Carrera Cabriolet, $140,000 of aluminum and steel that went zero-to-sixty in under 3.5 seconds. It was his baby. Derek was counting on his profits from the merger to pay for his latest turbo-engine toy.

The parking garage was dark, lit only by two rows of LED lights, which cast everything in eerie orange tones. As Derek made his way from the elevator to his car, each footstep echoed on the bare concrete, making him painfully aware of his isolation. He swiveled his head side to side, alert for danger, paying particular attention to the deep shadows, making sure he was alone.

At his car, Derek shifted his briefcase to his left hand and fumbled for the keys in his pocket, dropping them on the ground as he pulled them out. He glanced around before he bent to pick them up. Then, just as he pushed the button on the key fob to unlock the door, his cell phone rang.

Derek slid into the driver's seat of the Porsche, closed the door, and locked it. He answered the call as he pushed the ignition to start the car.

"Derek, it's Charles," said the voice on the other end of the line. "Elliot's dead."

"What? Hold on, Charles. It's switching to Bluetooth."

The car's engine revved. Ready to get out of the dark garage, Derek reversed out of the parking spot and sped down the ramp.

"Now, what did you say?" he asked Charles.

"Elliot's dead."

Derek stomped on the brakes, skidding to a stop and taking in a deep breath. He ran a hand through his oiled black hair. "What?" Surely he hadn't heard Charles right.

"Derek, Elliot's dead."

"What the hell happened?"

"Apparently, he was murdered."

It took a few moments for Derek to process the information. "When? Where?"

"Tonight, at the house in Vail. Victoria found him. Miles Preston just called me."

Derek loosened his silk tie and ran a finger around his neck. "Do they have any idea who did it?" He let off the brake and continued down the ramp.

"Miles didn't say." After a few beats, Charles added, "But I'm sure Victoria is a suspect."

Derek thought about the unlikely possibility that Victoria could have killed Elliot. Derek was in his mid-forties and had never been married, but had dated multitudes of women over the years and took pride in his ability to spot a crazy one from a mile away. Victoria was aloof, a bit cold for his taste, but he didn't think for a minute she was capable of murder.

Derek knew it seemed callous, but he couldn't say he would miss Elliot. He had always pegged him as a bit of a Boy Scout, never one to push the envelope on business ethics, but his death was definitely going to be a problem.

"What are we going to do?" he asked Charles. "About the merger?"

"I've got this under control. I'll start calling the board members first thing in the morning. Meet me at the office at seven. Plan on working tomorrow *and* Sunday." Charles hung up without saying goodbye.

At the garage exit, Derek looked both ways, then

pulled the Porsche out onto the deserted street. He sped through several blinking lights, headed north through downtown toward his condo in Riverfront Tower.

He thought of the million things that could go wrong now that Elliot was dead but realized there were a few things that might work in his favor.

Elliot's absence would leave an open spot on the board of directors. And Derek knew that, at least initially, there would be chaos. There would be documents to file with the Securities and Exchange Commission, reporting Elliot's death, documents for nominating and appointing a successor. And with the pending merger, they'd need to fill the empty board seat soon. Charles was CFO and already sat on the board. The thought crossed Derek's mind that maybe, as chief counsel, he could be the one to fill the empty seat. It was too late to bring in an outsider. The thought was tantalizing. He downshifted and hit the gas, sped through another blinking light.

As he neared the condo, his thoughts turned back to Elliot. *Murder?* He couldn't believe it had happened to someone he knew. He wondered how Elliot had been killed, then thought of Victoria. If she was in the house, surely she had heard something.

Derek looked at the digital clock on his dash. It was two in the morning. He was tired, but now he couldn't wait to get back to the office in a few hours.

By then Charles would have more details about the murder. It had occurred too late to make the morning edition of the *Denver Post*, but there might be something on the early news.

As he swung the car into the underground garage of the condo, his thoughts turned to Elliot's killer.

Derek still had on his suit jacket, but he shivered. He didn't believe Victoria murdered Elliot Banks, but he had his suspicions about who had.

CHAPTER 5

Sunday, June 17

THE DAY BEFORE was lost in a mental haze. Victoria had spent Saturday ensconced in her hotel room, refusing to come out. Miles had room service sent in, but she barely ate a bite. How could she? She was still reeling from finding Elliot in a bloody heap the night before.

When she asked Miles about going home, he had told her the police had not released the crime scene yet. *Crime scene*—she couldn't believe that's what her beautiful home was now. But later that day, they *had* released it, and Miles was ready. Someone with the Vail Police Department had given him the name of a company in Denver that would clean the study. They had worked through the night, and now Victoria was finally able to go home. But she had to get through the police interrogation first.

The detective across the table glared at her like she was his next meal. In response, Victoria lowered a cool gaze and willed herself not to blink. She wouldn't give him the satisfaction. She had answered all of his questions, even the same ones he asked in different ways, trying to trip her up. She was obviously not giving him the answers he was hoping to hear.

"Detective Conner, I've told you again and again, I don't know anything. I didn't see anything. I didn't hear anything. I wish I had, but I didn't."

Miles Preston laid a hand on her arm in an obvious attempt to keep her from getting frustrated, but it was too late. She looked at Miles and gave him a single nod to indicate she was fine. Yes, she was frustrated, but she would keep it in check—she knew how. She wasn't going to let the rude detective crack the veneer she had worked so many years to perfect.

Detective Wayne Conner leaned forward, resting his hairy arms on the edge of the table between them. "So that's it? He was working in his study, you went to bed, then you got up, and you found him dead."

Victoria nodded once. "That's it."

"And the blood on your robe and your hands?"

"I went to him when I found him on the floor."

The detective glared at her. "And the hatchet?"

Victoria met his gaze without flinching. "It's a tomahawk. Or you can call it a war club. But it's not a hatchet. It's from the Lakota Sioux tribe and was used in the Battle of the Little Bighorn in 1876."

Detective Conner leaned closer, spewing spittle as he talked. "I don't care if it was used in 1876 or 1976.

Thirty-six hours ago someone bashed your husband's head in with it."

Victoria winced for the first time.

Miles sat forward. "That's out of line, Detective."

"It's okay, Miles," Victoria said. "I'll answer the detective's questions."

She took a few seconds to collect herself, trying to avoid the mental image of Elliot being murdered with the tomahawk. She remembered how ecstatic he'd been when he'd won it at auction in Santa Fe a few years earlier. It was in near-mint condition despite being nearly a hundred and fifty years old. And it was beautiful. The metal blade was pierced in the shape of a Christian cross. A large strip of hide, beaded with various colors in a geometric pattern, hung from the bottom of the handle; along the shaft was an assortment of leather straps and feathers.

Victoria remembered how Elliot had taken great pains to hang the tomahawk at just the right angle, the hide and feathers falling down the wall just so. He hung it on the wall opposite his desk, above a Navajo lance he purchased years earlier from a dealer in Scottsdale.

Victoria took in a deep breath and looked back at the detective, waiting in defiant silence for his next question. She wanted nothing more than to be finished with the questioning, but she wasn't going to give him the satisfaction of appearing irritated.

Detective Conner cleared his throat and sat back in his chair. Victoria sensed he finally realized he wasn't going to rattle a confession out of her.

"The *tomahawk*," he continued in an even but passive-aggressive tone, "was found on your husband's desk, not on the floor." Victoria sat silent, and he continued. "Forensics is going to tell us it was the murder weapon—there was blood and hair all over it. The problem I have is, someone hit your husband on the back of the head with it, then laid it gently back on his desk before they fled the scene?"

Victoria let him stare at her a while before she shrugged.

He slammed a fist on the table. "Why was it there, dammit? Killers don't usually leave the murder weapon lying around, and they sure don't set it neatly on the corner of a desk. Hell, they set it down so gently there wasn't even a dent under it."

Victoria closed her eyes and pinched the bridge of her nose. "Again, Detective, I don't know why the tomahawk was on the desk."

Miles stood up. "I think that's enough for today. My client has answered all your questions more than once. It's obvious she has no idea what happened. We'll leave so you can get on with the business of finding out who *did* kill my client's husband."

Outside, a news crew from the CBS affiliate in Denver met Victoria and Miles on the steps to the building. A young female reporter shoved a micro-phone in Victoria's face while the cameraman filmed.

"Do you know who killed your husband, Mrs. Banks? Where were you when it happened?"

Miles took Victoria by the elbow, trying to steer her around them. But at the bottom of the stairs, she stopped and looked at the reporter.

Victoria took a second to collect her thoughts. "I have no idea who killed Elliot," she said. "I was at home, but I don't know what happened."

"Victoria—" Miles tried to pull her toward his Mercedes, parked at the curb.

"It's all right, Miles." Victoria turned back to the reporter and saw the cameraman step to the side to get a better angle. When Victoria spoke again, her voice was firm. "I don't know who came into my house Friday night and killed my husband, and it doesn't appear the police have any idea yet, either. But I can assure you, I won't rest until his killer is found."

The reporter brought the microphone back to her own mouth. "As an oil and gas company, is Banks Oil & Gas involved in anything contentious or illegal?"

Victoria frowned, confused by the question. "No."

Miles urged her toward the car again.

"Was your husband having an affair?" She stuck the microphone back in Victoria's face.

There was silence. Victoria stared down at the

twentysomething reporter, who seemed to instantly shrink in stature despite her high heels. The reporter nervously tucked a strand of blond hair behind her ear.

"No," Victoria answered in an even tone. "Elliot has never had an affair. My husband was an honorable and decent man who was brutally murdered. And I won't rest until his killer is found."

Victoria turned and walked toward the Mercedes. At the car, Miles held the passenger door open for her, waited for her to get in, then shut it.

As Victoria buckled the seat belt, the reporter shouted through the closed window.

"Victoria, did you murder your husband?"

Miles pulled away from the curb, and Victoria leaned back into the leather seat and closed her eyes. She realized now that talking to the reporter had been a mistake. It was only going to make things worse.

CHAPTER 6

HAROLD LAMKEN WAS a tall, lean man in his early fifties with graying strawberry-blond hair and fair skin that was perpetually burned from a life spent outdoors. He had worked for Elliot Banks for years, considered him like family. But it was different with Victoria.

From the first time he met her, Victoria had reminded Harold of a rare exotic bird, elegant but aloof, perched in her gilded cage to be admired from afar. He was fascinated by her, wanted to protect her, yet was intimidated by her as well.

Harold sat in his tattered recliner watching news clips of Victoria answering questions from the reporter outside the police station. Her voice was low but determined. Harold grabbed the remote from the TV tray next to the recliner and turned up the volume.

She looked beautiful in a light-gray dress that set off her dark hair and gray eyes. Harold watched her closely, taking in every word. He could tell the reporter's questions about Elliot had made her angry—they made him angry, too. Victoria tried masking her emotions in front of the reporter, but Harold had known her long enough to tell when she was upset.

When the segment was over, he turned off the television and set the remote on the TV tray, picked up his Keystone Light, and settled back into the chair. He drained the contents of the can, wiped his mouth with the back of his hand.

The guilt and fear that had haunted him since he'd first heard about Elliot's death had suddenly gotten worse. But he told himself there was nothing he could do.

Harold remembered when Elliot had first hired him. Elliot must have been just out of college. He remembered the affable but confident kid offering him a chance to work for his new company.

They had met on the side of the road off Highway 85, just north of Denver in Weld County. Elliot's late-model truck was steaming, and Harold had pulled over to help.

After a few minutes looking under the hood, Harold told him, "It's too hot to tell just yet, but it looks like you have a coolant leak."

Elliot explained he was on the way to check an oil well his company had just drilled. He asked Harold if he was busy, then offered him a hundred dollars for an hour of his time if he would shuttle Elliot out to the well and back. Harold was between jobs and told him he would be happy to oblige, despite being nervous his ancient Subaru wouldn't make it another hour without taking a break. But the afternoon had been fruitful.

Later, back at Elliot's truck, which was no longer steaming, Harold found the pin-size hole in the coolant line and pointed it out to him.

"Probably time for a new truck," Elliot said, then turned to Harold. "Hey, do you want a job?"

Harold was dumbfounded and stood staring at him. "Uh…"

"I need a pumper."

"A what?"

The kid laughed. "A pumper. You can call yourself a 'producer' if it makes you feel better. You check the operating wells, make sure they're still working." He gestured at the old Ford. "You fix this truck, and I'll give it to you to use."

Harold stood silent, thinking. He'd been looking for a job for months. Was this kid really going to hand him one, just like that? And a truck to boot?

"It's simple. All you have to do is drive out and check that the wells are pumping every day and that everything is okay. It'll be easy. I've only got one well so far, but I'm planning on drilling another soon. I'll have you make deliveries once in a while, stuff like that, too. How about it?"

And just like that, Harold had a job. He went on

to work for Elliot Banks in various capacities for nearly twenty years, morphing through several positions until he was made house manager of the Vail estate after Elliot married Victoria.

Having grown up nearby, in the small town of Minturn, Harold had jumped at the chance to move back home. He moved into his parents' old trailer just outside of town with his nephew, Tyler.

Managing the estate was a simple, trouble-free job, and Harold loved it. He watched over the house and grounds when Elliot and Victoria stayed at the condo in Denver and fixed any maintenance issues that weren't complicated enough to warrant a contractor. And when a contractor *was* needed, Harold oversaw the work.

Elliot was a great boss. Harold could remember only one time that Elliot lost his temper with him. A couple of months earlier, Tyler had taken Harold's key to the Banks house and used it to get in when he thought no one was home and was in the process of swiping a few bottles of liquor from the study when Elliot walked in. All hell apparently broke loose— Elliot and Tyler yelling at each other. Recounting the story later, Elliot told Harold that Tyler "was on a one-way street to no good and going to end up in jail like his mother."

To Harold, although the comment was likely justified, it was a sucker punch to the gut. Tyler's mother had been Harold's baby sister. Eileen had lost her way sometime after Tyler's birth, fell in with the wrong crowd, and was ultimately busted for meth. When she later got cancer and was dying in prison, she made Harold promise that he would raise Tyler as his own. Since then Harold had tried, but it hadn't always been easy. Tyler had inherited his mother's willful stubborn streak and was no stranger to the Denver County Jail. Harold thought the move back to Minturn would do his nephew some good. Now he wasn't sure.

But the last three years working in Vail had been some of Harold's best. Overseeing the estate was nowhere near full-time work, and in his downtime, he could hunt or fish for food like when he was a kid. Elliot Banks paid him like it was a full-time job, even though it wasn't. It was a good life. Until Elliot was murdered.

Now Harold wondered what would happen. He crushed the empty beer can in his fist and hurled it across the trailer toward the kitchen. He knew it was only a matter of time before the Vail police paid him a visit, and he wasn't sure yet what he was going to tell them.

CHAPTER 7

CHARLES STRATTON WAS standing in the walk-in bar just off the living room, pouring bourbon over ice into a short crystal glass.

"It's too early for that, darling, don't you think?" Katie asked him. She was sitting on the long down sofa, her feet curled underneath her, flipping through the pages of the latest *Vogue*.

Charles glanced at his wife and marveled at her ignorance. Katie gave new meaning to the epithet "bubbleheaded bleached blonde," but she was gorgeous.

Charles swished the liquor in the glass, chilling it. "It's Sunday," he replied. "And with the last two days I've had, I think I'm entitled to it."

Charles had gotten to the office just before seven Saturday morning and had been greeted at the door by a nervous Derek Lowe. Charles assured him that, despite Elliot's death, the merger wouldn't be in jeopardy.

They quickly made a list of documents that would need to be drawn up for the emergency board meeting in a few days. Then, with the contact list of the board of directors of Banks Oil & Gas, Charles had called each one to inform them of Elliot's murder. He spent two days fielding scores of questions— what he knew about the incident, about Victoria, and about the impending merger. He quelled most of their fears over the fate of the company, and by the time he left the office late Sunday morning, he was confident he had everything under control. All the directors were on board with his plans for the company going forward.

Charles sank into an overstuffed chair facing Katie and took a long swallow of the liquor. For a few minutes, he watched her flip through the magazine. They had been married for more than fourteen years. Katie wasn't tall and lithe like Victoria, but she was smaller and curvier. And where Victoria was fair and brunette, Katie was blond and tan.

Charles had been envious of Elliot when he dated, then later married, Victoria, but he'd quickly gotten over it. Victoria was beautiful, but she was smart, and Charles knew smart women could cause problems.

Katie closed the magazine and tossed it on the floor. "Done with that one," she said with unwarranted satisfaction.

Charles watched her, marveling how the two women couldn't be more different. Katie had spent three years as a bouncing cheerleader at the University

of Colorado at Boulder—he wasn't even sure what
her major had been before she dropped out. Victoria
had graduated with honors from Colorado School
of Mines with a degree in petroleum engineering.
Charles remembered being impressed with Victoria
until he realized what an inconvenience a cerebral
wife could be—too smart for their own good.

Katie stretched out her short legs, swung her feet
to the Aubusson rug, and looked at him expectantly.
Charles knew she wanted something. What was it
this time? he wondered. He'd just gotten her the new
Cadillac. Was it a trip? Jewelry? He waited for her to
speak, wishing he were anywhere else at that moment.
He had too much to deal with to be bothered with
the impulsive wishes of his capricious wife.

"I was thinking—" she began.

Charles's cell phone rang. Saved by the bell, he
thought. He saw that it was Luther Byrd, the on-site
production manager for Banks Oil & Gas. Luther was
a ruffian, an uncouth hoodlum, but his kind served a
purpose and Charles tolerated him.

"Did you see Victoria Banks on the news?" Luther's
voice was deep and tinged with apprehension.

Charles didn't know what he was talking about,
then remembered Miles Preston mentioning something about Victoria being questioned again by the
police that morning. "No, I didn't see it."

Luther let out a breath. "A reporter caught her

coming out of the police station. She said she's not going to rest until they find Banks's murderer. Then the reporter started asking questions about the company. I hope this isn't going to stir up any trouble."

Charles glanced at Katie and noticed her watching him. He got up from the chair and walked to the bar on the pretense of pouring himself another drink. He lowered his voice. "There isn't going to be any trouble."

"If they start looking into the business—"

"It won't get that far."

"But what about Victoria?"

"What about her?"

"She sounded determined to find the killer. She could stir up trouble."

"I'm telling you, Luther, it won't be a problem. If there are any issues, I'm sure you can deal with them. I'll let you know if it comes to that."

There was silence on the other end of the line. Then finally Luther answered, "You're the boss."

When he hung up, Charles noticed Katie still watching him. He poured a second drink, walked back into the living room, and sat down.

"You were going to say something?" He wanted to avoid talking about the phone call. She was easily distracted.

"Yes," she said, nervously smoothing the front of her silk dress. "I know you said to stay away, but I want to see Victoria, and I want you to be okay about it. I want to go to Vail…today."

Charles saw a momentary flicker of determination before Katie's insipid, pleading expression returned. He wondered what it would be like if she ever forcefully stood her ground. After fourteen years, Charles had honed his instincts about how far he could push her and knew when it was to his strategic advantage to give in.

He took a moment to think about it. Katie liked Victoria and would be genuinely concerned about her. Charles could keep them apart only so long. He swirled the liquor in his glass.

He thought about what Luther had told him and decided that if Victoria was going to cause problems, it could benefit him having Katie close to her, reporting back to him about what she was up to. The more he thought about it, the more he liked the idea.

Charles smiled. "Of course I'm okay with it." He got up, walked over to Katie, and bent to kiss her. "Will you be back tonight, or will you be staying over in Vail?"

Relieved, Katie practically bounced off the couch, picked up the magazine she had thrown on the rug, and gave her husband another kiss. "I'll be back in time for a late dinner. Don't start without me."

"I won't," Charles promised. He walked to the bar,

found one of his best bottles of wine, and handed it to her. "Here, take this. You might need it."

Katie took the bottle from him, her expression now sad. "Good idea. I'm sure it won't be an easy visit."

"Be careful on the interstate. It's Sunday. Traffic will be terrible coming back to the city."

"You worry too much."

"Give Victoria my love."

Charles watched Katie bound out of the room, his eyes narrowing at the possibility that Victoria Banks could cause problems he would need Luther Byrd to solve.

CHAPTER 8

ON THE DRIVE home from the police station, Miles tried making small talk, but Victoria was distracted, hearing only some of what he was saying. She stared straight ahead, barely registering the familiar street signs and houses as he weaved his way past Vail Village and turned onto Forest Road.

As they neared the house, she interrupted him. "Miles, I didn't kill Elliot."

He was quiet. Out of the corner of her eye, she saw him glance at her, then turn his attention back to the road. He let her continue.

"I'm beginning to believe everyone thinks I did, but I didn't." When he still didn't reply, she asked, "You don't think I killed Elliot, do you?"

"Of course not, Victoria. That's why I'm here."

She felt a weight lift and let out the breath she had been holding. "Thank you."

"We'll get through this. If the police don't come to the conclusion you had nothing to do with Elliot's murder in the next day or two, I'll hire you the best legal defense team in Denver. But in the meantime, I would advise not talking about the investigation with anyone."

Victoria looked at him apologetically. "Like a reporter?"

Miles offered her a gentle smile. "Yes, like a reporter."

Victoria turned her attention to the passing homes. A few seconds later they pulled into the driveway and wound their way around the back of the house.

"Is there anyone you want to call?" Miles asked. "To come be with you? Any family? I can call them if you want me to."

She wasn't sure how much Elliot had told Miles over the years, about her past and about her family. She suspected Elliot had loved her enough to keep it a secret, even from Miles. Victoria shook her head. "No, no one."

Miles turned off the ignition. Victoria could see his expression was etched with worry—or was it pity? She wasn't sure.

She opened the car door, then grabbed the morning's *Denver Post*, which had been set outside her room at the hotel that morning, and got out. "I got a text from Katie," she said in a cheerful voice, trying to lighten the mood. "She's on her way out from Denver."

Miles shut the car door and followed her toward

the house. "Good. I haven't seen Katie or Charles in forever. Katie is always good for a few laughs."

"Yes, she is," Victoria agreed, although she wasn't looking forward to the visit, but instead wanted more time alone.

"And she's good company," Miles added. "You need someone around you right now. Someone you can talk to, or lean on."

Victoria agreed again.

"If I miss her," he said. "Please tell her I said hello."

Victoria pulled her keys from her purse and unlocked the back door. "How about I make us some lunch? I can whip up a couple of turkey sandwiches with pesto."

"That sounds great."

Inside, Victoria locked the back door behind them, went into the kitchen, and placed her purse on the corner of the counter where she kept it, then set the newspaper down on the breakfast table. She stood next to the table, taking in and releasing a slow breath, her gaze sweeping the room. Everything looked the same as it had two days earlier, but so much had changed.

When she was finished making the sandwiches, she placed them on small china plates, then meticulously cleaned the kitchen, rinsing the knife and cutting board before putting them into the dishwasher.

She set her plate on the breakfast table and took the other into the dining room, where Miles was making phone calls about a legal defense team, should she need it.

He was in the middle of a call and mouthed a "thank you" as she handed him the plate. On her way out, she heard his side of the conversation. It was easy and friendly, obviously someone he knew.

Back in the kitchen, Victoria sat down in a chair facing the window and looked toward the mountains. The sun was bright. She could just make out the Gore Range in the distance, still blanketed with snow from the last spring storm nearly a month earlier. She then noticed a deer feeding on grass at the far end of the yard. It looked peaceful.

If she let herself, she could almost imagine life back to the way it was, but she knew it never would be. She pulled the *Denver Post* toward her and unfolded it, laid it back on the table, and immediately drew in a quick breath. A photograph of herself and Elliot taken at the Black Diamond Ball held in Beaver Creek the year earlier, the same photograph Elliot had framed and kept on his desk in the study, was splashed across the front page.

After her initial shock, Victoria looked at the picture fondly, remembering how handsome Elliot had looked in his tuxedo that night and how humbled he had been to receive the Citizen of the Year award for his commitment to local charities. Victoria drew a finger slowly over his picture as she recalled the closing line from his acceptance speech, which she'd helped him write: *There are no limits on what we can achieve when we all work together, because there are no limits on human compassion.*

Her gaze moved from the picture to the headline. ELLIOT BANKS MURDERED IN VAIL. She scanned the first few paragraphs, salacious details about the murder. She set the paper aside and massaged her temples in an effort to ward off an impending migraine, the image of Elliot lying dead in a bloody heap still stuck in her mind.

Victoria pushed the paper aside and stared down at the sandwich. She knew she should eat something, but she no longer had an appetite. After taking a few reluctant bites, she got up from the table and dumped the rest into the trash.

It had been a challenging morning being grilled by the belligerent Detective Conner, and now the negative publicity had begun.

She wasn't going to be able to sit by and let the police investigate Elliot's murder—not while they were focusing their investigation on her. In their defense, she thought, murder was nearly nonexistent in the rarefied world of exclusive Rocky Mountain resort towns. Then she remembered the murder cases in Aspen only a few weeks earlier. She remembered the news accounts on television and on the internet, stories about the victims and the police and their hunt for the deranged killer. The case had terrified Colorado and fascinated the country, and it gave her an idea.

In the dining room, Miles was busy scribbling something onto a notepad set in a leather binder, his head down. The large bronze chandelier in the room cast his downturned face in shadows. Victoria thought of the times he had come to the house and she had seen him and Elliot at that very table, usually after the three had had dinner together. Elliot and Miles would be in deep discussion, often agreeing on how to solve the world's problems. Victoria smiled faintly, remembering.

After a few moments, Miles looked up and saw her watching him. "The turkey sandwich hit the spot," he said, setting down his pen and leaning his back against the chair. "Thank you."

Victoria sat in the chair next to him. "Miles, I have an idea."

The easy look on his face tensed. "What is it?"

"I didn't kill Elliot. The police and at least one reporter think I did, and I can't sit around hoping they come up with another suspect. I think I need to be proactive about this."

Miles looked concerned, but he nodded in agreement.

Victoria set her phone on the table. "There's one person I think could help prove I'm innocent."

He frowned. "Who is that?"

Victoria didn't answer. He was skeptical, and it annoyed her. She pulled her phone closer and googled the number for the Aspen Police Department. When she found it, she looked back up at him.

"Trust me," she said as she dialed the number.

CHAPTER 9

JACK MARTIN WAS a forty-three-year-old ex-cop with a dog and nowhere to go. He knew it might depress him if he thought about it, so he didn't.

Home was an Airstream trailer parked at a campground at the south end of Shadow Mountain Lake, just north of the larger Lake Granby in the Arapaho National Forest. Jack had chosen a spot away from the water's edge but closer to the forest.

It had been a rowdy Sunday at the campground. A handful of kids playing kickball in an open field, a group of college students laughing and playing music as they guzzled gallons of beer. Two retired couples had hauled kayaks down to the lake, one of the women tipping over as she tried to get in. There had even been a domestic skirmish involving the flinging of hot dogs.

Jack kept to himself but had loved it all.

The first month at the lake had been quiet—too quiet, usually just Jack and one or two other campers. He'd thought he would enjoy the solitude, but he didn't. In the last few weeks, the summer tourist had finally shown up. They were an eclectic and lively bunch that kept him entertained just by giving him something to watch.

Jack knew the campground would work great for the summer, but he would need to move come fall. There was no way he was going to be caught so far from civilization in a winter snowstorm. He'd go east, closer to Denver, or maybe farther south in the Rockies, where the snowfall wouldn't be as treacherous.

Earlier that morning, Jack had logged on to the camp's Wi-Fi and checked his bank balance. He had resigned from his position as the senior detective with the Aspen Police Department two months earlier after he'd solved the Hermes Strangler case, and his funds were now running low. If he was careful, he'd have enough to last through winter and into the spring without having to tap his emergency fund. He knew he'd eventually have to pull the trailer back to Texas and look for a job, but the Rockies had grown on him, and he wasn't ready to leave just yet.

He sat in the trailer at a small table bolted to the floor, studying a large map of Colorado unfolded in front of him. After a few minutes, Crockett nosed up to him and set a hefty paw on his leg. He'd had the dog two months, long enough to know the dog wanted to go outside.

Jack tried turning his attention back to highways

and campgrounds, but his concentration was shot. He patted the dog on his head. "I'm trying to figure out where we're going next, Crockett. And you're not helping."

He leaned over and pulled a worn pair of hiking boots from the bench on the other side of the table, then bent down to put them on. The dog started to jump and pant.

"Calm down. I'm coming." Jack grabbed a water bottle off the counter, filled it at the sink, and threw it into his backpack.

When Jack opened the screen door, Crockett didn't bother with the step, but jumped to the ground in a single leap. Jack followed him, stepping out of the Airstream into the bright afternoon sun.

Leaving the campground behind, the two skirted the lake's eastern shoreline until they caught the trail leading to the summit of Shadow Mountain. Crockett stopped to stare at a moose wading in the shallow water near the lake's edge, but Jack called him back. He had been warned to give moose a wide berth. "From a distance, they appear friendly enough," an old camper had told him. "But don't let that fool you. They'd just as soon stomp you to death as look at you." Jack had taken the old guy at his word.

The trail turned away from the lake, and they walked farther into the forest, the trees closing in on them and engulfing them in their shadows. The wind kicked up as they climbed higher, reminding Jack the sun had already begun its afternoon descent. The hike to the summit and back to the campground was roughly nine and a half miles. It would be nearly dark by the time they got back.

A few hours later, near the top of the mountain, Jack leaned against a boulder and took in the view of the lake and mountains. Crockett sat at his feet, his ears alert and swiveling as he scanned their surroundings.

Jack took in a deep breath, smelling the pine. Across the water below, he could just make out the small town of Grand Lakes. The view was familiar. He and Crockett had made the hike dozens of times since they'd left Aspen and settled at the campground two months earlier.

He pulled a granola bar from his backpack and took a large bite, then reached down and gave what was left to Crockett. As he stuck the trash into the backpack, his cell phone rang. He dug it out and looked at it, but didn't recognize the number.

"Is this Detective Jack Martin?" The woman's voice was silky and sexy as hell. Jack was immediately intrigued.

"Speaking," he answered without his usual edge.

The woman sighed with what Jack thought sounded like relief.

"Detective Martin, my name is Victoria Banks.

You're a hard man to find. I hope I haven't caught you at an inconvenient time."

Jack didn't know what to think. Who was this woman? And how did she get his number?

She continued. "At your earliest convenience, I have a job offer I would like to discuss with you."

CHAPTER 10

KATIE STRATTON ARRIVED in Vail like a ray of sun shot through a storm cloud.

"Charles sends his love," she said, standing on tiptoes to give Victoria an air kiss, then handing her a bottle of wine. "He would have come, but he's so busy taking care of things at the office. There's so much to do now that Elliot is—"

Katie looked up with an expression of horror. Victoria gave her an understanding smile.

"I'm so sorry, Victoria. That sounds so crass."

It *was* crass, and the reminder that Elliot was gone shot a stabbing pain through Victoria's heart, but she knew Katie would never intentionally hurt her.

Victoria shook her head and gestured her inside. "It's okay," she said, then shut the heavy bronze door behind them and locked it. "Please tell Charles how grateful I am that he's there to pick up the pieces and keep the company going."

Katie held out a paper bag, beaming again. "I picked us up an assortment of cheeses from Delizioso on my way in—to go with the wine."

In the family room, Katie sank into one end of the large down sectional, kicked off her shoes, and tucked her feet underneath her. Sun filtered through the window behind her, setting off her helmet of blond hair like a halo. Although Victoria wanted some time alone and hadn't been looking forward to the visit, she was now glad Katie was there.

They talked for an hour, snacking on the cheese and sipping wine. Katie dominated the conversation as she mapped out the plans she had made for the two of them. First it was going to be a trip to New York in the fall—shopping and the latest Broadway show. Then somewhere warm in the spring. Katie talked out loud as she thought of the possibilities. The Bahamas, the Maldives, or Mykonos.

"Capri!" Katie said with exaggerated satisfaction, practically bouncing off the couch. "That's where we'll go."

Victoria let her continue to talk and plan.

Victoria hadn't had many close friends growing up. In fact, she could remember only one—Jennifer, who had lived across the street. The two had spent countless summer days playing outside until one or the other was called in for dinner. At Asbury Elementary, just south of downtown Denver, they had been inseparable. Until the day Victoria's mother was arrested and Victoria was put into the foster system. She'd never seen Jennifer again.

When the conversation slowed, Victoria thought it was a good time to change the subject. Miles probably already thought she was crazy for calling the detective from Aspen, so she hadn't mentioned anything to him. Victoria wanted to run her theory by Katie first.

When Katie stopped talking to drain the last of the wine in her glass, Victoria seized her chance. "I want to change the subject for a second. There's something I want to talk to you about."

Katie swallowed the wine and looked at her with concern or curiosity, Victoria wasn't sure which. But she continued. "You know Doris Reed, Elliot's long-time personal assistant?"

"The crazy woman with the red hair?"

Victoria liked Doris and knew Elliot had adored her, regularly commenting on her kind heart and her tenacity when it came to her work. But Victoria couldn't fault people who didn't know Doris for thinking she was a bit odd. She was.

Victoria looked at Katie and smiled, but she shook her head. "She's not crazy, Katie. She's…eccentric." Victoria picked her adjective carefully.

"If you say so."

Victoria took a deep breath and started again. "The night of Bob Hawkins's suicide—"

"The accountant?"

Victoria nodded. It never ceased to amaze her

that Katie could talk on end about subjects that were of no importance, yet the minute the conversation turned serious, she struggled to keep up. Katie was simple—some would argue shallow—but Victoria knew, deep down, she had a heart of gold.

"Yes, Katie, Bob Hawkins the company's controller." She gave Katie a moment to process the information. "The night Bob died, Doris told Elliot she was suspicious about it being a suicide."

"Suspicious about what?"

"She didn't believe it was suicide. She didn't think Bob could have done it, leave a wife and two children like that. Elliot said she went on and on about it not being like him. Bob was always happy and would never have done that."

"Well, if it wasn't suicide, what did she think it was?"

"Murder."

"Murder?" Katie practically spit the word out, wincing in disbelief. "What did Elliot think?"

"He didn't say. I could tell he didn't want to talk about it. Doris called him here at home the night it happened. That's the only reason I know about it. Elliot never talked about it again."

Katie didn't reply but sat watching her.

Victoria hesitated before continuing, but she decided she wanted her friend's opinion enough to risk a humiliating response. "Do you think there could be a connection with Elliot's murder?"

"Elliot's murder and Bob's suicide?" The look of astonishment on Katie's face spoke volumes. Victoria wished she hadn't brought the subject up.

Katie untucked her feet and moved to sit closer to Victoria, taking her hand. "Darling, you're still in shock—"

"I'm not." Katie was looking at her with pity Victoria didn't want. She got up, picked up the platter of leftover cheese, and walked toward the kitchen. "It's just a theory, but I'm going to look into it."

"Look into what?"

"Look into Elliot's murder."

"But the police are doing that."

"So far they're focusing their investigation on *me*. I'm going to hire someone to help find out who really did it."

"Who are you going to hire?" From the tone of her voice, pity had morphed into disbelief again.

Victoria walked back to the couch and sat down. "Jack Martin, the detective who solved the Hermes Strangler case in Aspen a few weeks ago. I'm sure you heard about it."

"Of course I heard about it." Katie looked at her in astonishment. "Have you talked to him? The detective? How did you find him?"

"It took a little finagling, but I got his cell number.

I called him this afternoon. He's coming over later. Hopefully, he'll agree to take my case and help find Elliot's murderer."

Katie's eyes bulged wider. "But that's the police's job."

"I can't count on that," Victoria said, sighing. The conversation wasn't going as she had hoped.

Katie looked at her, skepticism written all over her face. "You're probably wasting your time, darling— and your money." She then added, "But he sure won't be bad to look at."

Victoria remembered the pictures of Jack Martin in the press—tall, good-looking, wavy dark hair falling just above his collar. "He'll be here in about an hour. Would you like to stay and meet him?"

Katie contemplated the offer. "Meet the handsome detective that was all over the news for weeks, then up and disappears and no one has heard from him since—until *you* found him?" Katie thought about it, then shook her head. "It's tempting, but I need to get back." She got off the couch and carried the wineglasses to the sink. "I told Charles I'd be back in time for a late dinner. I should probably get going. Besides, I know I've talked your ear off."

"You haven't," Victoria assured her. "I've enjoyed the visit."

In the foyer, Katie looked at her, serious again. "You're alone," she said, glancing up and down both sides of the long corridor. "You're not nervous about staying here by yourself? I mean, after what happened to Elliot? And a strange man is coming over?"

"He's a detective, Katie, not a murderer. Besides, Miles is at the Four Seasons and is coming to meet him. He'll be here any minute." Victoria gave her a gentle hug. "Thank you for coming. You cheered me up."

"Well, I hope so," Katie said, slinging a giant Louis Vuitton bag over her shoulder and sailing out the door. On the sidewalk, she turned around. "I'll be back in a few days to check on you, but in the meantime, you call me if you need anything."

When she was gone, Victoria closed the front door and locked it, then leaned back on the cool metal, relieved that Katie hadn't shown any inkling she thought Victoria could be guilty of killing Elliot.

Katie had obviously thought Doris Reed's conspiracy theory about Bob Hawkins's suicide actually being murder was ludicrous, and it probably was. She wouldn't bring it up again. Victoria could also tell Katie thought the idea of hiring Jack Martin was ridiculous.

She thinks I'm crazy, Victoria thought, beginning to wonder the same thing herself.

CHAPTER 11

JACK MARTIN WOVE his way through the forested canyons along Interstate 70, headed for Vail. He had never been to Vail before, but he knew it was another swanky ski town like Aspen that swelled with as many well-heeled tourists in the summer as it did in winter.

Ten minutes later, when the highway made a sharp bend to the south, Vail came into view. Jack wasn't sure what he expected it to look like, but this wasn't it.

The town was stretched out along the interstate, hemmed in by mountains to the north and south. Clusters of houses were tucked off both sides of the highway, partially hidden in clumps of trees. A small group of tall buildings loomed in the distance, just off the highway. As he got closer, Jack saw that several of them had bell towers and were covered with balconies. Hotels or condos, he decided—nice ones.

He exited the interstate and drove slowly past the center of town. Vail Village, Victoria had called it when she gave him directions over the phone.

The buildings looked like they had been plucked

from the Bavarian Alps, with heavy timber accents and decorative moldings around the doors and windows. Everywhere he looked, he saw cobblestone streets and European-style architecture—and tourists.

Storefronts revealed many of the same glitzy shops he recognized from Aspen, but missing were the renovated old buildings from Colorado's mining era. Everything in Vail looked new.

Jack wound his way through the village streets, crossed over a creek, and took a right on Forest Road. He double-checked the address in his notebook.

The houses on Forest Road were enormous. He idled the truck down the street, looking from side to side. Soon, a modern behemoth emerged from the trees on the south side. Address numbers cut into a metal panel mounted to a stone monument near the street indicated he was at the right house. Jack pulled to the curb and shut off the ignition.

The house was huge. A mass of geometric shapes dominated by huge walls that looked like giant concrete panels. Metal beams ran in all directions, and there was lots of glass. Jack couldn't begin to guess how many square feet it was.

"I guess this is it," he said to the brown dog sitting next to him. "Watch the truck, Crockett."

Jack studied the house and grounds as he made his way to the front door. The landscaping was perfectly manicured. Native wildflowers were tamed in beds set against long stretches of the foundation. Large aspen and pine trees wrapped the perimeter of the property as if to punctuate the importance of the massive building.

Jack remembered the simple three-bedroom house in Baton Rouge that he had grown up in—a small one-story with red brick, bougainvillea vines encircling the front porch, and his grandmother's prized Southern magnolia tree out front.

He stopped on the sidewalk and took another look at the concrete and steel behemoth looming in front of him. Next to his quaint childhood home in Louisiana, he thought, this thing was downright ugly.

The front door was tall and bronze. Two rows of metal rivets in the same color bordered the edges. *It must weigh four hundred pounds*, he thought. Jack shook his head and knocked, then noticed the doorbell set in its own small bronze panel in the wall to his left. He was about to ring it, but then he heard someone inside.

The door swung open, and a balding man of medium height, about Jack's age, greeted him with an outstretched hand.

"Miles Preston," the man said, swinging the door open further. "You must be Jack Martin. Come in." He stepped aside and motioned for Jack to enter, then shut the door behind him.

Inside, Jack looked around, wondering who Miles

Preston was and why Victoria Banks was nowhere in sight.

"Give me a minute," Preston said. "I'll let Victoria know you're here." With that, he turned and disappeared down a long curving corridor that stretched out from either side of the entry. Jack watched until he had disappeared.

The foyer was square and large. The floor was limestone. In the center was a mosaic made of tiny colored tiles set in a geometric pattern in grays and browns that looked Native American. Jack looked from the shiny floor to the frayed cuffs of his jeans and his scuffed cowboy boots. A quick polish would have been nice had he known what to expect.

A long corridor extended out perpendicular from the foyer in both directions. It was curved but seemed to run the entire length of the house. The walls looked like concrete, but they had a funny sheen, like something had been rubbed on them. Jack resisted the urge to touch them and see.

On one wall was a tattered blanket. A small brass plaque attached to the frame identified it as Navajo. Probably old and valuable by the care that had been taken to frame and display it just inside the front door. On another wall was an animal skull. It had short upturned horns and a prominent curving snout too long for a bull. A buffalo maybe?

Other items were hung on the walls along both

sides of the corridor. The objects were sparse and spaced far apart, everything scrubbed squeaky clean. The inside of the house looked like a museum.

He thought of his Airstream trailer and how efficient it was. How he could stand in the center aisle, wash his hands in the tiny sink, grab a beer out of the mini fridge and set it on the table without having to lift a foot.

This place was massive. He looked up and estimated it was a good twenty feet to the steel beam and wood-planked ceiling.

Jack walked over to the animal skull and peered up at it.

An easy voice spoke from behind him. "It's from the Pleistocene Era."

Jack turned. She was standing behind him looking up at the skull. And she was gorgeous. Dressed in a cashmere sweater the same caramel color as her slacks. Her dark hair was parted in the middle, pulled back and twisted into a low bun. Her eyes were an almost translucent gray.

When Jack didn't reply, she looked at him and offered an emotionless smile. "The last Ice Age," she explained. "It's a petrified bison skull—an ancestor of our modern buffalo."

"Petrified?" Jack wondered aloud. "Like petrified wood?"

"Exactly." She was still looking up at the skull. "Over time, sediment replaced the bone."

She turned and stuck out a hand. "Victoria Banks," she said.

Her hand was smooth and soft but her handshake firm.

"Jack Martin."

"Thank you for coming, Detective Martin. You must be wondering what this is all about. Let's go into my husband's study, and I'll explain."

Jack nodded and glanced down the hall from where she came. She must have read his mind.

"Miles had to take a phone call. He'll join us shortly. Please come with me."

Jack followed her down the corridor to a set of tall wood doors that were opened against the thick concrete walls. They stepped inside. It was an impressive room. Steel beams crisscrossed the high ceiling. Between them were dozens of stained-wood planks. The walls were the same concrete he'd noticed in the entry. There was no Sheetrock in sight.

Along one wall was a stacked rock fireplace that stretched to the ceiling. Floor-to-ceiling plate-glass windows that looked toward Vail Mountain lined another. A long velvet sofa was set in front of it.

Two modern-style leather and chrome chairs that looked like they could be at home on the space station faced each other in front of the hearth. A small black marble-topped table sat between them. Victoria took a seat in one of the chairs and gestured for Jack to sit in the other.

She studied him for a moment. Jack wasn't accustomed to being overtly scrutinized, but he studied her back with the same intensity.

She spoke with a faint smile. "I'm going to take a guess, Detective, and say that after I called, you googled me."

She was testing him. Jack sat back in the chair and crossed a foot over the opposite knee. "You didn't give me much to go on."

"I'm curious what your initial thoughts are."

"About you, or your husband's murder?"

"Both."

He wasn't sure how honest he wanted to be with her yet, so he kept his answer to the basics of what he knew. "I only know what I read from the news accounts online—that your husband appears to have been brutally murdered"—he glanced around the room—"*here*, in his study. And that you found him."

He left out the part about her being considered a suspect. But that had not been a surprise to him; the spouse was always investigated first.

She sat watching him, studying his response. Was she toying with him? She was self-possessed and remote, maybe even cold. But there was no indication in the brief background search he had done that would indicate she was a killer.

She turned her head and looked down at the floor. He thought he saw a crack in her veneer; her face softened a bit. "He was lying there. I know it probably seems strange to you, but I still feel him in here—with his desk and his things. Elliot and I spent a lot of time in here. I wanted you to see where it happened." She waited before she continued. Her voice was slow and halting. "They took the rug away as evidence. It was a beautiful replica of an ancient Navajo pattern. We had it made especially for this room."

Jack turned to look at the spot on the floor and realized she had sat him within ten feet of where she had found her husband dead. He didn't know if he should pity her or be appalled. Was she looking for a response?

He turned back to her. "What happened that night?"

Victoria gave him the same details that he had read in the online news stories. No more, no less. Her voice cracked at first, then remained devoid of emotion. Victoria Banks was going to be a hard one to read.

When she was done talking, Jack sat forward in the chair and got right to the point. "Why did you call me?"

She didn't flinch at his directness. "I told you. I want to hire you."

"Hire me to do what?"

"You're a detective—"

"A *retired* detective."

"I followed the Hermes Strangler case in Aspen very closely, Detective Martin. It was fascinating."

It wasn't fascinating, Jack thought. It was *frustrating*—had taken longer than he had hoped to solve, and with a body count that still bothered him. No, the Hermes Strangler case wasn't fascinating at all.

When he didn't reply, she continued. "My husband was murdered, and I've been told it's normal for the police to focus their attention on the spouse of the victim. But I didn't kill my husband." She paused, probably assessing his response, before she continued. "And while they're focusing most of their attention on me, I don't have much faith in the police finding out who *did* kill him. I want to hire you to do that for me—find who murdered my husband. I'll pay you five hundred dollars a day plus expenses, as long as you're making progress on the case."

She had stopped talking and watched him as he mulled over the proposition. He had never done private work before and wasn't sure if he wanted to. After his forced retirement from the bureau following an incident in Houston, he was fortunate to have landed the job in Aspen within a few months. He'd always suspected his superior at the bureau had something to do with him getting the job in Colorado, but no one ever confirmed it and he hadn't asked.

He wasn't desperate for the money—not yet. He had done the math and knew he could get comfortably through the winter. But the extra money would be nice. And what was he doing anyway except hiking with Crockett every day?

Jack watched her—cool and gorgeous, and aside from the house, dripping with understated wealth. He wasn't sure if he wanted to run from her or kiss her. He looked into her emotionless gray eyes. He was intrigued but also suspicious as hell.

"Okay," he said, hoping he wouldn't regret the decision. "I'll do it."

She let out a short breath, obviously relieved—a momentary crack in the stone veneer. "Thank you."

"There are a couple of things I won't compromise on, though," Jack said.

She hesitated. "Yes?"

"First, you call me 'Jack,' not 'Detective' or 'Detective Martin.' And second, you have to be completely honest with me—no secrets, however ugly or embarrassing you think they might be. If you're not honest with me, I won't be able to do my job."

Victoria nodded. "That sounds fine."

With the initial tension alleviated, they both relaxed back into the leather chairs.

"What's next?" she asked.

Jack leaned over and pulled a small notepad from a front pocket of his jeans. "I need to ask you a few questions."

Victoria looked toward the corridor. "Should we wait for Miles?"

"You tell me," Jack answered. "Who is he?"

"Miles is my husband's best friend and attorney," she said. Jack thought he saw a brief hint of sadness. "*Was* my husband's best friend and attorney," she corrected herself. "Now he's *my* attorney."

"Is he criminal defense?"

"No. Miles is a general practitioner, but he said he would hire a defense team for me if it came to that."

Jack scribbled the information in his notebook. "I'll need his contact information."

Just then Miles Preston walked into the room. "Whose contact information? Mine? I'll get you my card."

"Jack has agreed to take the case, Miles. He was just going to ask me a few questions."

Jack noticed the attorney's jaw tense. There was something there. Was it hostility, or was he just being protective of his client? Jack couldn't tell.

As Miles pulled the desk chair over to join them, Jack continued. "On the phone, you mentioned you found your husband, then called the police."

"That's right."

"When they got here, they found you on the floor with him." She nodded, so he continued. "It was late. Would the doors have been locked?"

Her eyes widened when she realized what he was getting at. "They *would* have been locked. I lock them myself every night. A bear could find its way in if you don't, and it's a fear of mine. But they must have been unlocked when the police got here. I didn't let them in."

"Who has access to the house?" he asked her. "Keys, code to a keypad?"

"Besides Elliot and myself, just Harold Lamken, our house manager."

Jack wrote the name down. "I'll need his contact information, too."

"Harold has worked for Elliot for years," Victoria said, "since long before I met Elliot. He trusted him completely."

Jack looked up at her. "Do *you*?"

She hesitated for a second. "I do. Harold was a friend to Elliot, as well as an employee. He didn't kill my husband."

Jack nodded. "I still need his contact information."

Victoria got up, walked to the large marble and chrome desk, wrote a number down on a sticky note, and handed it to Jack.

"Thank you," he said. "No one else had access to the house?"

Victoria shook her head. "No."

"A housekeeper?"

"Hilda comes twice a week. She was here Friday. I called her this morning and told her what happened and asked her to take the next few weeks off."

"She doesn't have a key?"

Victoria shook her head. "No, I'm always here to let her in. If I'm not, I have Harold do it for me; then he locks up later."

Jack wrote the information down and looked back up. "Were you or Elliot expecting any visitors last night?"

"No. At least Elliot didn't mention anyone to me. But it was late. He would have told me if someone was coming over when I went to bed."

"You're sure he would have told you?"

"Yes. Sometimes I get up in the middle of the night and come to the kitchen for a glass of water, or I'll stop into the study to check on him. He would have let me know if someone was coming over."

Jack scribbled a few more notes. "What about personal relationships? Did he have any recent confrontations with anyone?"

Victoria frowned. "No. Elliot wasn't like that. Everyone liked him, didn't they, Miles?"

Miles Preston nodded slowly, his face cast down. "If you're asking if Elliot had enemies, the answer is no. We've been friends since we were kids, and I can count on one hand how many times I heard him even raise his voice with someone."

Jack thought he recognized genuine sadness in the man's eyes. It was clear he had lost a close friend. He turned back to Victoria. "Tell me about your husband's business."

"What do you want to know? Banks Oil & Gas has wells all over the DJ Basin."

"DJ Basin?"

"It's a geological structure, an oil-rich formation. It's northeast of Denver but stretches all the way north to Wyoming. Elliot started the company by drilling there nearly twenty years ago, a few years out of school."

"Have there been any business deals that have gone sour recently? Any disgruntled employees who'd been fired? Anything along those lines?"

Victoria shook her head. "None that Elliot mentioned. The company's controller recently committed suicide, but I don't think it had anything to do with the business."

"How long ago did this happen?"

"Just last week."

Jack raised an eyebrow. The suicide could be a coincidence, but he didn't usually believe in coincidences, so he made a quick note of it, then turned to Miles. "Did Elliot ever talk to you about the company?"

"He hired me on occasion when he needed a

personal attorney," Miles said. "I'm not involved with the business, although he would ask my opinion on business matters on occasion—as a friend. Elliot would have told me if there was something contentious going on with the company."

Jack studied him as he spoke. He was breathing easy, the expression on his face still sad. He was telling the truth.

Jack turned his attention back to Victoria. "Who can I talk to at the company?"

She didn't hesitate. "Charles Stratton is the CFO and the second in charge after Elliot. You can talk to him." Jack wrote the name down. "And Derek Lowe, he's the company's general counsel. Derek would know about any legal disputes, but Elliot hadn't mentioned any. I think he would have confided in me... or Miles."

"You know a lot about the business."

Victoria nodded. "I worked at Banks Oil & Gas for several years, then quit just before we were married."

"Do you still work?"

"I do, part-time. I write articles and technical papers for industry journals. And I occasionally guest lecture at Colorado School of Mines."

"So you work mainly from home?"

She nodded again.

Jack spent the next several minutes asking more

questions. When he was finished, Victoria walked him to the door.

"Where are you staying?" she asked.

"At a campground on Shadow Mountain Lake. Why?"

"Just curious," she answered. "There's a place for everything, and everything in its place, Detective— you've heard the saying. I just wanted to know where your place was. I hope the drive here wasn't too far."

He told her it wasn't. *She's an interesting one*, Jack thought. And he wasn't sure what to make of her yet.

She held the door open for him. "Thank you again for taking the case, Detective."

"That was one of my two conditions, remember?"

"What was?"

"Referring to me as 'detective.'"

She grinned apologetically. "I might have a hard time with that one."

He nodded once. "It might be a few days before you hear from me. I won't call every day, just when I have information I think you'd want to know about. But I'll call in a day or so. I'll have more questions for you."

"Anytime. Thank you again."

As Jack walked to his truck, he thought about Elliot Banks—wealthy businessman lying dead on the floor in his multimillion-dollar mansion in the middle of the night. Then Jack thought about

Victoria Banks—cool and composed, and completely unreadable.

If someone had asked him at that moment, Jack wouldn't be able to swear his new client was innocent of murder.

CHAPTER 12

WHEN MILES PRESTON left, Victoria had been standing at the back door looking tired and frail. But he knew appearances could be deceiving and that Victoria was anything but delicate. Heaven help the man who underestimated her. Despite everything that had happened in the last forty-eight hours, she seemed shook but determined and in complete control.

He was reluctant to leave her, couldn't shake the growing concern that he was leaving her in the large house alone. He had suggested she move into the Four Seasons temporarily, or maybe lease a condo. He had gone so far as to google Vail condos for rent, shown her the leasing information on a beautiful two-bedroom overlooking the center of Vail Village, but she politely informed him she wasn't interested.

He knew Elliot wouldn't be happy knowing she was alone in the same house where he had been murdered only two nights before. But there was only so much Miles could do without coming across like an overbearing big brother, and he didn't want her to think of him as that.

He made the turn off Forest Drive headed to the Four Seasons. He would need to be back in Denver in the morning, but he was already mentally going through his schedule to see when he could return to Vail in the next few days. Victoria would need him. Of course, if the police requested another interview, he would come back immediately.

When he suggested she give the police more time before hiring Jack Martin, she had remained silent. She listened to his arguments about letting them do their job, giving them time to rule her out as a suspect before spending her time and money hiring a stranger she had only seen on the news. He reminded her that, although she was extremely wealthy, most of her finances would be tied up until Elliot's will was probated, which could be months. And as her friend, he advised her to limit any unnecessary expenses.

When Miles was finished talking, Victoria stared silently out the study window into the growing darkness. When she finally turned back to him, Miles knew he had made a mistake.

When she spoke again, her tone had changed. "I've hired Jack Martin. I was hoping you would agree with the decision, but I'm okay with it that you're not."

Miles wanted to help her, implore her to be

reasonable, but he knew it would be futile. He let the conversation drop.

"Victoria, do you need anything before I go?" he asked just before leaving.

She laid a hand on his arm, and her expression softened. "No. You're already doing plenty. But thank you. It's been a long day. Get a good night's sleep and be careful driving back to Denver in the morning."

And just like that, he'd been summarily dismissed.

As he pulled into the Four Seasons parking garage and took the ramp down to a lower level, Miles remembered the first time he'd met Victoria. She had been Elliot's date. Miles was with some girl whose name he no longer remembered, but he remembered the impression Victoria made. Long and lithe in a silk slip dress. Distant, yet beautiful and classy. He remembered thinking that if Michelle Pfeiffer had been a brunette in *Scarface*, she would have resembled Victoria.

Even then, Miles knew short, squat attorneys never got women like that, but that was okay. She was with Elliot, and Elliot was his friend. Miles had been the best man at their wedding two years later. Now he had to keep Victoria from being arrested for Elliot's murder.

Miles still couldn't believe Elliot was dead. They should have had years of time together—skiing and fishing and just being friends. If only things had turned out differently.

He took in a long breath as he swung the car into an empty parking spot, shut off the ignition, and sat thinking. He mentally sorted through the evidence the police had lain out and thought about what else he knew about the case. It made him nervous.

Unless something came up, he knew Victoria was in a nearly impossible situation. He knew Victoria wasn't guilty of murder, but he was worried the police did.

CHAPTER 13

Monday, June 18

CHARLES STRATTON SAT at a round table in the breakfast room. Early-morning sunlight spilled through tall windows, casting faint patterns across the black-and-white marble floor. The chandelier overhead added the additional light Charles needed to read the morning paper.

He was almost finished when Katie walked in and plopped down across the table from him, throwing her legs over an arm of the chair. She was wrapped in a pink fuzzy robe, her hands cradling a steaming cup of coffee. Her hair was pinned back, and her eyes were puffy with dark circles underneath.

It never ceased to amaze Charles how, with hair and makeup, Katie could transform herself from the little troll she was when she woke up each morning into the blond bombshell he liked to show off to his friends—and a few of his enemies.

Their marriage had never produced children, despite their years of trying. He was grateful for it, but admitting that to Katie would be disastrous.

Katie was expensive, but keeping her happy was a lot cheaper than a divorce.

She yawned, and Charles looked away. He turned a page of the newspaper and held it aloft, blocking her from his view. A quick scan of the business section and he would be on his way to the office. But first he wanted to find out what Katie had learned from her visit with Victoria. He waited to ask, not wanting to appear eager.

Katie cleared her throat. "So, what's on your schedule today?"

"Full day at the office. I probably won't be home for dinner."

"No surprise," she said and took a sip of the coffee. There was a hint of resentment in her voice.

Charles was relieved she didn't push the subject any further. The night before, when she had gotten home from Vail, he hadn't been there. His excuse was always that he was at the office. Sometimes that was true, and sometimes it wasn't.

"So, how was your visit with Victoria?" he asked in a casual voice, turning a page of the paper.

"Interesting." Katie set the coffee cup on the table and picked at a small chip in the porcelain handle. "She seems to be doing okay. I was expecting her to be a little more upset—crying or something, but she wasn't. But you know Victoria. She's never been one to wear her heart on her sleeve."

That's an understatement, Charles thought. He marveled the two women had become such good friends despite being so different. Where Katie radiated her emotions like a beacon, Victoria was uncommonly aloof. Aside from her stunning good looks, Charles never understood what Elliot saw in her.

Katie still fiddled with the cup. "She's hiring that detective who solved the Hermes Strangler case in Aspen."

Startled, Charles looked up. "Hiring him for what?"

"To find Elliot's murderer. She doesn't trust the police to do it, I guess." Katie took another sip of coffee and set the cup back on the table. "And she thinks there might be a connection between Elliot's murder and Bob Hawkins's suicide."

"What in the world makes her think that?" Charles's concentration was shot. No longer interested in the paper, he shook it, then folded it in half and stuck it in his briefcase lying open on the table.

Katie shrugged. "That crazy Doris Reed. She said Doris called Elliot the night Bob died, insisting it couldn't have been a suicide." Katie frowned and shook her head.

"If it wasn't suicide, what does Doris think it was?"

"Murder."

"Doris thinks Bob Hawkins was murdered?" Charles leaked disbelief into his tone.

Katie shrugged again, lifted the cup to her mouth but stopped. "Maybe she's got a point. You know he had that young family, and right before the merger... He would have made a lot of money after the merger, wouldn't he?"

Charles stood up, smoothing the front of his pin-striped slacks. He grabbed the matching jacket off the back of the chair. "I've got to get to the office. I'm already running late."

Katie twisted in her chair to face him as he came around the side of the table. "But why would a man about to make a ton of money commit suicide? Usually it's the opposite—they've gone broke. Think about it."

"No more thinking, darling. It's not your strong suit." Charles bent and kissed her on the top of her head, then pulled his briefcase off the table. She glared up at him, opened her mouth to protest, but he continued. "There was no evidence that Bob Hawkins's suicide was murder. That's a crazy conspiracy theory I would expect from someone like Doris Reed, not Victoria—and *certainly* not you."

It was an indirect compliment, which seemed to appease her somewhat. He enjoyed toying with her. If she was still upset by the time he got home, he would promise her a dinner at LeRoux, one of her favorites.

He took several steps toward the door and turned back. It was now confirmed, Victoria was going to be a problem.

"You should go see Victoria again sometime soon," Charles said. "I'm sure she's hurting more than she shows."

Katie thought about it, then nodded. "You're probably right. I'll call her today." She swung her feet to the floor and stood up, following Charles to the back door.

When he turned to give her another kiss, she stopped him. "Maybe if I wasn't still mad at you."

He pretended to pout.

Katie smiled briefly, then let it drop. "Later—if you're lucky."

Charles stepped outside, and she shut the door behind him.

CHAPTER 14

As JACK MARTIN drove north toward downtown Denver, he could see Mile High Stadium looming in the distance. He'd been in Colorado two seasons now but hadn't made it to a Broncos game. If he was still in Colorado in the fall, he vowed to make it to one.

He missed football. He still watched it on television some, but he would love to suit up one more time. He'd started playing in middle school, didn't fully blossom until his sophomore year in high school, when he'd been pulled up to varsity. By the end of his junior season, he'd had his pick of Division I schools—Alabama, Michigan, UCLA. The list had seemed endless. And for once in his life—the only time in his life—the world was at his feet. In the end, he'd chosen Texas A&M. It had been a good fit for a boy from southeastern Louisiana.

For a split second he let himself wonder what could have been had he avoided the injury in the game against Florida his senior year. He just as quickly dismissed the thought—he had learned long ago not to go there. Looking back was always pointless.

He took the ramp off the freeway into downtown and caught a glimpse of the gold dome of the state capitol building glistening in the morning sun. At a stoplight, he checked the GPS on his phone to refresh his memory about how to get to the Heritage Plaza building.

When he turned onto Seventeenth Street, he saw it, a giant brown granite and glass building that rose at least sixty-two floors. He knew that because the sixty-second floor was where the Banks Oil & Gas executive offices were located. He was on his way to see the CFO, Charles Stratton.

Jack took one last look at the building as he pulled into the underground garage. A granite monument at the street proudly displayed the name of the building. Just below it was BANKS OIL & GAS spelled out in large brass letters. There were various other company names in smaller letters that Jack couldn't read.

Inside, the elevator opened onto the sixty-second floor like a revelation, the dark confinement of the elevator opening to a view of the snow-capped Rockies in the distance that nearly took his breath away.

He stood just outside the elevator, letting his eyes adjust to the flood of natural light. The lobby extended to the exterior wall of the building, floor-to-ceiling glass windows that looked west. To the left was a long reception desk made of the same granite that covered the floor. To the right were two separate seating areas with coffee-colored velvet couches and an assortment of leather chairs.

A petite redhead looked up at him and smiled. "How can I help you?" She had a Midwestern accent.

"I need to speak with Charles Stratton."

"Do you have an appointment?"

"No."

The receptionist's smile faded.

Before she could come up with an excuse, Jack added, "Tell him Detective Jack Martin is here to ask him a few questions about the murder of his boss."

She stared at him slack-jawed. After a few seconds, she recovered enough to take down his name and asked him to have a seat.

Jack chose a leather chair facing the elevators. Habit learned the hard way. He never put his back to the entrance.

After settling into the chair, he looked around. The reception area was a cacophony of browns— brown granite, brown velvet, brown leather. But to his left, three large portraits in bright colors hung in stark contrast along the wall.

He studied the one closest to him. The subject was unmistakable—even in profile. General George Custer, American military hero who died at the hands of a Sioux warrior at the Battle of the Little Bighorn in Montana.

The portraits on either side were of two Native American chiefs. Jack thought he recognized one of them. Geronimo, maybe? The same artist's signature was scribbled on the bottom of each of them. Jack leaned over and squinted and his eyebrows shot up. Andy Warhol.

The office decor was strikingly similar to the mansion's in Vail. Jack was impressed. Elliot Banks's collection appeared meticulously curated. It must have cost him a fortune.

He hadn't been sitting long when another pretty twentysomething came to retrieve him. He followed her down a wide hallway into a meeting room, where she asked him to take a seat at a long conference table.

"Mr. Stratton is just pulling into the parking garage. He will be right with you," she said as she closed the set of glass doors.

As he waited, Jack glanced around the room. He had never seen an office like this one before. Except for the glass doors and the large windows, the walls were a deep red. They looked weathered. He leaned over and touched one. Leather—leather walls. He gave a quiet whistle. Bank Oil & Gas had it going on.

There was a long marble-topped side table with all the accoutrements to make a cup of coffee, but no one had offered him any. He sat in silence, taking it all in.

He was seated in one of ten chairs positioned around the table. In the center were various plates of pastries and small cookies, baskets of protein bars and dried fruit. There was a telephone in the center of it all. It had a dozen buttons for different extensions. A faint green light was lit up next to one of them.

After a few minutes, a tall man in a dark pinstriped suit swung open one of the glass doors and unceremoniously took a seat at the head of the table. There were no introductions.

"I'm a very busy man, Detective. How can I help you?"

He seemed rushed. Whether he was or not didn't matter. Jack disliked him instantly.

"Charles Stratton?"

"That's me."

"I'm here regarding Elliot Banks's murder."

"You're not the police."

Jack took in a deep breath, holding his growing temper. "No, I'm not, but I've been hired by Victoria Banks to find Elliot's killer."

Charles Stratton jerked his chin toward the ceiling and stared down his nose, appraising Jack. But Jack ignored him. He dug a small notebook out of the pocket of his jeans, laid it on the table, and took his time opening it to a blank page. He looked around, then pulled a ballpoint pen from a container that held a dozen or so in the center of the table.

Charles Stratton sighed impatiently. "Can we get on with this, Detective? Legally, I don't have to answer any of your questions. You're not the police—"

"We've already established that," Jack replied.

The executive looked like he could chew glass. He sat heavy in his seat, staring at Jack.

"Just a few questions," Jack said with an easy smile, irritating the man further.

Stratton pulled up a sleeve and pretended to look at his watch—a giant gold Rolex. "I've got ten minutes max, and then I've got to be on a call. Things are crazy around here since Elliot's death."

"I want to ask you a few questions about the business."

"I'll tell you what I can. Banks Oil & Gas is a publicly traded company and a lot of information is public record, but a lot of it isn't."

"Are there any ongoing lawsuits?"

Stratton looked at him like he was stupid. "We're an oil and gas company, Detective. There are *always* ongoing lawsuits."

"Any particularly contentious ones?"

"They're *all* contentious. But if you're asking me if anyone related to one of them would benefit from killing Elliot..." He pretended to consider the possibility, then nodded with a smirk. "All of them would."

This wasn't going well. Jack decided to change his tactic.

"To your knowledge, has anyone made an overt threat to harm Elliot Banks in any way? A party to one of the lawsuits? A competitor? A disgruntled former employee even?"

Stratton shook his head. "No. None that I've heard of." He leaned back in his chair, stuck his hands behind his head. "And I'm second in charge around here—first in charge now. I would have heard about it."

If the man was upset over his boss's murder, Jack couldn't tell. "What about investors?"

"What about them?"

Jack's jaw went rigid, but he spoke in an even tone. "Any unhappy investors?"

"None."

"Not a single one? A public company must have hundreds—or thousands—of investors."

"We do, but most are institutional investors—held in mutual funds or by insurance companies. There are only a handful of substantial private investors. It's all in the public record."

"And none of those investors are unhappy with the price of oil…or your stock price? I notice it's fluctuated wildly recently." Jack had done his research. The price of the company's stock had been anything but consistent the previous year, not surprising considering the fluctuating oil market. He knew the energy business was cyclical. "No one unhappy with management or the state of the business?"

Stratton brought his chair back to an upright position, laid his hands on the table, and leveled an impatient look. "As I said before, Detective. None." He threw up his hands. "There are plenty of people who would benefit from murdering Elliot Banks, but I don't know of a single one who would actually do it. I wish I could help you, but I can't. I'm afraid I don't know anything that would help you." He pushed his chair back from the table and propped his hands on his lap.

Jack knew when an interview was over.

Charles Stratton stood up, pushed open one of the glass doors, and waited impatiently as Jack collected his notebook and replaced the pen.

"Could you direct me to the men's room?" Jack asked as he walked through the open door.

"There." Stratton pointed to a door just down the hall.

"There's a good chance I'll have more questions for you in the next few days."

"Call my secretary. She'll know if I'm available."

With that, the arrogant CFO—now CEO—turned on his heel and left.

Jack pushed open the heavy oak door to the men's room. Charles Stratton had intentionally been no help. Jack was convinced the now first in charge at Banks Oil & Gas knew more than what he was letting on.

Charles Stratton might think he was off the hook, but Jack wasn't finished with him yet.

CHAPTER 15

JACK DRIED HIS hands and pushed open the men's room door.

"*Psst.*"

He looked around but didn't see anyone.

"*Psst.*"

Then he saw it—a head stuck out from behind an office door. It was soft and round and topped with a bright red poof of hair that looked like an exotic flavor of cotton candy. And it was looking at him.

"Come here, Detective," she whispered, thrusting a fleshy white arm from behind the door and motioning him over with a finger. "I need to talk to you."

Jack looked around, but there was no one else in the hallway. He wasn't sure what to make of the situation, but he decided, what the hell?

He walked toward the floating head and fleshy white arm. When he got closer, the woman pulled the door open just enough for him to squeeze past her into an office.

It was small—a desk and two chairs. The desk was covered in stacks of papers, and a computer monitor sat to one side. A table behind the desk held a telephone, an assortment of framed photographs, and more stacks of paper. The smell of flowers was strong, but Jack didn't see any.

He turned around to look at her. She was a gnome of a little woman, probably early sixties. Short and round, with hair dyed the color of a Coke can. He wasn't sure he'd ever seen hair that red before. Large round earrings like hot pink gumballs hung on either side of her head.

She motioned for him to have a seat, then clambered around him, lowering her bulk into the chair behind the desk. She was breathless, struggling with her size or nerves, Jack wasn't sure yet which.

He sat down. He glanced past her at the clutter behind her desk. It was a mishmash of knickknacks and photographs.

Despite the two of them being alone, the woman leaned across the desk and whispered, "I heard what Mr. Stratton told you." Her eyes narrowed to angry slits, and she shook her head, sending her bubble gum earrings swinging furiously. "He didn't tell you everything."

Jack was curious but cautious. He watched her and waited for her to continue.

The woman suddenly heaved her weight back in the chair with a startled look on her face, like she'd just realized she wasn't wearing any clothes.

"Oh my, forgive me," she said, leaning forward again. "I'm Elliot's private secretary." Her face instantly grew sad. "I *was* Elliot's private secretary. Doris Reed," she said, extending her hand across the desk.

Jack suspected the woman was a screw short of being completely assembled, but her position in the company—and proximity to Elliot Banks—could prove informative. He wondered how she had heard his conversation with Charles Stratton, then remembered the single green light on the telephone. Doris Reed was a sly one, he decided.

"Jack Martin," he said, shaking her hand.

"Oh, I know who you are, honey. I know all about that case in Aspen you solved—the Hermes Strangler. And now I know Victoria has gone and hired you to help her find out what happened to Elliot. Bless her heart. Sweet thing, that one. Some people don't think so, but I do."

Jack wondered what she meant about Victoria, but he wanted to get the conversation back on track. If he needed to, he would ask her about Victoria later. "So, you think Charles Stratton was holding something back when I questioned him?"

With renewed excitement, Doris leaned across the desk toward him. "Was he ever." She dropped her voice to a loud whisper again. "Honey, he didn't tell you the truth about anything. The lawsuits, disgruntled investors—there's one in particular. But most importantly, he didn't tell you about Bob Hawkins."

"Who's Bob Hawkins?"

"Who *was* Bob Hawkins is more like it," Doris said, shaking her head, sending her earrings swinging again. "He was the controller for Banks Oil & Gas until last week…until he committed suicide." As she said the word "suicide," she made air quotes with her fingers.

Jack remembered Victoria mentioning the suicide, but she hadn't given him the guy's name. "You don't think he killed himself?"

"No. And I don't think Elliot did, either. Now Elliot's dead." She had raised her voice to a crescendo but dropped it back down and leaned in closer. "You want to know what I think?"

Jack wasn't sure if he did. He had hoped to pay Harold Lamken a visit before the end of the day. According to Victoria, as their house manager, Lamken had the only other key to the house besides her and Elliot, and Jack wanted to talk to him.

He checked his watch. Traffic on Interstate 70 would already be heavy. He knew he wasn't going to make it back to Vail and decided to hear her out.

"What do you think?" he asked Doris.

"I think Bob was murdered—just like Elliot. Bob didn't fit the profile of someone you'd suspect of suicide." She ticked the points off on her fingers.

"He was always happy—never depressed. He was a family man. He had a loving wife and two precious kids. He had a good job here, and Elliot thought very highly of him."

Jack knew outward appearances were rarely accurate and that seemingly happy people committed suicide every day. "How did he do it? Was there a note?"

She shook her head, sending the gumballs airborne again. "No note. He was out to dinner with his family, a little place on Colfax on the west side of town. The story his wife gave the police was that they were having dinner—the two of them and the kids—and Bob excused himself, saying he got a text and needed to step outside to make a phone call. She said he'd been working long nights and weekends on the merger with Centennial State Energy, and she wasn't surprised he would take a call while they were out to dinner. But he didn't come back. Then, a little while later, she said they heard all the sirens and commotion outside. The police kept everyone in the restaurant, wouldn't let them leave. She tried calling Bob, but he didn't answer. About twenty minutes later, a detective from Denver PD came into the restaurant looking for her and told her what had happened. They later ruled the cause of death as suicide."

"But you don't think it was?"

"No. Does that sound like a setup for a suicide to you?"

Jack agreed it didn't sound typical—then again, no suicide was *typical*. He knew all too well that they were all tragic, and devastating for the families left behind. But statistics showed around three-quarters of suicides occur at the victim's home. Why would Bob Hawkins take his family out to dinner first? He made a mental note to google the story when he got back to the trailer to find out more information than what was being filtered through Doris Reed.

"What was the evidence it *was* a suicide? How did he die?"

Doris grabbed an open can of grape soda on the desk and took a large gulp. "Gunshot wound to the temple. Sitting in his car."

"They found the gun?"

She nodded. "They found it on his lap."

"Any prints on it?"

"Bob's prints were the only ones."

"His wife didn't mention he'd been depressed or upset about anything? No financial problems? Marital problems?"

Doris looked back up at him with renewed vigor. "No. You see, that's just it. No depression, no health issues, no financial issues, no marital issues—and your beautiful young family only yards away, enjoying a dinner out together, and you don't even leave a note?"

They heard footsteps outside the office in the hallway. Somewhere, a door closed.

Jack waited for her to continue.

"Just a minute," Doris said as she wriggled out of her chair and went to the door. She opened it slowly, sticking her head out. She looked up and down the hallway, then closed the door and sat back down.

She dropped her voice again. "Here's my theory. Bob's death wasn't a suicide but was *murder*—just like Elliot. I don't know why, but my bet is that it has something to do with the merger, or the disgruntled investor I mentioned. Boots Hamer."

Jack pulled his notebook from the pocket of his jeans, glanced at the stacks of paper and reports covering the desk. "Do you have a pen?"

"Sure, honey. Just a minute." Doris slid open a desk drawer and rummaged around until she came out with a pen. It was red. "Here you go."

"Boots Hamer?" Jack repeated, jotting down the name in his notebook.

"That's it. I don't know what the story is with Boots yet," Doris said, "but he's one of Elliot's first investors. He's been with Elliot since the beginning. Banks Oil & Gas has wells all over his properties in Weld County, just north of town. But he and Elliot were friends, too. Everything was fine with Boots all these years, until about a month or so ago."

"What happened?"

"Like I told you, I don't know yet."

She watched Jack, probably trying to read his reaction, but Jack was an expert in making sure he had none. He waited for her to continue.

"Let me show you something," she finally said.

She pulled up rhinestone-encrusted reading glasses hanging from a chain around her neck and put them on, moved the can of grape soda out of the way, and turned the computer monitor toward him. She wiggled her mouse until the screen lit up.

"This is my schedule. See here?" She pointed at the monitor. "I always made a note on my schedule when Elliot was out of the office—so I wouldn't schedule any meetings or anything else for him. In the last month, Elliot was out of the office several times to meet with Boots Hamer. This wasn't typical. He'd usually only see Boots a few times a year—at stockholder meetings, or if Elliot made a special trip out to the wells. He still liked to do that every once in a while. He said it reminded him of the old days when he'd check the wells himself. Of course, now we have a fleet of producers who do that.

"Anyway…back to what I was saying." She pulled a keyboard from under a stack of papers and began typing, her stubby fingers and bright red nails flying over the keys. "See all these meetings? Here, here, and here?" she asked, pointing to different dates on the screen. "Elliot had three meetings with Boots in the last few weeks. That was highly unusual. Something was up, and now Elliot is dead."

Jack had run across conspiracy theorists before. As an agent in the FBI office in Houston, he'd come across no shortage of kooks suspecting their neighbors of planning government assassinations, bank robberies, or being in cahoots with a Mexican cartel. But initially they had to take all the allegations seriously, never knowing which kook might actually have a credible lead. And Jack took every lead seriously. He didn't want any disasters happening on his watch.

Doris leaned closer to the monitor. She was saying something else about the schedule, but Jack was drawn to the photographs on the table behind her. There were scores of them. Some were obviously family members, similar to Doris in size and shape. Some were younger—her children, or nieces and nephews maybe, since she wasn't wearing a wedding ring.

But then he saw a picture of Tom Selleck. It was the famous publicity photo for the television series *Magnum P.I.* Selleck was dressed in a Hawaiian shirt and flashing a dimpled grin from the driver's seat of the famous red Ferrari.

Doris must have noticed his stare. "Tom's my cousin," she said. "Well, distant cousin."

Jack scanned the rest of the pictures, then pointed to one of Angela Lansbury dressed as her character,

Jessica Fletcher, in the mystery series *Murder, She Wrote.*

Doris turned and saw what Jack pointed at. "Angela Lansbury." She shrugged. "I like her."

Jack turned his attention back to the woman across the desk, who smelled of cheap rose perfume and grape soda, a woman who obviously loved her family and friends but was also obsessed with television detectives and conspiracy theories.

Doris was chattering something about the schedules again, but Jack cleared his throat and pretended to glance at his watch. She stopped talking and looked at him.

"I'm sorry, I really need to get going," Jack said.

Doris struggled out of the chair, came around the desk, and held out her hand. "Thank you for hearing me out, Detective. I'm going to keep investigating this on my end. You look into Bob Hawkins and Boots Hamer. Honey, I tell you, there's something there."

Jack nodded. "I will."

As he made his way down the elevator to the parking garage, Jack thought about his conversation with Charles Stratton. Stratton was hiding something. Things at Banks Oil & Gas weren't as rosy as Doris Reed's perfume.

Could Elliot Banks's nosy former assistant, the

one with the cherry-red hair and a habit of listening in on company conversations, be on to something?

Jack wanted to dismiss Doris Reed as a crackpot. All the signs pointed to it. But something in his gut told him not to.

CHAPTER 16

HAROLD LAMKEN STOOD at the open doors to the study, a beat-up cowboy hat in one hand and a large wrench in the other.

Victoria was sitting at Elliot's desk, her back to him. There was a small stack of papers and an open laptop in front of her. She was bent over, reading something, and hadn't heard him come in.

Harold watched her. She looked pretty in her jeans and simple blouse, her long hair pulled back in a ponytail to keep it out of her way while she read. Harold preferred her that way—simple. Not made-up and in fancy clothes like she was in the photograph Elliot kept on his desk.

Harold couldn't see the photograph behind her, but he didn't need to—he knew it well. He had looked at it numerous times. He conjured the image in his mind—Victoria dressed in a fancy long gown and Elliot in a tuxedo, his arm around her. Elliot looked happy. But why wouldn't he be? Before he was murdered, he had everything—money, status, vacations, the giant house in Vail…and Victoria.

Harold gripped the wrench tighter and took a step into the room, one of his boots catching an uneven spot on the wood floor of the study. Victoria heard him and turned around.

"Oh, hello, Harold." She smiled at him briefly before turning back to what she was reading. "I didn't hear you come in."

"I—I hope I didn't scare you."

She turned back to him. "No, of course you didn't scare me. I feel safer when I know that you're here."

Harold dipped his head, embarrassed. He stuck the wrench in his back pocket. "Um, thank you, Victoria. About Elliot…" His voice trailed off, and he had to swallow, not able to continue.

Victoria got up from the desk, walked over to him, and laid a hand on his arm, offering him a wan smile. She didn't usually show emotion, but Harold saw both sadness and kindness in her eyes. At that moment, he thought she looked like an angel.

"You don't have to say anything, Harold," she said. "You've worked for Elliot a long time. You weren't just an employee. He considered you a friend. I know this is devastating for you, too."

Harold nodded and took a step back, twisting his hat in his hands. "I fixed that leak under the guest bathroom sink upstairs and replaced the loose rock on the outside wall that Elliot wanted me to. If you don't need anything else, I'll be leaving now."

"No, I don't need anything. Thank you."

He hesitated in the doorway. She looked thin, almost frail. The guilt and fear that had haunted him every waking hour for nearly three days intensified. He wanted to help her somehow, didn't want to leave her yet.

He cleared his throat. "Would you like me to pick you something up to eat? I can bring it back—"

"No." She shook her head.

"Are you sure? It would be no trouble. I could swing by—"

"I'm fine, Harold, really. I have some more work I want to get done tonight." When she saw him watching her, concerned, she added, "Really, I'm fine. But thank you."

That was all Harold could do. He said goodbye, told her he would be back on Thursday, and left.

Thirty minutes later, Harold set the twelve-pack of Keystone Light he had picked up at the convenience store next to his recliner. He dug through the seat cushions until he found the remote, then clicked on the television. The Rockies were playing the Dodgers, and he was determined to drink himself into oblivion before the third inning.

If just for the night, he wanted to forget about Elliot, about Victoria, and about what had happened three nights earlier.

CHAPTER 17

WHEN VICTORIA TOLD Harold she felt safer with him around, it had been the truth. Although she was fastidious about locking doors, she never considered herself a nervous person. She didn't constantly turn and look in parking lots, wondering if someone was following her. She knew people like that. Katie was like that. But Victoria wasn't.

But with Elliot gone, the house seemed even larger. And she was alone.

The sun had dropped below the horizon, and the sky was getting dark fast. She could just make out the twinkling lights at the base of Vail Mountain in the waning daylight and suddenly felt like a fish in a fishbowl. Anyone outside could look into the lit room and see her, but she wouldn't be able to see them.

She thought about the dream—the man in the forest watching her, waiting. She got up from the desk and pushed the button that electronically lowered the shades over the windows. She would have to be more careful.

Back at the desk, she returned her attention to the

stack of company papers. Production reports, lease contracts, letters, royalty estimates. They were the documents Elliot had been reading the night he was murdered. The cleaning crew had done a meticulous job. Except for a few documents with blood spatter, the room was spotless.

Victoria flipped through each page, willing herself to look past any blood and scanning the contents before placing it into an open folder. For another hour, she sorted through page after page, setting aside what she thought needed to be returned to Charles Stratton at Banks Oil & Gas, and placing the rest in the open file folder on the desk.

When she finished, she put her elbows on the desk and sank her head into her hands. The harmony of her life that she had fought so hard for had been obliterated in a single night. She needed to put it back together, put herself back together. Everything felt so out of control.

Finished with the paperwork, Victoria turned her attention to Elliot's laptop. There would be unopened emails, both business and personal, that Elliot synced with his computer at the office. She booted up his laptop, typed in the password, and went straight to his email account. There were almost a hundred unopened messages following Elliot's murder from people who, obviously, at the time they sent them, hadn't been aware of what had happened.

First, Victoria scanned for any messages related to their personal accounts—bank records, credit card statements. She would get all the financial records transferred to her own email address. There were a dozen investment accounts alone. It would take days to get it all straightened out, and she wanted to get started on it immediately.

There was an email from the insurance company that insured the Vail house and their condo in Denver. A payment might be coming due. She forwarded it to her own email address to check later. She kept scrolling and found a utility bill for the Vail house and a renewal contract for the hanger in Eagle, where Elliot kept the jet. She forwarded those as well.

Another email caught her eye. It was from a professor who taught petroleum engineering at Colorado School of Mines. Victoria had taken two of the professor's classes while she was in school and recognized his name. She clicked on the email to open it and saw that it was an invitation asking Elliot to speak to his class.

Victoria read the message. The professor thanked Elliot for his support of the school in the past—the guest lectures he had given, the financial donations. He praised Elliot for having changed the lives of so many first-generation and low-income students by paying their tuitions all four years, then giving several of them jobs at Banks Oil & Gas when they graduated. Victoria knew Elliot had made substantial financial contributions to the school, but she hadn't known the extent of it.

The professor went on to update Elliot on several students he had helped over the years—where they were living and working. One student had married and started a family. It was obvious the professor had contacted Elliot before, referring to previous emails and updates.

Through the professor's words, Victoria was struck by the depth of Elliot's generosity and kindness. His contributions to local and national charities were well known; he had received several awards for his philanthropy over the years. But Elliot had kept many of the details of his generosity private—even from Victoria.

She didn't realize she was crying until the letters on the monitor blurred. She wiped the tears away with the back of her hand and kept reading.

When she was finished, she decided to take a warm shower to regroup. There was a lot of work to be done, and she couldn't afford to spend any more time on sentimentalities. She made a note to contact the professor, offer to continue the support for any students Elliot was currently helping. She didn't want Elliot's death to disrupt the help he had been giving them. She knew it was what Elliot would have wanted.

In the bathroom, Victoria turned the water on hotter than normal, then stood under the showerhead and let the water fall over her. She wanted to wash away the pain and the grief, the memory of what she and Elliot had that was now lost. She still couldn't believe he was gone. Their life together had been nearly perfect. What had happened? Where had it all gone wrong?

Victoria looked down at the drain and imagined her life as she knew it swirling away with the water. Then she reached deep inside for the courage that had seen her through tragedy once before. She lingered in the steaming water, letting it melt away the tension.

After a few minutes, she decided that it had been enough. A half hour later, after pulling on her favorite silk pajamas and stopping in the kitchen for a glass of water, Victoria was back at Elliot's desk in the study.

She scrolled through his emails from the day he had been killed. He would have already deleted some of them, Victoria thought, filed others. She would check the email folders next. But she knew the emails that Elliot thought were important, the ones regarding unresolved business or personal issues, would still be in his in-box.

She scanned the subject lines. There were messages from Charles Stratton and Derek Lowe and one from an executive at a mutual fund—one of Banks Oil & Gas's largest institutional investors. All were regarding the upcoming merger.

Victoria read through an email from the investment banking firm Elliot used to take the company public years earlier. Elliot and the CEO had become friends, and Victoria knew the same firm was handling the merger with Centennial State Energy.

None of the messages seemed out of the ordinary, until she noticed one with the subject line "Significant Irregularities." She didn't recognize the name of the sender.

Victoria clicked on the message and opened it, glanced at its contents, then scrolled to the bottom of the page. She saw the sender's name and the name of his company.

At first she was confused. Then the possibilities came into focus, and she drew in a sharp breath. Her heart sank as she read the email a second time, careful not to miss anything.

There had to be a rational explanation. Victoria reached across the desk for her cell phone, found the number in her contacts list, and hit the call button.

She heard the call ringing on the other end and wondered aloud, "Oh, Elliot. What did you do?"

CHAPTER 18

BY NINE O'CLOCK, Clark Poindexter had been at his desk for more than fifteen hours. Outside, the sky had gone dark hours earlier, but he hadn't noticed.

He sat in the dark room. A single-bulb banker's lamp cast a pool of light over the secondhand desk, illuminating the piles of paper stacked in front of him. For hours, Clark had printed and sorted through reams of reports and audits, dug into the financial weeds of Banks Oil & Gas like only a forensic accountant could do.

Except for the whir of the window air-conditioning unit, the small, nondescript office perched above Jackson's Deli on the eastern edge of downtown Denver was quiet. The building's only other tenant, a middle-aged cell phone repairman with a proclivity for body piercings and tattoos, had left hours earlier.

Underneath him, the deli would be wrapping up the dinner shift. The smell of roast beef and onions had faded with the daylight.

Clark leaned back in his chair, propped his wire-rimmed glasses on the top of his tall forehead, and pinched the bridge of his nose, screwing his eyes shut. He knew it was time to call it a day, knew his cognitive analytical skills had reached the point of diminishing return, but he wasn't ready to quit just yet.

One more audit file, one more Securities and Exchange Commission report, maybe one more quarterly production report. *Something* would jump out at him and explain why the numbers weren't adding up. There was something fishy going on at Banks Oil & Gas, and it was just a matter of time—a matter of sifting through enough accounts and analyzing the right financial data—before he would put the pieces together and figure it out.

He decided to keep working. Just one more hour, he told himself, then realized that's what he had said an hour earlier. He stood up and stretched, wrenching his neck from side to side, trying to loosen the kinks.

Clark Poindexter was a sliver of a man, average height, receding hairline, and a plain face that looked like a million others. What set him apart was an uncanny knack for numbers. Able to multiply and divide by kindergarten, he had mastered calculus by the eighth grade and spent high school taking engineering classes at a nearby university.

Originally set on majoring in chemical engineering, he had changed his mind after taking a chance elective in financial forensics. He'd graduated in three years with multiple honors from the Sloan School of Management at MIT, and then the government had come calling.

Clark had spent a decade with the FBI, analyzing financial data and uncovering complicated illegal financial schemes, before resigning to open his own practice. It wasn't a lucrative business, but it was rewarding—combing through financial data, uncovering embezzlement schemes for local businesses, and regularly testifying in court as an expert witness.

He filled a chipped coffee mug with water, stood at the window behind his desk, and sipped as he watched a busboy from the deli throw a bag of trash into a dumpster in the alley below.

Clark thought about his current case. Boots Hamer, wealthy Colorado landowner, had hired Clark to look into his declining royalties from Banks Oil & Gas. A separate company, Energy Marketing, had taken over the sales business for Banks Oil & Gas a year earlier.

Energy Marketing was owned by two Banks executives—Charles Stratton and Derek Lowe. Boots Hamer didn't trust them, thought they were somehow stealing from him. And Clark knew Boots was expecting answers from him soon.

Clark sat down and turned his attention back to the papers on his desk. Just one more hour, he told himself again.

He took a document off the stack in front of him and scanned it, noticed Elliot Banks's signature at the bottom. His murder on Friday had come as a shock.

Clark had emailed Elliot that morning, but he hadn't gotten a reply. He now knew that he never would. He had questions about the separate marketing company, about production reports and the company protocols. Somewhere there was an information breakdown, and he had hoped Elliot Banks could shed some light on it.

At their first meeting, Boots Hamer had told Clark that Elliot Banks was a close friend of his. That if there were shenanigans going on, Elliot wouldn't be involved.

But Clark Poindexter wasn't so sure.

CHAPTER 19

DEREK LOWE WAS alone in his dark penthouse with the balcony doors open to let in the night air. He stood just inside, staring at the lights of the city in the distance and swirling a gin and tonic.

It had been a long but productive day. Scores of company documents had been drawn up and filed regarding Elliot's murder and the upcoming merger with Centennial State Energy.

As he had hoped, Derek was appointed to the vacant seat on the board of directors of Banks Oil & Gas. Despite his boss's murder, there was cause for celebration. He drained the remaining contents in his glass, walked across the marble floor to the stocked bar, and mixed another drink.

Outside on the patio, he sat down on a lounge chair, the night wind blowing through his oil-slicked hair. He pushed his fingers through it, then leaned back onto the chair, shut his eyes, and took in a deep breath.

Derek had met Elliot Banks through Charles. It had been a lucrative introduction. When the company's previous general council had decided to retire a year later, Derek had been poised to step into the position.

He knew he had Charles Stratton to thank for it. Derek and Charles had attended Harvard together. Following graduation, the two had gone their separate ways—Charles to Wharton for an MBA, Derek continuing at Harvard for a law degree. But the classmates had stayed in touch. And when the position opened at Banks Oil & Gas, Charles convinced Elliot that Derek was the right man for the job.

Derek had been on track to make partner at a regional firm in Charlotte, but the opportunities were nothing like what Elliot offered him. Derek jumped at the chance to step into the lead attorney role at a publicly traded oil and gas company.

But the move was made even more profitable after Charles talked Elliot into letting the two of them form their own company. Charles and Derek set up Energy Marketing, a company that would handle the sale of the oil after it was pumped from the ground by Banks Oil & Gas.

It was a common practice—large firms letting executives set up side businesses, making their positions more attractive and keeping them from leaving for more lucrative jobs. And for Charles and Derek, the new company had proved more profitable than Derek could ever have imagined.

Now the Securities and Exchange Commission was on the verge of approving the merger with Centennial. Everything was going as planned. They had jumped through all the regulatory hoops, convinced the board that, even with Elliot's death, the merger was still the right direction for the company.

But Derek knew the deal wasn't done yet. Charles had told him their only problem could come from Victoria. As Elliot's heir, she was now the largest owner of the company's stock and held the majority of the voting shares. If she wanted—or if she suspected something was amiss—she could bring the whole plan crashing down on them.

And Victoria was now a suspect in a murder investigation. The more noise she made, the more scrutiny she would bring down on them from regulators and the media. Charles assured Derek that he wouldn't let that happen. Derek didn't understand how Charles could be so confident. What could he do if Victoria started causing problems? But Charles was a ruthless man, and there were some questions Derek knew not to ask. He had let the subject drop.

Derek thought about the money instead. He was going to make millions. And it wouldn't come a second too soon. He'd purchased the Porsche on credit and had nearly maxed out his credit cards on his last trip to Vegas. It seemed that no matter what his income was, he managed a way for his expenses to exceed it. But he wouldn't have to worry about his finances much longer.

He brought his phone up and scrolled through his emails, the bright light illuminating his face and causing him to squint. After a few seconds, he found what he was looking for: a message he had received several days earlier from his Realtor in Aspen. He opened it and scanned the listings again.

He was about to click on his favorite—a two-bedroom, two-bath in Aspen's coveted Crandall Building—but was interrupted by an incoming call.

He read the caller ID, and his hand began to tremble.

CHAPTER 20

Tuesday, June 19

VICTORIA WOKE BEFORE sunrise Tuesday morning, struggling to breathe and damp from a cold sweat. It was the dream again, and this time she remembered every detail.

The man had been in the forest. She couldn't see him and didn't know why he was there. The pine needles pricked at her bare feet as she walked. She squinted into the darkness but couldn't see, the moonlight shrouded in drifting clouds. It was cold and she wanted to turn back, but he was coming closer. She could feel him closing in, and she started to run, pushing the tree branches aside that grabbed and tore at her thin gown.

Before the man caught up to her, Victoria woke. She always did. She wouldn't let herself wonder what would happen if the dream continued, if he reached her.

She took in a deep breath and got out of bed. Leaving the lights off, she pulled a chenille robe from her closet and stepped out onto the patio off the bedroom, where she sat in the dark. The cold morning air chilled her but felt good.

She pulled her phone from a pocket of her robe and checked the time. Six o'clock. She noticed a voicemail and realized someone had called her the night before. She sat in the dark and listened to the message. The police were requesting another interview.

Victoria dropped the phone in her lap and her thoughts turned to Elliot, to his murder. Her life had never been easy, but even in the darkest times, she could never have imagined the nightmare she was living now. It must be karma, the universe getting back at her for the last few years of happiness. She decided happiness for the rest of her life was too much to hope for.

And she was running out of people to turn to for help. She was grateful for Harold Lamken. He had called to check on her after he'd left the day before. He sounded tired, but the worry in his voice was endearing. She'd told him about the meeting scheduled with the funeral home on Wednesday morning and reassured him that as long as she kept busy, she would be fine. Harold asked her the time of the appointment, then offered to go with her, but she politely declined.

Victoria ran a hand down the side of the concrete wall, cool to the touch in the morning air, and thought about Harold's offers to help. She wouldn't need the house any longer and wondered what to do about him, but quickly decided that would be a decision for another day.

Next, Victoria thought about Katie. Her dear, sweet friend lived life in a rosy bubble. Katie liked to shop and travel; she loved her designer clothes and her lunches with girlfriends. She had come to visit, offering her condolences and support, but with the growing scandal, Victoria wondered how long she would continue to be there. She knew Katie couldn't handle controversy.

There had been friends like Katie in the past. Victoria could count on them when things were going well, but at the first sign of trouble, they would slip away—stop returning calls and texts. Victoria would hang on to Katie as long as she could, but she knew it was only a matter of time before she, too, pulled away.

Then there was Charles. He had worked for Elliot for years, long before Victoria came into the picture. The two couples had shared countless dinners and vacations over the years. Victoria knew he was busy. She hadn't expected him to make the drive to Vail to see her as Katie had, but he hadn't even bothered to call. But Victoria reminded herself he had been Elliot's friend, not hers.

Her thoughts turned to the conversation with Derek Lowe the night before. She had never liked

Derek, never liked his type—the sort of man who considered women conquests to be chewed up and discarded on a whim. She hadn't expected him to gush condolences, but she *had* expected him to be sympathetic, to at least say he was sorry, maybe offer to help her in some way. He hadn't done either.

But Victoria hadn't called him for sympathy. She'd called for information. When she'd read the email from the forensic accountant hired by Boots Hamer and found out that Boots was threatening a lawsuit, Derek was the first person she'd thought to call. As the company's attorney, she assumed he would know what the trouble was about.

She had never heard of Clark Poindexter and wasn't even sure what a forensic accountant did, but she had clicked on the link to his website, read the testimonials, and knew that Banks Oil & Gas was involved in something Elliot had kept from her.

When she mentioned the email to Derek, he'd dismissed it. He neither admitted nor denied knowing about Clark Poindexter, or even that Boots Hamer was threatening to sue for fraud. He was short with her. And from the tone of his voice, Victoria thought he was about to tell her to mind her own business. Instead, he asked for Elliot's computer.

"In case there's anything sensitive on it that could affect the merger," he said in a tight voice.

Victoria stared unblinking into the dark,

remembering her surprise and indignation at his dismissive response to her call. When he'd asked for Elliot's laptop, she had refused. The more she thought about it, the angrier she got.

The sun was still below the horizon but casting the mountains in silhouette. Victoria checked the time on her phone again. It was still early, but she couldn't wait any longer. She scrolled through her contacts and found Doris Reed's number.

"Victoria, honey." The kind voice sounded surprised and concerned. "How are you holding up?"

Victoria knew that Elliot had employed Doris at a low point in her life. She was just out of rehab and, with little experience, was virtually unemployable. At the time, the Banks Oil & Gas headquarters was a two-room office on the wrong side of town. The way Elliot had described it to Victoria was that it had been a leap of faith by both of them, him *and* Doris.

But it was a leap of faith that had worked out better than either could have imagined. As Banks Oil & Gas grew, Elliot kept Doris at his side. Victoria knew she was as much a mother figure as she was a trusted executive assistant.

Doris had called Victoria and left her a voice message the morning after Elliot was murdered. She now felt guilty for not having returned the call. After a few minutes of assuring Doris she was all right, Victoria got directly to the point. She told Doris about her conversation with Derek Lowe the night before.

"He's a snake in the grass, honey. He's not going to tell you the truth. You call me the next time you want information. If I don't have it, I'll investigate and find it for you."

"I was hoping since Derek was the company's attorney, he'd know about the lawsuit that Boots is threatening. There's a forensic accountant investigating it for him. I'm worried that Elliot was involved in something unethical…maybe even illegal."

Victoria struggled to keep her voice from shaking. The idea that Elliot could have been involved in something fraudulent was a question she wasn't sure she wanted answered. Had everything she had with Elliot—their life together—been a lie? She had to know.

"Honey, I've known Elliot for almost thirty years now. He wasn't capable of doing anything unethical, much less illegal, and I know you know that, too."

Doris's voice was soft and reassuring, but Victoria still had questions.

"Then why hire a forensic accountant?" she asked. "Why is Boots—who I know was one of Elliot's best friends, as well as an investor—why was he threatening a lawsuit? And over what?"

Victoria heard Doris take in and release a long, slow breath, thinking about what to say. "I don't know, honey. But I *do* know that if there is something fishy going on, Elliot had nothing to do with it."

Victoria hoped she was right, but she wanted to be sure. "How do we know that, Doris? Maybe I should contact the forensic accountant myself. Derek Lowe won't tell me anything."

Doris harrumphed. "Forget about him, honey. Derek Lowe probably hasn't told the truth in his whole life, wouldn't know it if it jumped up and bit him in his fancy-pants ass—excuse my French. You leave this up to me. There's been some other funny business going on that I want to get to the bottom of. I'll poke around and see what I can find out. I'll let you know. But in the meantime, I don't want you fretting over anything. You've got too much going on already right now. You forget about it for a while and let old Doris look into it. Deal?"

Victoria thought about it. "I do need to make the funeral arrangements."

"You take care of that, honey. You've got enough on your plate. I'll do some digging and see what I can find out."

Victoria agreed. She knew that Doris, as an insider, was in a better position to find out what was going on at the company anyway.

Victoria originally considered going to Jack Martin and telling him about the forensic accountant, having him help her find out what the lawsuit was all about, but she had decided against it. She couldn't risk him looking too closely at her and Elliot, looking into anything aside from the murder.

There were some things she wanted to keep secret.

CHAPTER 21

EARLY TUESDAY MORNING, Jack Martin drove west on Interstate 70 through the mountains. The sun was cresting the horizon behind him, painting the sky a deep mauve.

He drove through Vail and kept going, turning south on Highway 24 toward Minturn. He was on his way to pay an unexpected visit to Harold Lamken. It was early, but Jack knew Lamken had the day off and wanted to catch him at home.

As he got closer, Jack checked the address on his GPS, then turned off the highway onto a gravel road. He wound his way farther into the forest, dust boiling over the tailgate as the truck bounced along.

After a few minutes, the trees gave way to a small clearing. A faded blue mobile home was anchored next to a river, looking like it had been there for decades. The metal skirt that wrapped the bottom of the trailer had peeled back on one corner, exposing the concrete blocks it sat on. Tall summer grass threatened to choke the whole thing.

Jack parked next to a truck that was probably

worth more than the home and got out. He took the metal steps to a small landing, pulled open a torn screen door, and knocked. After a few second, he heard footsteps inside and the door swung open.

The man staring at him frowned. "Can I help you?"

"Are you Harold Lamken?"

"Who's asking?"

"Jack Martin. I want to ask you a few questions."

The creases in Lamken's forehead deepened. "About what?"

"Elliot Banks. His wife, Victoria, hired me to look into his murder."

The man was silent a moment. "You're a detective?"

"That's right. Can I come in?"

Lamken hesitated, and Jack knew he was debating whether or not to let him in. Finally, the man stepped aside and gestured for Jack to enter.

The front door opened directly into a small living room. An assortment of worn-out furniture was arranged on matted green carpet that looked as old as the trailer. The smell of beer and cigarettes was strong, even at eight in the morning.

Lamken swiped a stack of magazines and fast-food containers off the sofa onto the floor. "Damn kids." He looked embarrassed, or nervous. "Have a seat."

"Thank you." Jack sat to one side of the sofa,

careful to avoid a deep sag in the center. Despite the unkept appearance of the trailer, Lamken looked clean—just-showered hair and a shaved beard; his shirt and jeans appeared freshly washed.

Lamken settled into a recliner next to the sofa and cleared his throat. "How can I help you, Detective?"

"I'm sure you're aware Victoria is a suspect in Elliot's murder." Jack watched for a response from Lamken. When he didn't get one, he continued. "She thinks the police are wasting their time focusing on her, and they're going to let Elliot's killer get away."

Lamken nodded slowly, appearing to agree. "They came by here early yesterday morning. Asked me a few questions."

"What did they ask?"

"If I was at the house Friday or knew of anyone who might have been there other than Victoria. I told them I don't usually work Fridays—just Mondays and Thursdays. I check and clean the hanger in Eagle where the jet's at every Tuesday. I work other days if Elliot has something special for me to do, or there's an emergency. But there aren't many of those since the house is practically new."

"What else did the police want to know?" Jack was fishing for information, but also to see if the Vail police were doing their job.

"They asked me about Elliot and Victoria—if

they got along. And they asked about my job working for them."

"What do you do for the Bankses exactly?"

"I handle everything with the house and the grounds, except pay the bills. I do regular maintenance, oversee the housekeeper and landscaping company, clean the pool. If there's anything that needs fixing that I can't fix, I oversee the contractors."

"Do all these people have keys to the house?"

"No. Employees around here come and go with the seasons. Elliot wasn't comfortable with anyone but me having a key."

Jack nodded. He knew from the time he'd spent in Aspen that the workforce in mountain resort towns was transient. Lots of college students, or laborers from other countries.

Lamken got up from the recliner. "You want a cup of coffee?"

"No. Thank you, though." Jack settled back into the couch, resting an ankle on the opposite knee and picking at the tip of his cowboy boot. He knew the posture of a casual conversation—no notebook or list of questions, just two guys talking—could pay handsome dividends. He wanted Lamken to feel comfortable.

"Victoria told me you've worked for Elliot a long time."

"Right at twenty years, I'd say." Lamken returned

from the kitchen and sat back down with a cup of coffee that looked like syrup. "Elliot was a great boss. I worked for him out of Denver until he built the house in Vail and asked me to come take care of it for him."

"Then you know Victoria pretty good as well?"

He frowned. "Yes and no. I'm not sure anyone really *knows* her—except for Elliot. Kind of keeps to herself—one of those women you never quite know what they're thinking, you know what I mean? But she's always been nice to me—fair. Not like some of the demanding rich women around town that want you to work for nothing, then look down their nose at you. I've heard plenty of stories from the other guys working around here." Lamken shook his head. "Victoria's not like that."

Jack watched him take a drink of the coffee, then look out the window toward the river. Jack was still trying to figure Victoria out as well, but he wouldn't mention that to Lamken.

"Did Victoria and Elliot ever argue? Any disharmony in the marriage, or was it congenial?"

Lamken turned his attention back to the conversation. Jack could see the wheels turning. Lamken was wondering what to say—or what *not* to say.

He moved a set of keys and a remote that were on a TV tray next to the recliner and set the coffee cup down. "Police asked me that, too."

"What did you tell them?"

"That I thought they were happy. They got along for the most part."

"For the most part?" His answer left something unsaid, and Jack wanted to know what it was. "Did they argue regularly?"

"No, nothing like that." He paused. "I just saw it once, when some guy showed up at the door asking for Victoria. I was working outside, changing a bulb on a landscape light. I wasn't close, but I heard parts of the conversation. I don't think they knew I was there."

"Who was the guy?"

"I don't know. He asked for Victoria. Then she comes to the door, and they all start arguing. He never went inside. Later, after he left, I was working on another light—around the back of the house—and could hear Elliot and Victoria arguing through the windows in the study."

"Did you hear what they were saying?"

"No. I could just tell they were arguing."

"In all the years you worked for Elliot, that was the only time you witnessed an argument between them? Even a mild one?"

Lamken considered the question, searching his memory before he answered. "Yep."

Jack watched him, studying his body language, and thought he was telling the truth. But it wasn't much of a story, and it didn't give Jack much to go on. Probably a happier-than-normal marriage, if someone who worked at the house two or three days a week for three years heard them argue only once. But who was the guy at the door that started it all?

For another ten minutes Jack asked him a variety of other questions. Had Elliot had a confrontation with anyone recently? Was there anyone that Lamken thought was holding a grudge or wanted to settle a score? Had any companies or employees that had done work at the house been fired recently?

Nothing Harold Lamken told him was of any help.

Jack dropped his leg to the floor, smoothed the jeans over his thighs, and stood up. "I've kept you long enough—"

The front door suddenly swung open, slamming into the wall behind it. A twentysomething with pale skin and greasy black hair stumbled in, swaying and laughing. His shirttail was untucked. The fellow that came in behind him wasn't wearing any shoes. Almost immediately, Jack smelled booze.

The one who had opened the door came up short when he saw Jack. His smile faded, and he jerked a glance at Lamken, straining his eyes to focus.

Lamken got to his feet. "We've got company, Tyler. Behave yourself."

The one named Tyler looked back at Jack, pushed his hair from his eyes, and struggled to appear sober.

"This is my nephew, Tyler," Lamken said to Jack, then jerked his chin toward the other kid. "That there is his friend Patrick."

Jack took a close look at the second one who'd entered the room and stood propped against the open door. His eyes were slits, but Jack could tell they were bloodshot. He had the same sweaty complexion as Lamken's nephew, and greasy hair several shades lighter.

Lamken looked nervously from Jack back to his nephew. "Boys, Mr. Martin and I are talking business. Go on back to your room, Tyler. I'll let you know when we're finished."

Jack watched the two stagger down the hall and disappear behind a door with a torn AC/DC poster taped to it. They were an unsavory pair. Out all night and up to no good. Jack knew the type.

After they left the room, Jack glanced at the key chain on the table next to Lamken's chair. The key to the Bankses' house would likely be on it.

"Who has access to your keys?" Jack asked. "Besides yourself?"

Lamken stiffened, and Jack knew he had hit a nerve.

Lamken swallowed. "Nobody." He jerked a chin toward the front door and tried to laugh off the

question. "Did you see my truck? I'd never let anyone drive it. Nice, huh?"

"Very nice."

"Elliot got it for me. Last year. Got me a new one
every four or five years. I still haul stuff every once
in a while for him, pick up things in Denver for the
house. I take real good care of it. I don't let anyone
drive it."

Too much about the truck, Jack thought. Harold
Lamken was nervous. Jack considered pressing the
issue about access to his keys but decided to let it
go—for now.

Jack stole one last glance down the dark hall where
the two boys had disappeared, then walked to the
door that Lamken was already holding open for him.
He wants me out of here, Jack thought.

On the small metal landing outside the trailer, Jack
turned back. "I have a feeling there'll be more questions I need to ask you. I'll be in touch."

The muscles in Lamken's face tensed.

CHAPTER 22

WHEN THE DETECTIVE was gone, Harold shut the door and looked down at the floor. He stuck his hands on his hips and took in a deep breath, trying to calm himself down. Being interviewed by the police was bad enough, he thought. But for some reason, answering the detective's questions had been even worse. He needed to get ahold of himself.

Tyler and Patrick reappeared.

"What was that all about?" Tyler asked, swaying on his feet.

Harold shook his head, walked to the TV tray, and picked up the coffee mug. The coffee was cold. "It was nothing, Tyler. Mind your own business."

Tyler pointed an accusing finger at his uncle. "It *was* something. You just don't want to tell me. Probably something about your boss's hot wife, wasn't it? I saw her on television. The police think she killed him." Tyler laughed.

Harold poured the remaining coffee into the sink, then slammed the dirty mug on the counter, keeping his back to the living room and trying to ignore them.

But Tyler wouldn't quit. "I guess since her husband is dead, she's *your* hot boss now."

Patrick snickered in the corner.

Harold swung around. "Shut up, Patrick." He then turned to Tyler and spoke through clenched teeth. "Get out of here, and take Patrick with you before I do something I'll regret."

CHAPTER 23

"MR. STRATTON JUST pulled into the garage, sir."

Derek Lowe looked up from his desk and nodded. "Thank you." He had instructed his assistant to alert him as soon as Charles arrived. The call from Victoria the night before still had him rattled.

It had been a fitful night without sleep, and he had lain awake for hours, wondering if Victoria's suspicions would lead to his greatest nightmare coming true. Everything had been going smoothly before Bob Hawkins's suicide, then Elliot's murder.

Derek tried to reassure himself the merger would still go through despite the setbacks. It *had* to. He had racked up too much debt—the car, the private jet charters, and the women. If it didn't go through, he wasn't sure what he would do.

He wanted to talk to Charles. Make sure he could really tamp down any meddling by Victoria, prevent the financial media from sensationalizing the deaths, casting Banks Oil & Gas in a bad light. Derek needed to know for sure that they could keep the deal on track.

The company's investment bankers had indicated they were only two weeks away from being able to close on the deal. That meant Derek and Charles were only two weeks away from making more money than Derek had ever dreamed of. The last thing he wanted was news coverage of recent events catching the attention of the Securities and Exchange Commission.

Derek had tried to sleep, tried to convince himself that Victoria wouldn't find anything, wouldn't stir anything up. But her stubborn insistence that something nefarious was going on at the company had him worried.

He gave Charles a few minutes to get up the elevator and to his office. When he thought enough time had passed, Derek walked the short distance between their offices on the executive floor. He smoothed the sides of his oiled hair with both hands and took in a few deep breaths to steady his nerves. He wouldn't let Charles know he was on edge. He knew that to expose any weakness to Charles Stratton could be a tragic mistake. He had seen people make that mistake before.

Outside the door, Derek steeled himself one last time before he walked in. Charles was hanging his jacket on a coatrack in the corner. Derek cleared his throat, announcing his presence.

"How's it going this morning, Derek?" There was no friendliness in his tone, only acknowledgment.

Derek kept his voice in control. "Charles, we have a problem."

Charles scowled at him, sat down behind his large desk, and laid both palms down in front of him. "What now, Derek? Yesterday I came in and was immediately met by that detective Victoria hired. Today it's you? I think I'm going to start working more from home." He leaned back in his chair and crossed his arms over his chest. "What's the catastrophe?"

"It's Victoria. She called me last night."

Charles came forward and frowned. Derek now had his full attention.

"Again with Victoria. What did she want?"

"She asked me about Clark Poindexter."

"How the hell does she know about *Poindexter?*"

"Elliot's laptop. Victoria got on it and found an email Poindexter sent him."

"What did she say?"

"She knows about Boots Hamer threatening a lawsuit and knows he hired Poindexter to look into the numbers." When Charles didn't say anything, he added, "She suspects there's something going on with the company and wants to know what it is."

"What did you tell her?"

"Nothing. I didn't confirm or deny knowing

anything about Hamer's lawsuit. And I told her I didn't know anything about Poindexter."

"Did she believe you?"

Derek had learned to control his facial muscles, not reflect emotion in his expression. He was nervous but was determined not to show it. "I think so."

Charles took in and released a long breath, watching him, then looked out the window toward the mountains and rubbed his jaw. "She's getting to be a problem," he finally said, turning back to Derek.

"What do we do? I can give her false information, something innocuous that will buy us some time, keep her busy while we close the merger."

"Do that. Elliot's murder is a problem—it's negative publicity we don't need right now. We need to keep Victoria quiet. In the meantime, I need to figure out what to do about Doris."

"Doris?"

"Doris Reed. I found out she told Elliot that she didn't think Bob's death was a suicide. She suspected there was more to it. If she's still talking, she could be a bigger problem than Victoria."

Derek stood frozen in place, a rush of adrenaline threatening to cut off the oxygen to his brain. No good would come from *anyone* rehashing Bob's suicide—especially a nut like Doris. "Maybe you should fire her."

Charles tapped a legal pad with his Montblanc

pen. "Possibly. But we have to watch out with Doris. Firing her could cause more problems than it solves. Where are you with Boots Hamer?"

"I haven't heard anything from him since Elliot was murdered."

Charles nodded. "Good. Maybe he'll drop the threat now—but we can't count on it. Let me know if he or Poindexter contacts you again. My guess is that they will."

Derek agreed. This close to the merger, any interference from Hamer could be disastrous.

"The ball's in your court on that one, Derek. Make sure you squash any potential lawsuit. I don't need to tell you how much screwing that up could cost us."

The men stared at each other. Derek swallowed and was the first to break eye contact. "I'll take care of it."

"We've got to sweep any potential problems under the rug. I've kept everything in motion since Elliot's death, and now we're only a couple of weeks away. We can't let the guys at Centennial get jittery—not to mention the SEC."

Derek nodded and started to leave. At the door, he turned back. "I'll let you know what happens with Victoria."

"Do that. We can't let her become a problem."

CHAPTER 24

JACK MARTIN LOOKED down at his frayed jeans and scuffed cowboy boots, shook his head, and pulled open the leaded-glass door to Ludwig's. When he had agreed to meet Miles Preston that morning for breakfast, he'd expected it to be at a diner or a café, something akin to a Denny's or an IHOP. What he hadn't expected was a fancy restaurant that looked like it belonged in the Swiss Alps.

Jack noticed the maître d' glance down at his feet. One of these days, he really needed to polish his boots. But in his defense, Jack reminded himself, he hadn't planned on having breakfast anywhere when he'd left the trailer that morning. It was going to be a quick trip to interview Harold Lamken. But while Jack was questioning Lamken, Preston had left him a message asking to meet. Curious, Jack had agreed.

He stood just inside the doorway and glanced around the room. Bleached hardwood floors and walls with matching furniture made the place feel like a Swiss chalet. Not that Jack had ever been in a Swiss chalet, or had any plans to.

He saw Preston sitting at a back table and made his way over. He was on the phone, a cup of coffee and a plate of croissants already sitting in front of him. When he saw Jack approach, he hung up.

"Thank you for coming," Preston said, rising from his chair to shake Jack's hand.

"Your timing was good. I was already in the area and planning to call you for a meeting myself. You saved me the trouble."

"Have a seat." Preston gestured toward an empty chair and sat back down.

"Victoria's not joining us?"

"No. I thought we could be more frank if she wasn't here. I'm meeting with her later to discuss the defense team I want to hire—if necessary. Hopefully, there won't be a need."

A waiter appeared at the table and handed Jack a menu.

"I've already ordered," Preston said. "Get something if you'd like."

Jack scanned the prices and nearly choked. It was like being back in Aspen. But he hadn't eaten anything all morning and decided to treat himself. He would eat out of the refrigerator at the trailer for the next few days to make up for it. He ordered a full breakfast with coffee and orange juice.

After the waiter had left, Jack got right to the point. "You wanted to talk to me about something?"

"I do. We didn't get a chance to talk Sunday when you were at the house. Since I'm Victoria's attorney—and friend—now that she has hired you to help find who killed Elliot, I thought it was a good idea if we talked."

Jack nodded.

"I read about your case in Aspen—catching the Hermes Strangler. Very impressive. I can see why Victoria reached out to you, but quite honestly, I wish she had given the Vail police more time to investigate Elliot's murder before she hired you." He lifted his hands off the table. "But I can see why she wouldn't want to—the police still consider her a suspect, as ludicrous as that is."

"Is it?"

"Is what?" Preston looked confused.

"Is it ludicrous that Victoria could have killed her husband?"

Miles raised his eyebrows, surprised by the question. "Well, of course it's ludicrous." He adjusted the napkin on his lap, regaining his composure before he continued. "Why would you ask something like that?"

Jack shrugged. "The spouse is always the first suspect. I don't know Victoria or the deceased, but you do."

"I do, and it *is* ludicrous to suggest Victoria had

anything to do with it." He eyed Jack suspiciously. "What is it that you want to know?"

"Tell me about them. Their relationship, how they met. How *you* met them."

Miles Preston sat back in his chair, eyeing Jack suspiciously. "I guess this is about your investigation. The more you know about the victim and your client, the easier it will be to catch the killer."

Jack remained silent.

Preston came forward in his chair. "They met at Mines—"

"The university?"

Preston nodded. "Yes. Victoria was still a student. What Elliot told me at the time was that he was there as a guest lecturer for one of the classes—he did that from time to time. Anyway, Victoria was there, the two got to talking after the class, and well..." He lifted his hands from the table, then placed them back down again. "The rest is history."

"It was a happy marriage?"

"It was."

"How would you know?"

Preston appeared affronted by the question, but Jack needed to get to the bottom of things and didn't have time to beat around the bush. He had his suspicions about his beautiful client and hoped Miles Preston would put them to rest.

"I know it was a happy marriage because I was

Elliot's closest—and oldest—friend." The hard look on Preston's face softened a bit. "He confided in me about everything over the years—school, work, women. I assure you, it was a very happy marriage—at least for Elliot, it was."

"How did the two of you meet?"

"How did I meet Elliot?" Preston looked wistfully to the side of the room, as if trying to pull fond memories front and center. "We grew up together. I first met Elliot through Little League sports."

"You went to the same schools?"

Preston shook his head. "Not until high school."

"Regis Jesuit?"

Preston raised an eyebrow. "You've done your homework, Detective." When Jack didn't reply, he continued. "We knew each other before high school but went to different elementary and middle schools. I went to private schools. Elliot went to public schools the rest of us considered on the wrong side of the tracks, if you know what I mean?"

"How did Elliot afford Regis Jesuit for high school?"

"His father. He was sick—cancer, I think—but he knew how smart Elliot was and wanted to give him the best education he could. I think Elliot had a few small scholarships, but I know his father used his pension from Mobile Oil to send Elliot to Jesuit. It was a smart gamble that paid off. After high school,

Elliot got a full scholarship to Mines. And again"—
he lifted his hands off the table—"the rest is history."

"So Elliot's father was also in oil and gas?"

Preston nodded. "He was a lineman—a company
man. It was Mobile Oil back then. They later merged
with Exxon. It didn't pay much, but when he retired
early because of the cancer, he got a decent pension.
I think he used it all on Elliot."

Jack thought about the information and mentally
filed it away in case it proved valuable later. From
years of investigating homicides, he knew learning
as much as you could about a victim often helped in
finding their killer. Murder was rarely random, and
the circumstances surrounding Elliot Banks's murder
guaranteed his wasn't. The more Jack could find out
about Elliot and the people around him, the quicker
he would find his killer.

And the more Jack learned about Elliot Banks, the
more intrigued he was. Banks had gone from needing scholarships to get through school to owning one
of the largest energy companies in the state. Not bad
for a kid whose dad had been a company man on a
meager salary. Jack's admiration for the dead Elliot
Banks was growing.

"His mother? What about her?"

Preston shook his head. "Not in the picture. Left
them when Elliot was just a kid. He barely remembered her."

"Siblings?"

Preston shook his head again. "He didn't have any."

"What about after high school? Did you go to college together?"

"No. We went our separate ways but never lost contact."

"And after college?"

"Elliot worked for a small company for several years, then started Banks Oil & Gas. I went to law school and eventually joined one of the largest law firms in Denver. Banks Oil & Gas had its own legal department, but Elliot would hire me whenever he needed personal legal work or advice outside of the business. But mostly we were just friends."

"You didn't want to work with him? At the company?"

Miles shook his head. "No. I don't think it's a good idea to work with friends…if you want to stay friends. I did personal for Elliot—wills, real estate contracts, small stuff like that."

"But your father was in oil and gas. You never considered going into the business, too?" Jack had done cursory research on Miles and knew his father had once owned his own company.

Miles raised his eyebrows. "You've done your homework, Detective." He nodded. "Yes, my father was in the business years ago. But he expanded too quickly in 1990, when the price of oil surged because of the Iraq War. He lost the company when prices plummeted the next year. I was a teenager, and I guess that soured me on the business. It's probably why I went into law instead."

The waiter reappeared with their order. Jack looked down at his plate of food and was struck by the incongruity. Although the china plates had large purple and yellow flowers all over them and looked dainty and feminine, the breakfast did not. Jack was impressed—and hungry.

The two men continued to talk as they ate.

"Have you had a chance to meet with Charles Stratton or Derek Lowe yet?" Preston asked, then stuck a bite of omelet into his mouth.

"I met with Charles Stratton yesterday. He wasn't much help."

"I'm not surprised." Preston had a strained look on his face.

"You don't like him?"

"No, I don't. Not many people do. The guy is a pompous ass."

Jack nodded. Miles Preston had pretty much summed up the way Jack felt about Charles Stratton as well. "Let me ask you something, then. If there was anyone who had it in for Elliot—a disgruntled employee or a competitor—would Stratton know about it?"

Preston laughed, stabbing another bite of egg. "Stratton knew when Elliot took a shit. Yes, he'd know about it. That guy has his finger on the pulse of everything at that company. I still don't know why Elliot hadn't gotten rid of him."

"Were there disagreements between the two?"

"Elliot and Stratton? There were plenty. The two men had totally different management philosophies."

"Then why did Elliot keep him around?"

Preston shook his head and thought about it. "I think they were in too deep. They were too close to getting the merger done." He wiped the corners of his mouth with his napkin and sat back in his chair. "It's not like Stratton is an idiot—he isn't. It's just that the guy is a jerk. *Nobody* likes him."

And everyone liked Elliot Banks, Jack thought to himself. Except for whoever killed him. "What about Harold Lamken, the house manager?"

"Harold?" Preston adjusted the napkin in his lap, taking time to think about the question. "Harold worked for Elliot for years. I know Elliot trusted him completely, but…" His voice trailed off.

"But what?"

"I don't know, something always seems a bit off with him."

"Off?"

Preston shook his head. "I don't know. I can't

point to anything in particular, but if I were you, I would definitely give him a hard look."

"He has a key to the house."

"He does, and he knows Elliot's and Victoria's schedules—their comings and goings—better than anyone."

Jack agreed with Preston's assessment again. Something *was* off with Lamken—there was something he was hiding. Whether it was murder was left to be determined. Jack decided to pay Lamken another visit soon.

Preston put both hands on the arms of his chair and leaned back. "Detective Conner with the Vail police called me. He said they found fingerprints in Elliot's blood on the handle of the tomahawk used to kill him."

Jack raised his brows. Fingerprints could change everything. His temporary employment might come to an end sooner than he thought. "Are they running the prints through the national database?"

"He said they were going to but wasn't sure if they were clear enough to get an accurate match. He said he would get back to me. I'll let you know when he does."

If the police couldn't make a match, Jack knew his investigation would continue. It wasn't time to make retirement plans just yet. "Did Elliot ever mention anyone by the name of Boots Hamer to you?" Jack asked.

"All the time. Boots was Elliot's original lease-holder. He let Elliot drill on his land when nobody else could."

"Did Elliot mention anything about him being unhappy with their partnership?"

Preston searched his memory. "No, nothing that I can remember."

Jack would have to look further into the matter. For some reason, despite being friends, Boots Hamer was threatening to sue. And Miles Preston either didn't know about it or wasn't telling.

"What about Bob Hawkins? Did Elliot talk to you about his suicide?"

"He did. He was shocked. He didn't think Bob had it in him to do something like that. He had a family, and it happened right before the merger. Hawkins was about to make a ton of money." Preston shook his head. "It didn't make any sense."

Jack set his silverware on the empty plate and sat back in his chair, wishing the conversation had been as satisfying as the breakfast. But the longer Preston talked, the more credible Doris Reed's theory seemed.

Could there be a connection between Elliot's murder and Bob Hawkins's suicide? And if so, what was it?

CHAPTER 25

WHEN DORIS HAD hung up the phone with Victoria earlier that morning, she couldn't wait to get to the office. She was determined to put her investigative skills to work, find out what in the world was going on at Banks Oil & Gas. Why would Boots Hamer, Elliot's old friend, hire a forensic accountant and threaten a lawsuit? Something wasn't right, and she was determined to finally find out what it was.

She put the finishing touches on her makeup, smearing on bright red lipstick, then grabbed her car keys and slammed the door behind her. She revved the car's engine, backing out of the driveway, then left tire tracks as she screeched down the street headed toward downtown.

As she drove, Doris replayed the conversation with Victoria in her mind. She didn't tell Victoria about meeting Jack Martin. It might have upset the poor girl even more than she already was—get her hamster wheel to spinning something crazy, wondering what it was all about. Beautiful thing should be living the prime of her life, still happily married, not burying her husband.

Doris thought of Elliot and felt a lump form in her throat. She was more determined than ever to find out what the heck was going on. She wasn't going to let anything—or anyone—sully her sweet Elliot's good name.

When Doris got to the office, she was disappointed to find Charles Stratton already there. She sat down at her desk, booted up the computer, and pulled up Charles's schedule. Seeing that he would be out of the office for a lunch meeting, she decided that was when she'd make her move.

Doris spent the morning mapping out the details of her strategy. The day before, Charles had the company's IT technician block employee access to Elliot's online schedule. He also had the tech lock Doris out of Elliot's email account. It would be more complicated to get to the information she needed now, but it didn't matter. Doris had a plan.

She'd get into Elliot's office, print out his schedule from the month before he was murdered. Then she would scan his emails, print any that looked unusual. Afterward, she would take everything home and go through it all again, leaving no clue left undiscovered. If there was anything incriminating, depending on what it was, she'd tell Victoria.

Doris knew in her gut that Elliot hadn't done

anything illegal, but it was possible whoever murdered him was blackmailing him or framing him for something. Just the week before, Doris had watched an episode of *Forensic Files* where the poor schlub that was murdered had been framed to take the fall for something he didn't do. The killer mistakenly thought he would get away with it because the fall guy was dead. Doris wasn't going to let Elliot be somebody's fall guy.

He *had* been acting strange lately though. Distant. Elliot had regularly confided in her over the years, but whatever had been bothering him before he was murdered, he'd kept to himself. Doris remembered thinking his elusive behavior was unusual, but she had dismissed it at the time. Had she known the gravity of the situation—that Elliot was about to be killed—she would have pushed him for an explanation.

But she hadn't, and now it was too late. She owed it to the kindest man she'd ever known, the one who'd given her a job when no one else would, to find out if there was anything going on at Banks Oil & Gas that had gotten him killed.

At a quarter to noon, Doris's phone buzzed. She saw that it was Charles Stratton and pushed down the lump that caught in her throat.

"Doris, I've got a lunch meeting down the street. I shouldn't be long, but cancel my appointment afterward, just in case. It's with a pesky banker I don't have time to talk to anyway. Let the next CFO deal with him. I'm CEO now."

Without waiting for a reply, he hung up.

Doris couldn't stand Charles Stratton. After being promoted to CEO, Charles had started treating Doris like his personal assistant, bypassing his own assistant, who also reported to two other executives. But what Doris knew that Charles didn't was that she wasn't going to stick around. After years of working for Elliot, she was not going to answer to a snake like Charles Stratton. She would bide her time, stay at the job until she found out what was going on, then split.

Doris got up from her desk, cracked open her office door, and peered out. She watched as Charles disappeared around the corner headed to the elevators. When she heard the elevator doors slide shut, she slipped out.

In Elliot's office, she gently closed the door behind her, leaving the light off. It was a spacious executive suite with its own bathroom. Elliot regularly worked late into the evening, often cleaning up at the office before meeting Victoria for various social functions, or attending dinner meetings or other business events.

Everything in the office had been left as it was following Elliot's murder. Charles made it clear that, as the new CEO, he planned on moving into the suite, but he didn't want the company to incur the expense of remodeling it until *after* the merger with Centennial State Energy.

How benevolent of him to think of the company first, Doris thought with a sneer after Charles instructed her to close off the space and keep everyone out. Of course Charles couldn't be expected to move into the suite the way Elliot had it—simple but classic, smooth leather furniture with a smattering of tasteful Native American artifacts. Charles would want to bring in the tacky gilt furniture and Oriental rugs similar to the ones the Strattons had furnished their home with.

For a moment Doris thought she saw Elliot sitting behind his large desk. She imagined him looking up at her and smiling as he had done hundreds of times over the years. She pushed down the heavy lump in her throat and squeezed her eyes shut. When she opened them, Elliot was gone.

This was not the time for tears, she told herself. She had a job to do.

She scrambled across the office and around Elliot's desk, taking a seat in his chair. His computer was on the credenza behind her. She swung around and booted it up, tapping her fingers rapid-fire on the keyboard as she waited.

"Come on, come on," she said under her breath, looking behind her to make sure no one had seen her or followed her in.

When the monitor lit up, Doris typed in Elliot's password and pulled up his schedule. She scanned the entries. There were meetings with bankers and contractors—all names she recognized. Nothing seemed out of the ordinary.

She went back farther, and one entry caught her eye. Elliot had a scheduled meeting with Bob Hawkins the day after Bob died. The meeting would have included Boots Hamer and someone named Clark Poindexter—she didn't recognize the second man's name but decided it was probably the forensic accountant Victoria had mentioned.

Doris scanned several days farther back, then sent all the entries to the printer, wincing at the beeping sounds the printer made as it spit out the pages.

Next she pulled up Elliot's emails, sifting through the ones still in his in-box. Doris knew from years of working with Elliot that he was meticulous about his filing system, leaving any emails regarding unre-solved issues in his in-box, quickly deleting or filing the rest in an elaborate series of folders.

She printed out the messages still in his in-box. They would give her something to start with. There wasn't time to go through all the emails he had already filed. If she needed to, she would come back and search through the maze of folders later.

As Doris was shutting down the computer, she heard talking outside the door. She listened, then realized whoever was in the hallway was coming in. She leaped from the chair and ducked into the nearby bathroom, pulling the door shut just as two men walked into the office.

She caught a glimpse and recognized them as two guys from the building maintenance crew. Why would they be in Elliot's office? she wondered. Whatever their reason, she needed to stay hidden. Praise the Lord they hadn't noticed her. Then she looked down and realized the bathroom door hadn't closed completely. Too late to do it now. They would hear the latch.

Doris's heart beat heavy under her polyester blouse. To her horror, she could hear the two men getting closer. Were they coming for the bathroom? Was there a work order she didn't know about? Maybe a leak?

She drew in a breath and held it, waiting to be discovered. She stared down at her orthopedic shoes, then the marble floor beneath them, and was sure that when the men opened the door, she would pee all over it.

But they stopped just feet from where she stood quaking. She heard them move furniture—the desk or the credenza? She wasn't sure which. What were they doing?

One of them spoke in a deep, husky voice. "You

grab the processor. I'll get the monitor and the keyboard."

They were taking Elliot's computer.

There was more rustling.

"That's weird," the one with the husky voice said.

"What?"

"It's warm, like someone's been using it."

The room was quiet. Doris's plump shoulders heaved with every breath as she struggled to keep quiet, pressing her hands to her mouth.

Finally the other one spoke. "Probably from being plugged in."

"Yeah, you're probably right."

She heard them pull power cords from the wall.

"What are we doing with this stuff anyway?"

"Don't know. Mr. Stratton says he wants it. Said not to say nothing to nobody, just put it all in his car."

"Huh."

"I don't ask no questions. I just do as I'm told. Weird folk, these rich people."

"Yep. Ain't that the truth? Does he want the printer?"

Shoot, shoot. Doris remembered the copies of Elliot's schedule and emails she had left on the printer when she hid in the bathroom and strained to hear if they were taking it.

The husky voice answered, "Nah. He didn't

mention anything about no printer, so leave it. If he wants it, we can come back."

"Suits me."

When Doris heard the door finally shut, she waited a few more seconds, then peered out. They were gone. She let out the breath she had been holding and came out of the bathroom.

Why would Charles Stratton want Elliot's computer?

She grabbed the copies off the printer and on a hunch decided to check Bob Hawkins's office next. She would print out Bob's schedule and cross-check the entries with Elliot's. Nobody could convince Doris that Bob's death was a suicide, and in her gut she knew Elliot's murder was connected in some way.

Doris peered into the hallway. When she didn't see anyone, she slipped out of Elliot's office.

Bob Hawkins's office was much smaller. The first thing Doris noticed was that his computer was gone, and her heart sank. But as she was turning to leave, she saw the leather-bound book on Bob's desk and remembered the accountant was fastidious about keeping a backup copy of his schedule in a planner. Doris grabbed it.

Back at her desk, Doris pulled a package of strawberry Twizzlers from a desk drawer. She tugged a handful of the licorice from the package and chewed on it as she riffled through the printouts of Elliot's schedule.

When she found the one she was looking for, she read the name again. Clark Poindexter. Then she turned to the same date in Bob's schedule and saw the same name printed in Bob's handwriting. The meeting would have included the four men—Boots Hamer, Clark Poindexter, Elliot, and Bob. It was a meeting Bob would never be able to make. He had committed suicide the night before.

Doris thumbed back through the book and noticed Bob had had a meeting with Clark Poindexter several days before. He had met Poindexter at a café south of downtown. The meeting appeared to have been just between the two men—there were no other names listed.

Doris googled "Clark Poindexter."

"Forensic accountant," she muttered to herself. It was just like Victoria said. But what would Boots hire one for? And Boots was threatening a lawsuit.

Doris racked her brain, wondering why Boots would sue Elliot. Elliot never mentioned anything about it before he died. Then it dawned on her. It couldn't have been Elliot he was upset with. It had to be Energy Marketing, the company owned by Charles Stratton and Derek Lowe. It was the only answer. Elliot was as clean as fresh winter snow in the Rockies. If there was anything unethical or illegal going on, it would be with the company Elliot let the two snakes set up.

"It's a common practice," Elliot had reassured Doris at the time. "A way for top executives to make a little extra money, keep them happy so they're not recruited away by higher-paying jobs. Plus, it keeps me from having to manage that part of the business."

"Humph," Doris said aloud. She had told Elliot then that it was a mistake, and she believed it now more than ever. Damn those Ivy League hucksters.

Doris looked at Bob's planner again, scanned the entries, and noticed a meeting he'd had scheduled with Elliot in the office. That wasn't unusual, Elliot had meetings with his controller all the time, but Doris stared at the date of this particular meeting, and something about it nagged at her.

Her eyes grew wide when she remembered what it was. She heaved her purse onto her lap and rummaged through it for her cell phone. She needed to make a call, and there was no way she was going to make it from an office line.

CHAPTER 26

Wednesday, June 20

IT WAS EARLY. The parking lot of the Sunshine Café in Silverthorne was empty except for a delivery truck and an early-model brown Subaru wagon, the back covered in bright-colored stickers.

Jack assumed the Subaru would be Doris. She had called him the afternoon before to meet her at the diner. Something had her spooked enough to want to meet with him at a location more than an hour's drive outside of Denver.

Jack got out of the truck and walked across the parking lot toward the diner's entrance but heard a loud rumble and turned back. A red Camaro lurched off the highway and practically fishtailed into a parking spot. Jack couldn't see the driver, the sun glaring off the windshield, but he heard the music and saw the car's windows pulsate to the beat of KISS's "Rock and Roll All Nite."

If Doris weren't already waiting for him, Jack had half a mind to walk over and tell the idiot he was going to kill someone driving like that. But he reminded himself he wasn't a cop anymore and needed to work on minding his own business.

Jack turned away and took a few steps toward the diner but stopped and looked back. He watched as the Camaro's heavy door was pushed open by a fleshy white arm. Then he saw the hair—the same cherry-red color as the car.

Jack stood in disbelief as Doris got out and lumbered across the parking lot toward him, a giant bag for a purse draped over one shoulder.

By the time she got to him, she was out of breath. "Honey, wait till you hear what I've got for you."

Jack was still processing the Camaro. "Nice car."

She puffed with pride and nodded. "Thank you. It's the new ZL1. Fully loaded, 650 horsepower, 6.2 liter supercharged V-8. That baby can go zero-to-sixty in three and a half seconds. Not that I would know that personally." She winked at him. "I read it somewhere."

Jack raised his eyebrows. People rarely surprised him, but Doris Reed had—twice. He shook his head and laughed to himself. The meeting with Doris might end up being a complete waste of his time, he thought, but it promised to be interesting.

Inside, Doris settled into the booth and grabbed the menu that was lying on the table, her bright red hair and turquoise blouse clashing against the diner's canary-yellow walls. For a moment Jack thought he was caught in some psychedelic nightmare.

After he was seated, Doris set the menu back down and leaned across the table. She spoke in a loud whisper. "There's something fishy going on at the office. Wait till you see this."

She then rifled through the giant bag, pulling out a set of papers and laying them on the table.

Jack pulled the pages closer. "What is it?"

"Schedules," she said, stabbing the pages with a manicured nail. "This one is Elliot's." She reached back into the bag, pulled out a leather book, and opened it. "And this one is Bob Hawkins's."

"The controller who committed suicide?"

Doris nodded. "Right. Except I told you, it wasn't suicide."

A waitress appeared to take their orders, and Doris closed the leather book and sat up.

When she was gone, Doris leaned back in. "Bob had a meeting *here*," she said, pointing to an entry in the leather book. "It was with Clark Poindexter—a forensic accountant. The next day, Bob had a meeting with Elliot. See *here*." She pointed to another entry. "I remember the meeting because they were practically yelling at each other. I was outside Elliot's office."

Jack had no idea where she was going with it all.

She must have sensed his uncertainty. "Hang in here with me, Kojak. I'll connect all the dots for you in a minute. The heated meeting with Elliot was on the same day Bob died. I heard it because I was going to Elliot's office to ask for the afternoon off—it was my sister's birthday, and a group of us were planning a girls' night out that night.

"But, as far as I know, Elliot and Bob had never had any heated arguments before. It was out of character for either of them to be yelling. Then that night Bob supposedly committed suicide—the day *before* he had another scheduled meeting with Poindexter, the forensic accountant. Except that meeting was also going to include Elliot and Boots Hamer—the disgruntled landowner I told you about—the one Charles Stratton *didn't* tell you about when you asked him if there was anyone unhappy with Elliot or the company."

"Wait a minute." Jack sat back and lifted his palms from the table. If he understood her correctly, the whole theory sounded crazy. He was trying to keep it all straight. "You think Bob's death had something to do with the meetings with a forensic accountant?"

"Yes. And Elliot's murder, too."

Jack thought his initial impression of Doris as looney toons was probably on the money. He shook his head. "I'm not seeing the connection."

Doris let out a long breath and lowered a frustrated gaze, regrouping to come at him again.

This time she ticked off the points on her fingers, her ample bosom rising and falling under her blouse as she spoke. "Something is going on with the company for Boots Hamer to hire a forensic accountant. Something at the meeting Bob had with the forensic accountant didn't sit well with Elliot when Bob met with him the next day. That night—one day before they were *all* going to meet with the forensic accountant—Bob turns up dead. Now Elliot is dead."

Doris leaned back into the booth, crossed her forearms in front of her, and laid them on her abdomen. The look on her face dared him to dismiss her theory.

Jack wasn't convinced the threads of Doris's timeline meant anything, but he had to admit they were intriguing. He wanted to hear more. "So something the forensic accountant told Bob Hawkins upset Elliot. Then Bob dies. Help me further, Doris."

"Something is going on at the company that's got one of its largest private investors hot to trot enough to hire an investigator. But if there's something fishy going on, it won't be with anything Elliot was involved with. Elliot wasn't like that. He would never have done anything wrong intentionally. It's got to be something with the marketing company owned by Charles Stratton and Derek Lowe."

Doris explained the connection between the two companies. Banks Oil & Gas drilled and produced the oil. Then Stratton and Lowe's marketing company bought that oil from Banks Oil & Gas and sold it to refining companies at a markup, making Stratton and Lowe a tidy profit.

"Those two snakes in the grass are behind this somehow," Doris said. She glanced around the diner before digging into her bag again. "Take this," she whispered, sliding several folded sheets of paper across the table. "It's the police report on Bob's suicide. Maybe it will help."

Jack pulled the report toward himself. "How did you get this?"

"I've got my sources."

She didn't elaborate, and Jack didn't care. He recognized what she was implying and got right to the point. "You think Stratton and Lowe are behind Bob's death, and somehow it's linked to Elliot's murder?"

The waitress appeared at the table, and the two fell silent. They waited as she set Doris's breakfast platter and Jack's coffee in front of them.

When she was gone, Doris shook her head and continued. "I'm not going to sit here right now and say that out loud. But there's a good chance something they're involved in *resulted* in Bob's and Elliot's deaths." She skewered a bite of pancake with her fork and pointed it at Jack. "That's why I called you."

For the next fifteen minutes, Jack drank his coffee and watched Doris put away a breakfast fit for a linebacker. In between bites, she extolled Elliot's character and accomplishments and Stratton's and Lowe's personal shortcomings.

While they waited for the check, Doris admitted that Victoria was the one who had alerted her about the forensic accountant. But when Doris realized the sequence of events coincided so closely with Bob's death and Elliot's murder, she decided the situation warranted a call to Jack instead.

Doris asked him not to mention anything to her. "At least until we have some proof. No sense in upsetting the poor girl any more than she already is."

Jack wondered why Victoria hadn't called him about Clark Poindexter. Victoria had hired him to find out what happened to her husband, yet she was calling Doris about suspicious information she had dug up. It didn't make sense.

Jack assured Doris he wouldn't mention anything to Victoria. What he didn't tell her was that his suspicions about his beautiful client were growing, and he wanted to find out what she was up to.

Back in his truck, Jack watched Doris drive away, her tires spitting gravel as she lurched out of the parking lot on her way back to Denver.

He sat with his hands on the steering wheel. He still needed convincing Doris wasn't a raving lunatic, but he felt there was merit to some of what she'd said and wasn't ready to dismiss her crackpot theory just yet—not before he talked to a few more people.

And as much as it pained him, he knew just where to start.

CHAPTER 27

VICTORIA STILL COULDN'T believe she was making funeral arrangements. Just a few days earlier, she and Elliot had been planning their annual trip to the Bahamas. They'd decided to spend a week boating from island to island. Elliot had even put down a deposit on the *Temptation*, a 123-foot yacht that could accommodate eight guests, even though it was going to be just the two of them.

Back home from the funeral parlor, Victoria set her purse on the corner of the kitchen counter. She stood staring at it, mindlessly squaring the purse's corners with the edges of the countertop.

The meeting with the funeral director had been a blur. She knew he was being sympathetic and not pushing her, but he had more questions than Victoria had been prepared to answer. She needed more time.

Victoria had decided what she could—the date and the music. The funeral would be Friday morning at All Faiths Chapel. Elliot loved old church hymns, so they would sing "Amazing Grace" and "The Old Rugged Cross." But that was all she had. The director's remaining questions had been too much. Elliot's clothes? Who would give the eulogy? Did she want any specific readings or Bible verses included?

Victoria had made her apologies and cut their meeting short, asking to schedule another the following day. She knew she needed to pull it together and make the rest of the decisions by morning. The funeral was just two days away.

Her purse tipped to the side, bringing her back to the present. Without thinking, she pushed it upright, squaring its edges with the corners of the counter again.

She walked slowly through the kitchen, running her hand along the stone countertop, then along the back of a sofa in the family room. Next she walked out into the corridor and into the foyer, where she lingered. She stood staring up at the antique Navajo rug and remembered how excited Elliot had been when he'd won it at auction. She looked at the date of its origin engraved on a small brass plaque attached to the frame and watched the numbers come in and out of focus before she turned away.

She paused at the doors to Elliot's study, taking it all in. The large stone fireplace, the leather chairs in front of it. Her gaze swept past the windows, with their view of dark clouds gathering in the distance, and settled on the Dolan Geiman collage of a buffalo hanging on the opposite wall. Her eyes dropped to Elliot's desk and the objects sitting on top of it. All familiar and all waiting for him to come home. Elliot's laptop, the picture taken the night of the Black Diamond Ball, his engineering books, and his grandfather's slide rule in a shadow box perched in the corner.

It was as if Elliot were still there, but then her gaze settled on his empty chair—a stark reminder that he was gone.

But for a moment she indulged the dream, imagined him sitting there, turning and smiling at her as he always did when she entered the room. She looked over it all again, drinking it in with her eyes, but something nagged at her. Elliot was gone, but something else wasn't right, something with the room or his things.

Victoria closed her eyes and shook her head, shaking herself back to reality. It wasn't the time to start imagining things. There was too much to do.

A gentle ache in her feet reminded her she was still dressed for the meeting at the funeral home. She pulled off her heels and walked barefoot down the corridor to the master bedroom.

After changing into more comfortable clothes, Victoria pulled the drapes shut and sat on the edge of the bed. She checked her phone and saw that it was only ten o'clock. Although she rarely took naps, the morning had drained her. Just a few minutes, she told herself.

Lying in the dark with her eyes closed, Victoria listened to the faint patter of summer rain and gradually fell into a deep sleep.

Sometime later, from somewhere in her slumbering darkness, Victoria heard a chime. There was something familiar about the sound, but in her rousing sleep, it confused her.

Victoria stirred, waking slowly. She pulled her phone from the bedside table and realized she had slept for over an hour. She lay there a minute longer. Then, still groggy, she sat up and put her feet on the floor.

The chime sounded again, and Victoria realized it was coming from the security keypad mounted just inside the bedroom. Somewhere in the house, a door had been opened. Twice.

Victoria immediately stood up and started for the kitchen, wondering if she had forgotten to lock the back door behind her when she came in. Maybe the afternoon storm had blown it open. But she was sure she remembered locking it. She always did. She noticed it was no longer raining and knew it couldn't have been the storm.

Her heart beat faster as she made her way to the kitchen. She was almost there when, through a small window with a view to the driveway, she saw a man getting into a truck. She watched as it disappeared around the side of the house, headed toward the street.

Harold. Victoria thought for a moment, making sure she had the days correct. It was Wednesday. Harold wasn't supposed to be back at the house until the following day.

She remembered the two chimes. Harold had let himself in, then a few minutes later had let himself back out.

It wasn't like him to show up unannounced. Even when he had forgotten something—a jacket or his tools—he always called before he came back.

Victoria frowned.

What was he doing?

CHAPTER 28

JACK VEERED OFF the interstate and wove through Clear Creek Canyon toward the town of Golden.

Before he left the diner in Silverthorne, he'd googled Bob Hawkins's address and put it into the GPS on his phone. There was a good chance Doris Reed was a crackpot, but her theory intrigued him, and he wasn't going to dismiss it just yet.

Although he didn't relish the idea of showing up unannounced, he knew from experience that if he called first, Bob Hawkins's widow would likely refuse his visit. Jack would take his chances, hoping she was both at home and willing to talk to him when he got there.

He followed the directions on his phone, finally turning into a quaint middle-class neighborhood a few miles north of town. There was a park at the entrance with playground equipment painted in primary colors. A group of young mothers were gathered on benches watching children play. There was a lone jogger on a gravel path that wound around the park and up through trees toward the highway.

Everything looked new—the park, the houses, even the asphalt streets. The houses were two-story, freshly painted in various shades of gray or tan and sat just off the curb, each wrapped by pockets of green grass planted with trees and shrubs all the same size.

Jack drove slowly, avoiding a young woman pushing a stroller in the direction of the park. At Fifty-Ninth Drive he turned left, onto a long cul-de-sac with a dozen or so houses on either side.

GPS led him to a house near the end of the street. It was a two-story, painted khaki with rust-colored shutters. A child's tricycle was turned over in a small patch of grass near the curb. Jack righted it as he made his way to the front door.

On the landing, he paused, regretting what he was about to do. But he needed the information only Bob Hawkins's widow could give him.

He heard the sound of children playing inside, took in and held a deep breath, then knocked on the door. It took a while, but when the door finally opened, a pretty blond woman in her early thirties stood looking at him.

"Can I help you?" Her voice was soft and pleasant, but a slight frown creased the area between her eyes.

"Mrs. Hawkins?"

"Yes."

"My name is Jack Martin. I'm a detective." Her expression didn't change. Jack was sure she had talked to several detectives since her husband's suicide, and she probably assumed he was with the Denver police. He didn't want to mislead her.

"Mrs. Hawkins, I've been hired by Victoria Banks to help find out what happened to her husband, Elliot." Jack saw her frown soften. A good sign. "Would you mind if I asked you a few questions?"

She hesitated, and a boy of three or four came bounding down the stairs and wrapped his arms around one of her legs. She bent down, tousled his hair, and told him to go play with his brother.

When the child was gone, she looked back at Jack. "I don't know how I can help you, Detective. I only know what's been on the news. My husband…" She stopped and swallowed. There was an overwhelming sadness in her eyes.

"I'm sorry about your husband," Jack said. Such a young, beautiful family, he thought. What a loss. "If I could just ask you a few questions about him. I won't take much of your time."

She frowned again. "But you're investigating Elliot's murder. Why do you want to know about Bob?"

"I understand he worked for Elliot before he died. I'm talking to several people who work for Banks Oil & Gas, and I would like to get an idea of what your husband's perspective was—or what, if anything, he might have mentioned to you."

She thought about the request for what seemed like an eternity. Just when Jack thought he was going to strike out, she nodded.

"Okay," she said in a tentative voice.

Jack let out a slow breath, not realizing he had been holding it. "Thank you. I can't imagine how difficult this has been for you. I apologize in advance if anything is painful for you to talk about."

"It's okay, Detective. How can I help?"

Jack had always hated the job of talking to the family of a victim. It was an intrusion, and he knew from personal experience that it forced the family to relive memories they were often fighting to come to terms with, or to forget.

Jack knew the conversation would be difficult for both of them. She would still be processing the shock of her husband taking his own life. He felt a stab of guilt at having to ask her to relive his last few days. He needed to get as much information out of her as he could, but he didn't want to hurt her any further than what had been done by her husband's suicide.

Jack cleared his throat and nodded his gratitude. "Did your husband happen to mention anything out of the ordinary to you before he died?"

"About what?"

"Maybe problems he was having—financial or health-wise?"

She shook her head. "No."

"Any problems with family or friends recently that you know of? Maybe a co-worker?"

She shook her head again.

"Did Bob talk to you about his job? Things that went on at work?"

She finally nodded. "Sometimes."

"Was there anything going on at work that had him upset?"

"The only thing he talked about recently was the merger."

People kept bringing up the merger, and Jack's interest was piqued; he wanted to know more. When she didn't elaborate, he asked, "Do you remember what exactly Bob said about the merger?"

"Just that everything was going smoothly. He was looking forward to it. He said the controller at the other company was older and was going to retire after the deal closed, which meant Bob would have been controller of the new, bigger company."

"He was happy about that?"

Her eyes got glassy with tears, and she nodded. "He was very excited. We were going to pay off the house and the cars. Bob said we would have enough money to put away for the boys—for their college funds." She cast her eyes down and stopped talking.

A financial windfall just around the corner, a family that loved him, no contentious issues with family or friends. None of it was a motive for suicide. Then Jack remembered something Doris had mentioned—the heated argument between Bob and Elliot.

"Did Bob like the people he worked with?"

She remained silent but wiped her cheek with her hand and nodded. Jack could tell she was fighting back more tears. He gave her a moment before he continued.

"What about Elliot Banks? Did Bob like working for him?"

She finally looked up, smiling wanly. "Very much. Bob thought the world of Elliot." The veil of sorrow fell over her again. "It's horrible what happened to Elliot. He was such a nice man. Bob would tell me stories. Did you know that Elliot gave Thanksgiving meals to over a hundred needy families in the Denver area every year?"

Jack shook his head.

"Every year," she repeated. "And there's no telling how many students he put through school at Mines—kids who never knew where their scholarship money was coming from. Bob said Elliot even hired a few of them once they graduated—but they never knew he was the one who paid their tuition."

"How was he as a boss?"

"He was a great boss. He was always kind and

generous to his employees." Her eyes lit up as she remembered. "In fact, when Bob and I got married, we didn't have any money, and Elliot knew that. He paid for our honeymoon."

Jack was taken aback. "That's quite a wedding gift."

She laughed softly and seemed embarrassed. "I should back up and explain."

Jack was glad to see the memory was a happy one.

"Elliot hired Bob when no one else would," she said. "When Bob graduated from Colorado State, he went to work for an accounting firm downtown. But about a year later, he felt he needed to join the fight in Afghanistan. I didn't want him to, but he enlisted. He served just over a year when, one day, his Humvee hit a land mine. Everyone was killed except Bob. He survived but was burned over forty percent of his body—his face disfigured on one side. When he came home, the accounting firm he had worked for told him his position was no longer available—at least that's what they said. So Bob interviewed with other firms, then with private companies. But nobody would hire him. There was always some excuse. Bob suspected it was the burns, that his disfigurement scared people away. Then he interviewed with Elliot."

"That's when he went to work at Banks Oil & Gas?"

She nodded. "He was hired as the assistant

controller, but a year or so later, the woman who was the controller retired and Elliot gave Bob the job. Bob loved that job." She was lost in her memories for a while before she came back. "And he loved working for Elliot."

Jack knew he had to tread lightly, not wanting to offend her. "Did your husband have any lingering issues with the accident in Afghanistan? PTSD maybe?"

"No. Not on the outside, at least. Nothing that affected his work or his life with us at home. He *did* have dreams—nightmares really. They would wake him in the middle of the night sometimes, but he dealt with it. He wouldn't let it affect the family. The boys never knew."

Jack knew he was venturing into sensitive territory and hoped she wouldn't shut down. "Did he take any medications?"

She admitted that Bob had been on prescription medication for pain, but insisted he never showed signs of psychological problems and was never violent. In fact, she told Jack, it had been the opposite. She went on to describe Bob as a kind and caring husband and father. From the depth of her grief, Jack knew she was telling the truth.

"Did you notice a change in his behavior the days before he died? Was he acting differently in any way?"

She thought about it. "The last few days he seemed...distant."

"How so?"

She took her time to think about it. "Like he was distracted," she finally said. "He wasn't as attentive to the boys or me. The boys would want to play when he got home, but he said he was too tired. He told them he had something to do, but then I would find him in the bedroom watching television. He was always very involved with the boys when he came home from work—playing with them outside if the weather was nice, or inside if it was too cold or wet. He *always* played with them when he got home from work...except for the last few days."

"Could it have been financial troubles?" When she didn't reply, he added, "I hate to get so personal, Mrs. Hawkins, but it's very important that I understand Bob's suicide."

Her voice was soft but firm. "He didn't do it."

"Do what?"

"Kill himself, like they said."

Jack felt his pulse quicken. "What makes you think that?"

"I know him...*knew* him." She looked down, and Jack gave her time. When she looked back up, there was a steely resolve in her eyes. "He wouldn't have done that to me and the boys. I don't care what the police say."

Jack knew it was true that law enforcement was often quick to rule a death "suicide" if there was even the slightest indication that the victim might have taken their own life. It was a fast and clean way to close a case.

But Jack also knew that law enforcement often got it wrong.

"Detective, can you answer something for me?"

Jack hesitated, but the desperation in her eyes got to him. "I can try."

"Is it typical for police to dismiss the fact that a victim's cell phone was missing—from the scene?"

Jack stared at her, not sure what to say. That information changed everything. Unless the death was the result of a burglary, it would be very unusual for a suicide victim's cell phone not to be found on the body—or at least in the vicinity—especially when the victim's excuse for leaving his family alone in a restaurant was to return a phone call. The information about the missing phone hadn't been in the police report Doris had given him.

She stood watching him, pleading with her eyes for Jack to agree with her that her husband *hadn't* taken his own life, leaving her to raise their boys alone.

Jack knew what she wanted to hear, knew it would help ease her pain. But as much as he wanted to, he couldn't tell her that—not yet.

But he had to tell her something. "That *is* unusual,"

he finally admitted. "And I promise you, I'll look into it."

Jack reflected on the turn of events as he drove out of the neighborhood and away from the young family left alone to bear so much sorrow.

Doris Reed had insinuated that Bob's suicide was faked—that he had been murdered. Jack now strongly suspected that she was right.

CHAPTER 29

FROM THE RED patches on her face, Charles knew Katie was getting angry, but he didn't care.

They were having dinner in the dining room at opposite ends of the long table, the crystal chandelier casting shadows over Katie that Charles thought accentuated the wrinkles starting to etch her face in recent years. Next time he would suggest adding candlelight. He didn't want any reminders his trophy wife was aging. He was in no position to look for a replacement yet.

He kept eating, wanting to finish his meal. Luther Byrd was coming by the house later. Charles had told him to come around eight. They had problems to take care of.

But first Charles wanted to talk to Katie about Victoria. Victoria had refused Katie's offer for another visit, but Katie needed to push harder, even insist. Charles had to know what Victoria was up to. Had the detective she hired found out anything? Was he poking around in the company's business or running in circles looking for Elliot's murderer?

"Charles, I can't help it if she didn't want me to visit again. I can't hold a gun to her head and force her to let me in."

Charles considered the idea. Tempting, he thought, but it would never work. "Call her again."

Katie heaved a sigh. "I'll call her in a couple of days. I don't understand why this is so important to you. Who cares if she's hired that detective?"

"I care!" Charles barked at her. "And if you had any sense, *you* would care, too. I've told you—a detective meddling in company business right now could cost me millions. And we both know how important my bank balance is to you."

The look on Katie's face was a mixture of shock and humiliation. Her eyes were glassy. "What's going on, Charles? You're not usually this cruel."

He breathed in through his nose, turning his face toward the ceiling. "Katie, you have to understand. I've come too far to lose it all now. This merger falling apart is not an option."

It seemed to placate her some. He knew the money was almost as important to her as it was to him. Almost. "What about Doris Reed?" he asked.

Katie looked confused. "Doris? What about her?"

"Has Victoria talked to her?"

"Yes. She mentioned talking to Doris. Why?"

"Did she mention talking to her about Bob Hawkins?"

Katie frowned. "Why do you care if she talked to Doris about Bob?"

Charles slammed down his wineglass, spilling some. "For once in your life, Katie, just answer a damn question."

"Yes! She said she told Doris that she believed now that there was something to her theory that Bob's suicide and Elliot's murder were somehow connected. Doris offered to look into it for her."

Charles grinned, a feeble attempt to make amends. "See, now, that wasn't so hard, was it?"

Katie looked down at her full plate of food, then back up. "May I be dismissed now?" she asked in a sarcastic tone. "I've suddenly lost my appetite."

They stared at each other.

Charles spoke first. "Darling, if you could see the look on your face. I bet if I handed you a tomahawk, you would attempt to do to me what Victoria did to poor Elliot."

Katie paled, then glared at him. "You really are a monster." She pushed her chair from the table and stood up. "And since that caveman buddy of yours is coming over again," she said on her way out of the room, "I'll be at the company's apartment at the Ritz-Carlton tonight. I don't want to be any part of whatever the two of you are up to."

CHAPTER 30

LUTHER BYRD RESENTED the large mansion in the gated community that Charles Stratton lived in. And he resented being summoned to it at his boss's whim.

Luther lived in a small wood-framed house on the northeast side of Denver. Built in the early 1970s, it had thin walls and little insulation. It was cold in the winter and hot in the summer. And it was a forty-five-minute drive from Luther's home to the Stratton mansion. He was having to make the trip more often than he used to, more often than he thought was necessary. Tonight he had been content, watching a Rockies game and draining the last of a six-pack when he'd gotten the call.

At least he'd make the drive in his new black Ford Raptor. Luther looked over the leather interior with pride as he drove, running his calloused hand over the smooth dash.

If only his son-of-a-bitch father had lived long enough to see what Luther had made of himself. *You'll never amount to nothing.* Luther had heard it a thousand times. The proclamation usually came with a slap up the side of his head.

Luther swerved to miss a slow-moving Lexus, flipping the driver the bird in the dark as he drove past.

He told himself not to waste any more time thinking about his dead father. A heart attack seven years earlier had come at just the right time. Had the old coot lived any longer, Luther might have had to kill him himself. Luther wound down his window and spit into the wind.

There were bigger fish to fry now, new resentments to keep from festering. He had learned long ago to keep his anger in check.

His thoughts turned back to Charles Stratton. There would be time to settle the score later. For now he'd go along with it, taking his orders as they came. But he should at least be paid more than the paltry sums Stratton threw at him like scraps to a dog. As soon as the time was right, he'd ask for more.

Why shouldn't he make more? Luther did as much work as Stratton for the damn company, maybe more. And he sure as hell did more work than the slick attorney Derek Lowe. Thinking about the high-and-mighty Lowe with his cocky attitude and shiny sports car, Luther wound down the truck window and spit again.

Just because Luther didn't have their Ivy League education didn't mean he wasn't as smart. Although

Luther barely got out of high school, the principal practically throwing his diploma at him to get him gone, he had street smarts. And Luther knew that's what counted.

Luther had been a roughneck, working on a Banks Oil & Gas drilling rig when he met Charles Stratton. Roughnecking was going to be a temporary gig, just until he could get enough money together and move, but that had been eight years ago. It was backbreaking work, but it paid well.

Stratton had small side jobs for him at first—riding along when the executive needed him to intimidate someone or break up a feud between other roughnecks. There had even been a few side jobs that had nothing to do with the company.

Charles Stratton always made it clear that if Elliot Banks ever found out what he was doing, Luther would be fired. But Stratton made the risk worth it by slipping him extra cash after each job.

Over the years, Luther proved valuable. The jobs Charles Stratton gave him had been simple in the beginning, but they got more complex as time went on. But after a couple of years, Stratton had him promoted to production manager, which meant more money.

Luther knew the latest job was one that could get him arrested, but he had enough on Charles Stratton and Derek Lowe to ensure he'd take the two crooked executives down with him if it ever came to that.

Luther was fed up with the shiny-shoes executives, but he'd keep his temper in check, biding his time until he could take what was owed him—more if he could figure out a way—then get out of town. California probably. His sister was out there. He could shack up with her until he found something better.

He swung the truck off the residential street onto the Strattons' long driveway, his lights sweeping the vast estate. Even in the dark, he could see the crisscross pattern of the meticulously manicured lawn. Closer to the house was an array of shrubs clipped into perfect round balls. A stone fountain with a woman pouring water from a pitcher sat in the center of the circular drive. Luther swung around her and parked.

He got out of the truck and looked over the estate. The place was lit up like Fort Knox—inside and out. No telling what the bill was just to light the place. Luther shook his head, then spit on the brick-paved driveway.

At the front door, he wiped dried mud from his work boots on the iron mat and was about to ring the doorbell when a black Escalade tore around the side of the house headed for the street. It was dark, so he couldn't see who was in it, but he hoped it wasn't Charles Stratton or he had made the trip for nothing.

He turned back and rang the doorbell and heard an elaborate chiming like church bells somewhere inside. He waited and was about to ring the bell again when the door swung open.

Charles Stratton was a tall man, but to Luther's satisfaction, Luther dwarfed him. Being able to look down on people was an advantage Luther had used on numerous occasions. He would probably never have to use his size to rough up Stratton, but he knew being physically imposing gave him an edge.

"Come in, Luther." Stratton's face was tense, and there was fury in his eyes.

It was immediately apparent that he was in a bad mood. From experience, Luther knew that meant their meeting would be short. Fine with him.

He followed Charles through the foyer, his boots clomping on the black-and-white marble floor. To his left, a marble staircase with brass railings in an elaborate scroll pattern swept up to the second floor.

In the library, Stratton turned to him and got right to the point. "There's an issue with an employee. I need you to be ready to deal with it."

Luther assumed it would be another roughneck, or maybe one of the truck drivers was caught stealing gas again. It didn't matter. He would take care of them like he had done numerous times before.

Luther jerked his chin. "Who is it?"

Charles's face was an icy mask. He hesitated before he answered. "Doris Reed."

The name hit Luther in the gut like a sucker punch. "A woman?"

The expression on Charles's face didn't change. "She's a problem for us."

Luther shook his head and looked down at the floor, stuck his hands on his hips. "I don't know, man. A woman?"

"It's irrelevant that she's a woman—she's a problem. I need you to be ready to take care of it when I say." When Luther didn't reply, Stratton added, "She's been nosing around where she shouldn't and could destroy everything we've been working for…if we let her."

Luther had never hesitated taking a job before, even though some had been pretty nasty. In fact, he found he liked the nasty ones best. But this was different. A woman. He didn't know if he had the stomach for it.

Luther shook his head again, ran his giant hand through dirty hair as he shifted his weight from side to side, thinking about it. "Man, I don't know. I've never beat up a woman."

Charles lowered his voice to a growl. "I don't want you to beat her up."

Luther froze. Charles Stratton was an evil man he

would never turn his back on. Luther knew Stratton would slit his throat if it served his purpose. But Luther was too smart to ever let him do that. He was going to screw Stratton first, then get the hell out of Dodge.

He thought about the job. It wasn't beating up a woman. It was getting rid of a problem. Charles didn't have to say anything more. Luther knew what he meant.

He felt a flicker of anticipation start to grow in his gut, and he thought about it a moment longer, his pulse quickening. "What's her name again?"

CHAPTER 31

Thursday, June 21

FIRST THING THURSDAY morning, Jack called Victoria and gave her a cursory update on the progress of his investigation. He told her he had questioned Charles Stratton and Harold Lamken and, so far, hadn't uncovered any concrete clues about who might have had a motive to kill Elliot.

He didn't tell her about his meeting with Doris Reed or his visit with Bob Hawkins's widow. For the time being, he would keep his word to Doris, not mention anything to Victoria about her suspicions that Bob's death and Elliot's murder were somehow connected.

Jack tried to convince himself that his motive for keeping the information from Victoria was the same as Doris's—to keep from hurting her further, at least until they knew something more definitive. But deep down he knew that wasn't the reason. There were secrets Victoria was keeping from him, and he didn't trust his own client.

Jack sat outside in a folding chair, his back against

the cool metal of the trailer. As he drank coffee, he watched the sun begin to break over the horizon, streaking the sky shades of orange and pink.

He thought about the day before and couldn't shake the image of the sad young widow with the toddler clinging to her leg. Jack was more determined than ever to find out what was going on.

Crockett suddenly darted toward a rabbit that had emerged from the forest, and Jack called him back, getting up from the chair.

"We don't have time for that this morning, Crockett." He poured the remaining coffee onto the ground and bent to pet the panting dog, then took the step into the trailer and grabbed the keys to his truck off the counter.

Back outside, the excited dog danced around his feet as Jack walked to the truck and opened the door. He turned back, and the dog sat patiently waiting.

"Have you ever been on a drilling rig?" Jack asked. The dog cocked his head to one side, listening. "Me neither. Get in."

The night before, Jack had phoned Clark Poindexter, the forensic accountant Doris had mentioned. Jack wanted to meet Poindexter, ask him a few questions about Banks Oil & Gas. Poindexter had agreed to talk on the condition the meeting included his client Boots Hamer, and Jack had readily agreed. He wanted to talk to Hamer as well.

Poindexter contacted Hamer, and a meeting had been set up for later that morning on a Banks drilling rig located on Hamer's property.

After the meeting was arranged, Jack had done some digging and found out Boots Hamer was one of the wealthiest men in Colorado, owning just over twenty thousand acres on the western edge of the oil-rich DJ Basin, an area stretching from northeast Colorado into southeast Wyoming and west into parts of Nebraska.

Hamer was a very rich man who, for some reason, according to Doris Reed, was unhappy with his partnership with Banks Oil & Gas.

Leaving the mountains behind, Jack drove through Denver, then turned north on Highway 85 toward the town of Greeley in Weld County. As he drove, the countryside changed drastically. Gone was the lush green grass of the tree-covered mountains. Outside Denver, the land grew flat and brown.

Jack drove on, watching small towns slide by that seemed familiar. The parking lots of local diners were crowded with long-haul trucks, their drivers asleep in their cabs or inside having breakfast. Resale shops and beauty parlors in strip malls were opening for morning business. He passed small gas stations, many with U-Haul trucks or trailers sitting out front ready to be rented.

The small towns looked like dozens of others he'd

been through in Texas and Louisiana. For a moment he felt the dull ache of being homesick and alone. He wanted to stop, walk into one of the diners, and have a cup of coffee, talk weather and politics with the locals. Jack pushed the absurd feelings aside and refocused his concentration on the road.

He checked his GPS and saw that the drilling rig was almost two miles from the highway, off a dirt road. The truck bounced over rock and gravel, kicking up dust that swirled in the bed, the sound reverberating loudly in the truck's cab. Crockett sat on the passenger seat, his pink tongue hanging out, staring straight ahead and loving every minute of it.

A few minutes later, Jack saw the oil derrick looming in the distance, a metal behemoth on a raised platform, pointed at the sky. At its base was a cluster of small buildings. Even from a distance, Jack saw the flurry of activity, men and machinery moving every which way.

He pulled through a wide opening in a fence. Overhead, a metal sign read BANKS OIL & GAS, HAMER 23H.

A small building off to one side looked like it could be the office. Jack parked next to it, wound down the windows, and left Crockett in the truck. Just before he got to the door, it swung open. A short, weathered old man in a giant cowboy hat and boots stepped out.

"You that detective?" The old man squinted up at him, a toothpick balancing on his lower lip.

"Yes, sir," Jack answered. "Jack Martin."

The old man looked him up and down, pulled the toothpick from his mouth and tossed it aside, stuck out a hand for Jack to shake. "Boots Hamer. Nice to meet ya."

He was a leathery little man with a happy face, giant white teeth that caught your eye when he smiled, and a grip that felt like it could crush a bowling ball.

A thin man with wire-rimmed glasses had emerged from the building behind him. He was significantly younger and paler than Hamer. Dressed in khaki slacks and a button-down shirt and carrying a cheap leather briefcase, he looked ridiculously out of place at the rig.

The thin man pushed his glasses higher on his nose and stuck out his hand.

Jack shook it.

"Clark Poindexter," he said.

Jack nodded. "Thank you both for agreeing to meet with me."

"What's this all about?" Boots Hamer asked in a raspy smoker's voice.

Jack was relieved there was no animosity in his tone. "As I told Mr. Poindexter on the phone last night, I've been hired by Victoria Banks to investigate her husband's murder."

Hamer looked down at the ground and shook his head, then looked back at Jack. "It's a cryin' shame what happened to that boy. Elliot was a good kid."

Jack saw real sorrow in the man's eyes. He needed to square that with the fact Hamer was threatening a lawsuit. "I would like to ask you a few questions, Mr. Hamer, about your relationship with Elliot Banks and Banks Oil & Gas."

Hamer nodded toward Jack's truck. "That yours?"

"Yes, sir," Jack answered.

"Mind if I have a seat on the back? This might take a while, and my old legs don't like standin' that long—especially in this hot sun."

Without waiting for an answer, Hamer turned and walked toward the back of the truck, and Jack followed. The old guy was about five feet six in boots, but he walked with the swagger of a man twice his size.

Hamer let the tailgate down and hopped up. "I know you called Poindexter here because you must have found out somehow that I'd hired him to look into some business for me."

Jack nodded.

Hamer took off his hat, wiped his forehead with the back of his arm, and put it back on. "Well, if you're trying to find out who murdered Elliot, then you're a friend of mine, and I'm gonna tell ya. I didn't have no problem with Elliot—that I'm sure of. But somethin' is going on around here that ain't on the up-and-up."

"What do you think it is?"

"My profits," Hamer replied. "They've been going down at a steady pace, and somethin' isn't right." Hamer looked over at the rig site.

Jack glanced around, too, and from where he stood, could see at least a dozen men working different parts of the rig.

Hamer continued. "There's just as many men working, just as many trucks coming and going, the price of oil is up, yet somehow my royalties are *down*."

"Did you talk to Elliot about it?"

The old man nodded. "I did. Elliot said he was going to look into it. Maybe he did. Maybe he didn't. I'll never know. Poindexter here and I were supposed to have a meetin' with Elliot and that company accountant, Bob Hawkins. But the day before the meetin', Hawkins up and kills himself. Another good kid, that one. Who would have figured?" Hamer shook his head again. "Anyhow, I was going to get with Elliot again sometime soon—with Poindexter here—but now Elliot's dead."

"So Elliot Banks never gave you an explanation for the declining royalties?"

The old man's face grew hard. "He didn't. He said he didn't know anything about it but would look into it. But let me tell you, the problem wasn't with Elliot."

"But you didn't get a chance to confront him with your suspicions?"

The old man frowned hard. "I didn't. I talked to him a couple of times about my royalties declining and asked him to look into it so I wouldn't have to sue to get to the truth. It liked to have killed me to threaten that, but I had to get the kid's attention. But Poindexter here met with that accountant who killed himself—Hawkins. Told him what I suspected."

"And what was that?"

"That, somehow, those slick ol' boys he had working for him—Stratton and Lowe—were shortchanging me out of my royalties. This didn't start happening until they took over the selling of my oil for Elliot."

"You don't believe Elliot could have been behind the drop in royalties somehow?"

Hamer screwed up his face and shook his head. "No, I don't. I wouldn't believe that for a minute. Let me give you a little history." He took off his hat and wiped his forehead again, then shifted his weight on the tailgate, getting more comfortable.

"When I met Elliot Banks more than twenty years ago, he was a kid right out of Colorado School of Mines with a dollar in his pocket and a million-dollar dream in his heart. All these city-slicker guys from Denver to Houston—Exxon, Chevron, you name it—had been all up in my business, trying to lease my land to drill. But my pappy never allowed no drillin' and my grandpappy never allowed no drillin', so *I* never allowed no drillin'. We were, and always have been, a ranching outfit."

A smile cracked the old man's leathery face. "But one day this kid shows up. And for some reason I like him. I didn't give in right away—no, sir. But this kid was persistent—and friendly as hell. He kept it up for over a year. We ended up friends—fished the Poudre River together most Sundays. Then one day I thought, *What the hell would it hurt to let the kid punch one well?* That was the Hamer 1. That damn thing ended up blowing out might near the size of Spindletop. Made us both rich as hell. My wife, Betsy, liked her new clothes and the Cadillac Seville I bought her so much that I let the kid drill one more—the Hamer 2."

The old man looked around, raised his arms. "This here's the Hamer 23H. *H* for horizontal. They've been drillin' 'em sideways for about a decade now, go figure. So you see how the story went." He shifted again on the tailgate. "The point of me telling you all this is to say, whatever is happening to my royalties has nothin' to do with Elliot." He jerked his gray stubbly chin at Jack. "You look into Stratton and Lowe. I'll bet you a bottle of Jack Daniel's you'll find something there. Ain't that right, Poindexter?"

Jack looked from Hamer to the accountant, who

appeared to be melting fast in the hot sun, the pale skin on his cheeks having turned a bright red and sweat beading on his tall forehead.

"What have you found out?" Jack asked him.

Poindexter took a handkerchief from his pocket and dabbed at his face. "There are irregularities in the production reports." He stuck the handkerchief back in his pocket. "It does appear output has been declining, yet there are no indications in the projections based off recent seismic reports that would indicate they should be doing so. It's an anomaly. I'm still looking into it."

Hamer cut in. "You keep lookin' into it, Poindexter. Jack, I'm gonna give you the direct number to my personal mo-bile telephone." Hamer slid off the tailgate, patted the pockets of his jeans, then the pockets of his shirt. "I'd be obliged if you'd keep me informed of anything you find out about Elliot's murder. In turn, I'll have Poindexter here let you know what he finds." Hamer frowned, still searching his pockets. "I'm always losing that damned contraption. Must have left it in the office. Hold on a minute, boys."

He left Poindexter and Jack standing alone.

"Level with me," Jack said when the old man disappeared inside the office. "Hamer's not here. I understand his loyalty to Elliot Banks, but if there's fraud in the distribution of Hamer's royalties, do you think Banks could have had something to do with it?"

The accountant nervously squeezed and released his grip on the handle of his briefcase. Jack knew he was probably wondering if he could trust him.

Jack repeated his question. "Do you think Banks could have been behind something fraudulent? Stealing from Hamer?"

When Poindexter finally spoke, it came out as a squeak. "Maybe."

Boots Hamer flung open the office door and marched over to them, flipped open a cell phone—a model Jack hadn't seen in almost a decade. "You call me if you find out somethin' about who killed Elliot," he told Jack. He gave him his number, then flipped the phone shut and jammed it into a pocket of his jeans.

Not in the habit of sharing information about an investigation, Jack hesitated, then gave Hamer a quick nod to satisfy him. For some reason, he liked the old guy, hated lying to him. But if his investigation proved that Elliot Banks was stealing from his friend, Jack didn't want to be the one to break the old guy's heart.

Back in the truck, Jack cranked the air-conditioning on high. "Sorry about that, buddy. I didn't know how hot it was going to be," he said, patting Crockett on the head. "Next time I'll leave you at home."

On his way through the gate, a black Ford Raptor nearly ran him off the road. Jack swerved and braked to a stop, glaring at the guy as he sped past, kicking up a small tornado of caliche-colored dust.

Jack's FBI training kicked in, and he did a quick assessment. Large man, head nearly touching the roof of the cab. Black hair that seemed to match the paint color of the truck.

"Jerk," Jack said aloud, pulling onto the gravel road, leaving the drilling rig behind.

As he maneuvered the dirt road toward the highway, he thought about Boots Hamer and Elliot Banks. The old man had been adamant—Banks wouldn't be behind any fraud. He had insisted it would be Charles Stratton and Derek Lowe.

But could the old guy be wrong? Jack hoped like hell he wasn't.

He didn't want to have to tell his grieving client that her murdered husband was stealing from his best friend.

CHAPTER 32

IT WAS ALMOST noon. Harold Lamken's stomach growled, alerting him that it was time for lunch, but he didn't have time to stop. He needed to finish planting the lavender.

Victoria had asked him to plant it in the beds around the swimming pool several weeks earlier, before Elliot had been killed. The shrubs had just come in from the nursery in Denver. Harold knew it would make Victoria happy to see them, and he wanted to get them in the ground right away.

"I read that hummingbirds like lavender," she had said. "Elliot didn't want me to hang a feeder. He said it would look tacky. So I thought this might be a way to attract them. And I love the smell of lavender, don't you?"

Harold carried the last pot around the side of the house and set it down on the grass, remembering their brief conversation. He didn't dare tell Victoria he thought lavender smelled like weeds but had assured her he would find some and plant it around the pool to attract hummingbirds.

He picked up the shovel and dug into the dirt, carefully setting the loosened soil aside so as not to disturb the annuals he had planted for her at the beginning of the summer.

As he dug, Harold glanced through the windows at the back of the house. He had been there for hours but hadn't seen Victoria all morning. He wanted to talk to her.

It was typical for Victoria to keep to herself, not have much to say. Elliot was the one who usually gave Harold a list of what needed to be done around the house, but now Elliot was gone. Harold was anxious, knowing how much things had changed. And as much as he didn't want to, he knew there was no way around it. He needed to keep his distance; he had to quit.

When Harold was satisfied with the hole, he set the shovel aside, grabbed one of the plants near its base, and carefully wiggled it side to side, sliding it out of the plastic pot. He set the lavender down and pushed dirt up around it. Something about doing it made him think of Elliot. They would bury him the next day. Thinking about it made Harold sad.

After the last shrub was planted, he stood up, brushing soil from his jeans. His thoughts turned from Elliot to his nephew, Tyler. "He's a good kid, just high-spirited," Harold would tell people when Tyler was young. He'd tried to put a good spin on it, but even back then Harold knew his nephew was trouble.

Over the years, Tyler had grown from a "high-spirited" kid into a dangerous and stubborn adult. Two arrests for assault and battery, one for shoplifting, and one for attempted murder. Luckily, the judge had dropped the case of attempted murder for lack of evidence. But Harold wasn't sure his nephew was innocent and feared he was capable of it—and maybe worse.

He dumped the last bit of mulch around the plants and bent to spread it. He needed to move, take Tyler with him. But where would they go? Minturn was Harold's home. He had grown up in the blue trailer and liked being back. Tyler was an adult, and every year since he'd turned eighteen, Harold hoped he would decide to go his own way. But to Harold's frustration, Tyler showed no signs of wanting to move out. If only Harold hadn't made the promise to Eileen.

He stacked the empty pots and carried them back to the garage. Out of the corner of his eye, he saw Victoria slip past a window in the corridor that looked out over the driveway. The pangs of guilt he had felt since Elliot's murder grew stronger.

He shouldn't be there. It was too dangerous. While he had a key to the house, there was always the risk that Tyler would use it to get in—to steal something again, or worse.

Harold set the plastic pots down next to his truck and started back across the yard for the shovel and empty mulch bag. He didn't want Victoria to see him looking, but as he walked by each window, he strained to catch a sideways glimpse of her. He was disappointed she was nowhere to be found.

He carried the shovel and bag to his truck, stuffed the empty pots in the bag, and threw it all into the bed of his truck. He looked toward the back door and felt a pang in his stomach he knew wasn't just from hunger.

When he finished cleaning up the yard, Harold drove to Stop N Save, filled up his truck with gas, and grabbed a burrito and a bag of chips. He spent the rest of the afternoon winterizing the exposed water pipes around the house. It was only June, a long way from the first freeze, which probably wouldn't come until September, but he didn't have anything else to do, and if he was going to quit soon, he didn't want to leave Victoria in a bind. He would take care of what he could for her first.

As he worked, he thought about leaving her. There was no other way. When the time was right, he would quit, but he decided to wait until after Elliot's funeral.

When he was done for the day, Harold took one last look at the back door, hoping Victoria would see that he was leaving and come outside. But she didn't, and he was disappointed. He hoped she would see the lavender he had planted that morning and that it would make her happy.

Back at the trailer, Harold found Tyler lying on the couch watching television, McDonald's trash was scattered across the coffee table and the floor in front of him.

He didn't bother to look up when Harold walked in. "Been working for your hot boss?"

"Shut up, Tyler." Harold threw his keys down on the TV tray next to the recliner, sat down, and started to pull off his boots.

Tyler craned his neck to look over his shoulder. He grinned, hamburger bun or french fries still stuck in his teeth. "What day do you work next? Maybe I'll go over there and help you out."

Harold shot off the recliner, reached down, and grabbed his nephew by the collar. He was close enough to smell the onions on his breath.

"If you ever go back over there," Harold said through clenched teeth, "I'll kill you."

CHAPTER 33

JACK SAT IN a folding chair outside the Airstream with a Shiner Bock and a small stack of paper set on a flimsy card table in front of him. Crockett lay at his feet, watching the forest for any movement that would send him darting off to investigate.

When Jack had gotten back from meeting Hamer and Poindexter at the drilling rig, he had dug out his small printer from the compartment under his mattress and printed out his research.

Most of the detectives he knew would have a hard time working in such a confined space. While at the FBI, Jack had had a good-sized office and his pick of various conference and briefing rooms. Even while in Aspen, he'd had a decent-sized desk and two small interrogation rooms to choose from if he needed more space.

He didn't have that luxury anymore, but it didn't bother him. He leaned back in the folding chair and glanced toward the summit of Shadow Mountain. Small patches of snow still clung to the recesses in the rocky crags near the top. Nowhere he had worked before had offered these kinds of views. The realization that it wouldn't be much longer before he would have to head back to Texas and find a job was a sobering reality.

He dropped the chair back onto all fours, pulled the beer bottle from the table in front of him, and popped the cap off with the underside of his college ring.

It bothered him, but there wasn't time to get sentimental. The future would take care of itself like it always did. He would worry about moving later.

Jack took a long draw on the bottle, pulled the stack of paper toward himself, and started with the page on top.

Charles Stratton. Forty-five years old. Married to Katie Stratton, thirty-six. Both lived in Cherry Hills Village, which Jack knew was one of the ritziest areas in Denver. There was a smattering of other information on the page printed from the Department of Motor Vehicles database. Jack would thank Luke McCray for the information again later. Luke had been his partner at the Aspen Police Department when they solved the Hermes Strangler case.

Next, Jack read through the executive bio he'd printed off the Banks Oil & Gas website. Charles Stratton had attended Harvard, earning an undergraduate degree. Then he'd earned an MBA from Wharton. There were a handful of accolades from previous positions he had held in Boston before joining Banks Oil & Gas as its chief financial officer.

Jack thought it was interesting that Elliot Banks hadn't been dead a week and the company's website already listed Charles Stratton as the CEO. He suspected Stratton had a hand in getting the website updated so quickly.

Jack set the company bio aside and started in on the more in-depth research he had done into Stratton's past. There were mentions of a handful of promotions over the years, published in Boston's local financial news.

A wedding announcement in the *Denver Post* included a picture of Katie Stratton. Pretty, Jack thought. Short and curvy, long blond curls spilling down the open back of a lace wedding dress. The announcement mentioned her family. Jack googled her father and found out he was a wealthy local surgeon, her mother a prominent local philanthropist. Jack turned his attention back to the announcement and read that Katie had graduated from a private girls' high school in Denver, then was a cheerleader at Colorado Boulder before becoming a substitute schoolteacher. But the announcement made only cursory mention of Charles and nothing about his past except for his Harvard education.

There were articles about Banks Oil & Gas that included scores of quotes from Stratton. Jack read them all. The only one of real interest was an article following the death of Bob Hawkins. A financial reporter with the *Denver Post* had asked if Hawkins's death would affect the impending merger with Centennial State Energy. Stratton had replied simply, "No comment."

Noticeably absent was any mention of charitable contributions. It was in stark contrast to the long list of donations Jack found when researching Elliot Banks. Over the years, it appeared Charles Stratton had made none.

Jack flipped to the older information—Charles Stratton *before* Harvard and the high-powered financial jobs. Stratton had grown up a poor kid in a blighted area of Springfield, Massachusetts. There was no mention of a mother, but his father had obviously been a town drunk, in and out of jail for public intoxication several times during Stratton's formative years.

There was a second son. Charles had an older brother. Jack read about Bruce Stratton's deliberate hit-and-run, which had killed a guy he'd fought with outside a Springfield bar. The brother had been incarcerated in the maximum-security prison at Lancaster and had been serving a life sentence ever since.

But it wasn't just the father and brother who had gotten into trouble. Jack was surprised to find that the almighty Charles Stratton had his own skirmishes with the law growing up. There was a ticket for vandalism when an eighteen-year-old Stratton had been caught throwing a brick through the window of a convenience store. A month earlier, the same store had filed charges of theft against Stratton, who had been an employee for only a few weeks when cash started disappearing from the register. Lucky for Stratton, the judge had thrown the case out for lack of evidence.

But through it all, Charles Stratton had been a stellar student, somehow managing to graduate valedictorian of his high school class and earning a spot at Harvard.

His early skirmishes with the law were obviously a side of Stratton he had since worked successfully to hide. There were no mentions of the impoverished upbringing or questionable family members in any of the news stories or corporate press releases. No mention of the accusations of theft or vandalism in the announcements of his wedding to Katie or his appointment by Elliot Banks to CFO of Banks Oil & Gas.

After just one meeting, Jack's initial impression of Charles Stratton had been that he was a selfish, power-hungry SOB. The research Jack had on him seemed to affirm it.

The question was, just how far would Charles Stratton go to reach the top?

CHAPTER 34

CHARLES WAS READY. It had been nearly twenty-four hours since Katie had stormed from the house, angry with him. But earlier that day, he had pulled one of the small baubles from the safe he kept to placate her on occasions such as this.

Katie was sitting at her vanity table, looking into a gold-framed mirror hanging in front of her. "I love it, Charles," she said, her fingers brushing the circle of diamonds hanging from the silver chain around her neck. "It's perfect."

"I'm glad you like it." Charles leaned over to kiss the top of her head. "Let's go downstairs. I'll help you fix dinner."

She turned on her velvet chair and looked up at him. "I wasn't planning on dinner together—I was still mad at you from yesterday. I wasn't going to cook."

"We'll find something."

She shook her head. "I didn't feel like going to the market today. I don't think we have anything."

Charles couldn't imagine how Katie could

consistently waste days with little to show for them except discarded fashion magazines and the occasional lunch with girlfriends. People without ambition were enigmas he didn't understand. But he was tolerant of them when they served his purpose.

"Then let's go to the club for dinner."

Katie beamed. "That's a great idea." She sprang from her chair and started toward the large closet they shared. "Just give me a few minutes to get dressed."

Charles leaned back against the bathroom counter, pulled his phone from the pocket of his slacks, and scrolled through emails. He could hear Katie furiously opening and closing drawers in the closet.

"Charles, you do remember that Elliot's funeral is tomorrow, don't you?"

Charles looked up from his phone and toward the open closet door. Katie had slipped on a silk dress and was adjusting it in the full-length mirror. He had forgotten about the funeral. He wasn't interested in going but knew it would look bad if he didn't.

"What time?" he asked.

"Ten o'clock at All Faiths Chapel."

"In Vail?" He knew he had to go to the damned thing but hadn't planned on losing a whole day.

"Yes, darling. Of course in Vail. Elliot almost never spent time in Denver after he and Victoria built the house—you know that."

She had positioned a stepstool below the shoe

rack that stretched floor to ceiling. Charles watched her balance on her tiptoes, reaching for a pair of stilettos. She wavered, momentarily losing her balance before catching herself. Charles knew he could easily reach the shoes she wanted without the stool, but he turned his attention back to his phone. He'd let her feel the satisfaction of accomplishing *something* before the day was over.

When Katie finally emerged from the closet, she stood looking at him, her head cocked at an angle. "Well?"

She was fishing for a compliment. *She's nothing if not consistent*, Charles thought. The woman thrived on compliments and adulation—the hallmarks of low self-esteem.

He stepped toward her and pulled her close. "You look amazing."

On the way down the marble staircase, they continued the conversation.

"Did you get a chance to call Victoria today?" he asked.

"I did, actually. I asked if there was anything we could do for her tomorrow—for the funeral. She sounded so tired, or maybe she was depressed."

He tried sounding sympathetic. "She might be, and with good reason."

They had reached the bottom of the stairs. Katie's stilettos clicked across the black-and-white marble floor as they made their way through the foyer. "I'm worried about her."

"Why?" Charles hesitated at the entrance to the kitchen and let Katie walk through the swinging door ahead of him.

"She's not herself. She's always been an introvert. I know that—everyone knows that. She's always been ridiculously private. But since Elliot's death, it's something more." In the kitchen, she stopped and turned around. "She's trying to hide it, but I can tell she thinks there's merit to Doris Reed's crazy theory that Elliot's death could be connected to Bob Hawkins's suicide."

The financial press had already hounded Charles for information on Elliot's murder. The questions were mostly regarding how Elliot's death would affect the merger, but a couple had touched on the ongoing investigation. Charles knew that if the scandal-hungry journalists caught wind of Victoria hiring the celebrated detective who had just caught the Hermes Strangler in Aspen, there would be renewed interest that could further endanger his plans.

"Talk to her at the funeral," Charles said. "Go see her in a day or two and take her to lunch—on me."

Katie looked at him with a wry smile. "You're so benevolent, Charles. Lunch? On you? How kind."

Her sarcasm grated on him, but he forced the irritation aside. "Ask her what's going on with the police's investigation. Hopefully, after the funeral she'll drop her investigation with that detective."

"Why?"

"Nothing good can come from it except bad publicity."

"What difference would that make?"

The limits to Katie's inductive reasoning never ceased to astound him. He drew in a deep breath. "Darling, any bad publicity could risk crushing the merger—I've told you that. We can't let the fortune I'll make slip through our fingers." Charles gently guided her down the hallway toward the door to the garage. "Find out what's going on with the investigations—both of them. We can't let Doris Reed's delusions—now Victoria's—put things at risk. For all our sakes—Victoria's included—she needs to drop the case. This has to be wrapped up quickly."

They stepped out of the house onto the textured floor of the garage. Charles pushed the button to open the garage door, then punched the key fob to his black Mercedes, unlocking it.

Katie's heels clicked as she walked past her Escalade toward Charles's car. "I want the merger to be a success for you, Charles—I do. But I'm still very concerned about Victoria. She's not herself, and she looks so tired."

Charles walked behind her toward the Mercedes.

"Take her some of those sleeping pills of yours. Maybe she'll slip up and take too many."

Katie wheeled on him. "Charles!"

He laughed. "Darling, of course I'm kidding," he lied.

CHAPTER 35

MILES PRESTON SAT in a patio chair on the balcony of his suite at the Four Seasons in Vail. The air was crisp, the sun having dropped below the mountains an hour earlier. The swimming pool several stories below was large and illuminated a glowing blue-green. He could hear people chattering by the pool, the sounds muffled by the faint whir of traffic on Interstate 70 on the other side of the building.

He sat watching the crowd. People dining at outdoor tables, kids laughing and yelling to one another as they splashed in the water. It all seemed so frivolous and innocent. He vacillated between wanting to join them and wanting to hurl himself off the balcony. He had to pull it together—for Victoria.

He emptied what was left in the crystal highball, then set it down on the concrete floor of the balcony. He wouldn't refill it again. The contents of the minibar had been significantly depleted in the two hours since he'd gotten the call from the Vail detective.

"Mr. Preston, we need your client to come in for further questioning."

Miles had known the call would come. It was a regular occurrence for suspects to be interviewed more than once before police ruled them out. But what the Vail detective said next had come as a complete shock.

"Our forensics team has identified the bloody fingerprints on the tomahawk used to murder Elliot Banks. The prints are those of his wife, Victoria."

It was a blow he hadn't expected. He would call the defense team in the morning—get them involved. They had been consulted and were already on retainer. But they had been his backup plan. Miles never expected to have to call them into action.

At least the police had agreed to wait until Monday after Miles pointed out the indecency of having her come in on the day of her husband's funeral. To his relief and somewhat surprise, the detective had agreed.

But he and Victoria had to be there first thing Monday morning. Miles would have the very best attorneys on the defense team there as well. He had everything lined up, ready to go, but he still felt like he had failed her. The detective had only mentioned her coming in for *questioning*, but with her fingerprints on the murder weapon, Miles feared it could end up being more.

He continued to stare into the hypnotic blue-green of the pool below. The drone of the freeway in the distance had grown louder. In the back recesses of his mind, he knew he needed to get up, go inside, and shower. The funeral was the next day.

He needed to call Victoria, tell her the police had found her fingerprints on the murder weapon and that she was wanted again for questioning, but he couldn't bring himself to do it—not yet.

He mentally ran through several scenarios on how to ask her about the fingerprints, but was unsatisfied with any of them. He wanted to know how they'd gotten on the tomahawk, but he wasn't sure how to ask her without sounding like he thought she was guilty.

Along with the whiskey, the questions ate at his gut. How could she have been so careless? How would she explain her fingerprints in blood on the murder weapon? Miles would confront her—he had to; he was her attorney and her friend—but not yet.

The whiskey made him feel heavy in the chair, and he welcomed its numbing effect. He would tell her about the fingerprints *after* the funeral, not before. The decision—or maybe it was the whiskey—helped dull his nerves.

He closed his eyes, letting the cool night breeze chill the thin layer of sweat that had formed on his brow. As he drifted off to sleep, his final thoughts were of the impending events of the following day.

Elliot's funeral.

And having to tell Victoria she could be arrested for murder.

CHAPTER 36

Friday, June 22

JACK MARTIN GOT to the chapel early. The sky was overcast and dreary, dark clouds threatening rain. He stood near a cluster of aspens at the base of the steps that led up to the sanctuary. A set of large wood doors had been propped open for the arriving mourners.

Jack stood quietly to the side, watching funeral-goers ascend the steps, and was struck by the vast cross-section of people who'd come to mourn Elliot Banks. They were young and very old, black, white, and Hispanic. There were executive types in suits and ties, but also scores of people from the working class. The cross-section of cultural and socioeconomic statuses was striking. It deepened Jack's curiosity about the man whose murder he investigated.

When it looked like the last of the mourners had arrived, Jack made his way up the concrete steps and into the church. The small chapel was standing room only. He found a spot to one side near the back and stood against the wall.

He scanned the room, his eyes sweeping from side to side, then drifting up to the ceiling. It was a beautiful church, with heavy bent timbers that stretched from the floor on either side and curved overhead, finally meeting above a wide center aisle. The arched beams and planked ceiling reminded Jack of the inverted hull of an old ship.

Behind the altar was a tall window with clear panes of glass set in a striking geometric pattern, a view of pine trees through it. Somewhere, music was playing softly. The setting was peaceful.

Jack hadn't been to a church service in years—hadn't wanted to, not since the death of his grandparents. But the overwhelming sense of peace he felt being in the pretty little chapel in Vail had him reconsidering. It could have lulled him into a state of relaxation, but he couldn't let it.

Jack shifted on his feet, repositioning himself along the wall. There was work to do.

He scanned the crowd.

Unless a murder was random—which they rarely were—the killer always had a motive. And Jack knew that solving a murder wasn't so much about figuring out *what* had happened as it was about figuring out *why*.

Jack needed to find out why someone would kill Elliot Banks, and he had a deep suspicion that whoever had done it was now somewhere in the chapel.

The thought was sobering yet invigorating at the same time.

A man in a dark suit and holding a Bible took the steps at the front of the church and began speaking.

Blessed are those who mourn,
for they will be comforted...

Jack continued to scan the crowd, his gaze settling on Charles Stratton, newly minted CEO of Banks Oil & Gas. Stratton sat in the second pew, just behind Victoria. A short, good-looking blonde sat next to him—Katie Stratton. Jack recognized her from their wedding announcement.

He watched Stratton's body language as the preacher continued to speak. Stratton sat relaxed, not looking at the preacher, but shifting his gaze to various spots in the church, then brushing something from his shoulder.

The new CEO of Banks Oil & Gas looked anything but upset that his former boss was dead. He looked bored. Stratton had a lot to gain with Elliot Banks out of the way. Was that motive enough for murder?

Derek Lowe sat on the opposite side of Katie Stratton. Jack had not met with Lowe yet, but he recognized him from his picture on the company website. Lowe sat ramrod straight and extended an arm down the top of the pew. He had one foot resting on the opposite knee, his leg extending out into the aisle. Lowe was more formal than Stratton in his demeanor and dressed like a slick Wall Street type—dark-gray pin-striped suit, hair greased back in a way that reminded Jack of Gordon Gekko.

Greed is good. Jack contemplated the famous line from the movie and wondered if Derek Lowe had as much to gain from the murder of his boss as Charles Stratton did. He remembered what Doris Reed had called the two—*snakes in the grass.* By the looks of them, and the short amount of time he had spent with Stratton, Jack was inclined to agree.

Miles Preston sat across the aisle from Stratton and Lowe. Preston looked nothing like the composed attorney Jack had met at the fancy restaurant only a couple of days earlier. His suit was wrinkled, like he had worn it the day before. He had a ruddy complexion and a pained look on his face, almost as if he was sick—or hungover. Jack watched as Preston used a handkerchief to dab once at each eye, then drag it across his forehead.

Jack hadn't heard back from Preston about the fingerprints on the tomahawk. If he got a chance to speak to him in private, he would ask. If the police were able to identify the prints, then Jack's temporary employment would end as quickly as it had started.

The preacher introduced Preston to give the eulogy.

Jack watched as Preston stood up and approached the dais, looking visibly distraught.

At the pulpit, Preston cleared his throat. "Elliot Banks was one of those rare men gifted with both a magnetic personality and a brilliant mind. I've watched him draw someone into his circle many times over the years, regale them with witty conversation, and make the person feel like they were the only one in the crowd. He had a knack—a gift. He was the guy everyone wanted to be around, the guy everyone wanted to be. And I was honored to call him my best friend…"

Jack continued to study the crowd. Several rows behind Stratton and Lowe sat Harold Lamken: employee for many years, knew Elliot's comings and goings—his habits—and he had access to the house. Lamken was the only one other than Elliot and Victoria who had a key. Did Lamken let himself in that night and murder his boss? When Jack questioned him at the blue trailer by the river, Lamken had been shifty, acting nervous. But would he kill his employer? Cut off the hand that fed him?

Lamken sat motionless in the pew, a cowboy hat in his hands. He appeared to be looking down at it. Jack watched him for a while. Lamken never looked up, wasn't shifting in his seat or bouncing a leg—nothing to suggest he was nervous. Jack continued to study him closely but couldn't decide if his body language suggested profound sadness or guilt. There was still more to Lamken's story than what Jack knew.

To the right of Lamken, on the same pew, sat Doris Reed. Her bright red hair, jarring against the black polyester pantsuit she wore, was the first thing Jack had seen when he'd entered the church.

Doris was visibly distraught, her heavy bulk quaking with silent sobs. She was quirky, maybe crazy, but she was also a kind woman whose heart was obviously broken by the death of her longtime boss and friend. The enormous depth of the woman's sorrow was palpable. Jack could only watch her for a little while before he had to look away.

Miles Preston had finished talking, and the preacher returned to the pulpit. Jack continued to scan the crowd.

Sitting behind Lamken was Boots Hamer. The old man was dressed in a dark suit with one leg kicked sideways into the aisle, exposing a black alligator cowboy boot. He held a cowboy hat in his hand and looked down at the floor, nodding slowly with whatever the preacher was saying.

Jack's gaze shifted to Victoria Banks, alone in the front pew. He hadn't seen her walk in and assumed she must have gotten there early. She was wearing a simple black dress, her dark hair pulled low and twisted into a knot at the nape of her neck. She wore a simple strand of pearls. She looked beautiful. The fact that she was alone, no family or friends accompanying her, was painfully obvious.

From where he was standing, Jack couldn't see her face, but he watched her shoulders and long slender back for any signs of grief. She sat still, looking straight ahead, her posture erect. Jack couldn't tell if she was staring at the preacher or at Elliot's dark mahogany coffin, which sat directly in front of her, covered with a bouquet of Colorado wildflowers.

One at a time, the preacher introduced several people who got up and spoke, all of them extolling the virtues of their friend or boss. For a man with no biological family of his own, Elliot Banks hadn't lacked for love and admiration. Not the sort of guy you would expect to be a target for murder.

When the last speaker had taken their seat, the minister approached the dais again, held a single hand aloft, and bowed his head.

Even though I walk through the valley
of the shadow of death…

At the end of the service, Victoria rose and silently approached the casket. Jack watched as she laid a hand on the dark wood, then bent forward and gently kissed it. She straightened one of the blooms in the bouquet that had fallen to the side, then turned and made her way quietly down the aisle.

If she had slept any the night before, Jack couldn't tell. She didn't have on any makeup, and there were dark circles under her eyes. But even in the starkness of her sorrow and fatigue, Jack could see the underlying beauty. As she made her way down the aisle, mourners stood silent, most of them watching her until she was out of the sanctuary.

Jack was one of the first to follow her out of the church, but he kept his distance.

Outside, the sun had broken through the morning clouds and was shining down in large milky streaks. Jack took his position in front of the cluster of aspens and watched the crowd file out of the church, many opting to mingle in the yard.

A man approached Victoria from behind, putting a hand on her shoulder. When she turned around, he leaned in to kiss her cheek, but she pulled away. Jack watched as they talked, the conversation appearing tense. Victoria glanced around as if looking for help, or to make sure no one would overhear, Jack wasn't sure which. She pulled the man several steps away from the growing crowd outside the chapel.

The guy looked to be in his early thirties. He was thin and taller than Victoria by a few inches. He was dressed in faded jeans and boots and wore a plaid shirt untucked. From a distance, Jack thought he resembled a tall Brad Pitt and would probably be attractive to women, but Victoria was obviously not glad to see him.

As they talked, the guy ran a hand through a mop of dirty-blond hair and looked frustrated. Jack watched closely as they continued their tense exchange. If it looked like Victoria needed help, he was ready to step in.

After a few seconds, the guy threw up a hand in apparent surrender and turned to leave. Victoria reached for him but let her hand drop short, letting him go.

She turned her attention back to the crowd still lingering in the churchyard. Several mourners approached her and took turns offering their condolences. Jack watched her greet each one, amazed at how quickly she had regained her cool demeanor following the encounter with the Brad Pitt look-alike.

Doris Reed walked past, turning her head in Jack's direction long enough to give him a quick nod. No words were spoken. Charles Stratton and Derek Lowe could still be nearby, and Jack knew Doris wouldn't risk them seeing her talk to him.

As the crowd slowly dispersed, Jack debated approaching Victoria to offer his condolences for the loss of her husband. He wouldn't bring up the investigation—the funeral wasn't the time or place. But he felt compelled to speak to her, if only to let her know that he was there.

Jack took a step toward her but was immediately clapped on the back. He turned to see Boots Hamer offering a wan smile.

"Right nice service, don't you think?" Hamer asked.

"Hello, Boots." Jack shook his outstretched hand. "Yes, it was very nice. Elliot seemed like a good man."

Hamer nodded in agreement, and Jack saw the sorrow again in the old man's eyes.

"He was, and I'm going to miss him somethin' fierce." Hamer was lost in his sadness a moment, then clapped Jack on the back a second time. "I think I'll go say hello to the widow. You keep me posted on that investigation of yours."

Jack watched Hamer approach Victoria, who seemed genuinely happy to see him. She smiled and let Hamer take her hand in his and kiss it. They spoke for only a few seconds.

When Hamer had moved on, Jack took a step in Victoria's direction, then stopped. Miles Preston appeared and gave her a quick hug. The two talked for a bit, then turned and walked together in the direction of the parking lot.

Jack wanted to talk to both of them—but *separately*. He wanted to find out from Preston if the bloody prints on the tomahawk had been identified, but he wanted to question him privately. To ask in front of

Victoria—immediately following the funeral—was an insensitive affront Jack wouldn't risk.

He also wanted to talk to Victoria, but she looked spent. She needed time. Jack decided to let her mourn today; he would call her tomorrow.

He wasn't sure yet how he would approach the subject, but he was now determined to find out the identity of the blond man—the man who had tried to kiss Victoria on the day of her husband's funeral.

CHAPTER 37

FOLLOWING THE FUNERAL, Charles Stratton went straight to his black Mercedes parked on the street next to the church. He couldn't get out of Vail fast enough.

There was still work to do on the merger, but by the time he got back to the office, most of the day would have already been lost. He would work late to make up for it and expected Derek Lowe, who was somewhere behind him, also headed back to Denver, to do the same.

He was relieved Katie had driven herself to Vail, saying she wanted to stay an extra day or two, have lunch with friends, and do some shopping before she returned to Denver. Charles was glad to have her out of the way for a few days. He suggested Katie call Victoria, keep him informed about the progress of the investigations. Katie had reluctantly agreed to *think about it* but made no promises. The blasted woman still didn't understand the significance that bad publicity from Victoria's meddling could cause. If the financial press really sank their teeth into the story of Elliot's murder and started snooping around the company's business, it could spook the investors or their counterparts at Centennial State Energy. Or worse, it could ignite an SEC investigation that could bring all of Charles's plans crashing down around him.

Charles accelerated up the ramp to Interstate 70, headed east. It would be two hours before he'd be back at the office. As he sped his way through the mountains, he thought of all the possible scenarios that could derail the merger. His biggest problem at the moment was Doris Reed.

The day before, the IT technician at Banks Oil & Gas had alerted him that someone had logged onto Elliot's computer and accessed his schedule and email account. When the technician had gone to check on the computer, he discovered it was missing. Charles knew the computer was tucked safely away in his library at the mansion but let the technician think it had been stolen.

Charles maneuvered the Mercedes around a Subaru wagon, cursing the old woman who drove it for going slow in the fast lane. People in general irritated him. And from experience, he'd learned that most of them weren't worth a damn.

He thought about the one he needed out of the way. The one he suspected of accessing Elliot's computer, snooping through his schedule and emails. No one else would have Elliot's passcode. He wished he had thought to change it.

Charles used the touchpad on the car's dash to access his contacts, then found Luther Byrd's number and punched it. As he listened to the call ring on the other end of the line, he maneuvered the last turn before the Eisenhower Tunnel, where he knew he would lose service and the call would be dropped. He would make it quick.

The voice that finally answered was deep and gruff. "Yeah."

Luther Byrd was vulgar and crude. Charles was often repulsed by him, but he served a purpose. He needed to put up with Byrd a while longer; then he would figure out a way to get rid of him.

"Luther, it's Stratton."

"Yes, Mr. Stratton?"

Charles took in a deep breath, knowing what he had to do. It was a drastic measure, but it had to be done. "Do you remember the problem we talked about at the house Wednesday night?"

"The woman?"

"Shut up, Luther." The guy was as dense as granite. "Not over the phone, you idiot."

There was silence on the other end of the line, then finally, "I remember the problem." The voice sounded indignant, but Charles didn't care.

"Take care of it ASAP."

The black Mercedes slipped into the tunnel, and the call went dead.

CHAPTER 38

LUTHER BYRD'S DAY had gone from bad to worse. He was at a well, recalibrating a busted meter when he got the call from Charles Stratton. He had stepped away from the two men working with him to answer it.

When Luther hung up, he glanced over at the two guys, decided to let them finish the job, and walked to his truck. He would readjust the calibrating later, when the two were finished and gone. In the meantime, he had more important things to do.

He opened the door to his truck, reached in, and pulled a stainless-steel flask from the console. Turning his back to the pump and the men, he twisted off the cap and took a long draw of the whiskey, letting it burn the back of his throat as it slid down his gullet, then wiped his mouth with the back of a dirty hand and replaced the cap.

When he thought of Stratton's call, he leaned over and spit into the dirt, barely missing the side of his steel-toed work boot.

Nothing bothered Luther as much as being barked

at like a junkyard dog. He'd served in the army long enough to know he didn't like taking orders—especially not from uppity superiors—military *or* civilian. To hell with the dishonorable discharge, Luther thought. It hadn't held him back one bit. And he had finally been rid of the arrogant SOB officers that lived to insult him.

He might not be in the army any longer, but now he had Charles Stratton to deal with, and Stratton's imperious manner was becoming intolerable. Luther would bide his time a little longer—but not much. Stratton had promised him a big payday when the damn merger finally went through. Luther would wait until then, but not a day longer.

As soon as he got what was coming to him, he'd split, and take whatever else of value he could load into his truck. He'd already swiped a few of handling tools lying around one of the rigs. Stashed safely in his garage, they would be easy to fence when the time came. He had also pulled copper wire from a conduit when no one was watching. That would be an easy sell at the scrap metal yard. But Luther knew he deserved more and would figure out a way to get it before he headed to California.

In the meantime, there was another job to do.

CHAPTER 39

BACK HOME AFTER the funeral, Victoria lingered just inside the front door. She looked around the foyer, then down the hall toward the kitchen and the master bedroom. She turned slowly and looked in the other direction, toward the dining room and Elliot's study. The house was quiet. Although it was empty, she felt Elliot everywhere.

Before Miles had dropped her off, he had offered to take her somewhere for lunch, or to bring her dinner later. When she refused, he asked if she wanted him to come inside. Victoria told him she appreciated his concern, but she wanted to be alone. She was glad he said he understood, telling her to call him if she changed her mind. Then he left.

For a few minutes following the funeral, the sun had broken through the clouds. But on the short drive home, the darkness had swallowed the light once again.

Inside, the house was dark. Victoria thought the darkness gave the house a dreary feel that mirrored her mood. She left the lights off.

At the doorway to the study, her eyes swept the room and the objects in it: Elliot's books and art, the things he kept on his desk. She studied it all, feeling him in all of it. He smiled at her from the picture of the two of them on his desk; it had been a wonderful night for both of them. She remembered how proud she had been that night as he accepted the Citizen of the Year award, and her sadness deepened.

Her gaze slid across the desk to Elliot's engineering books. His laptop. She noticed the large chunk of gold pyrite and remembered the story Elliot had told her about finding it one summer while a student at Mines. He had dug it up somewhere in the mountains while on a geology field trip. A four-pound chunk of jagged rock that looked like gold but wasn't. As long as Victoria had known him, Elliot had kept it on his desk.

Something about the pyrite bothered her. She had worked at the desk several times since Elliot died but hadn't remembered seeing it. But that was crazy, she thought. Where else would it have been?

She looked out through the large windows at the far end of the room. Vail Mountain was now shrouded in dark clouds that threatened rain.

To her left, a Native American lance hung on the wall, slender and elegant, wrapped with leather straps and feathers, the flint rock tip honed to a sharp point. Above it was the empty spot where the tomahawk should have been. Its absence was a brutal reminder it had been used by Elliot's killer a week earlier. Victoria shuddered and turned away.

In the kitchen, she placed her purse on the corner of the counter and walked slowly to the windows that looked out onto the backyard. In the distance, she noticed lavender in the beds around the pool. Harold must have planted it the day before. Even in the overcast gloom, the lavender was beautiful, its long flowering shoots of soft purple. A lone hummingbird buzzed around the blooms for several seconds before darting away. Victoria stared at the lavender, wanting the bird to return, but it didn't. It was then she noticed a section of the purple blooms looked dry, as if they were already dying, and her heart sank.

She pulled off her shoes and carried them with her down the dark corridor to the master bedroom. In her closet, she placed them in their spot on the shelf, arranging them so they were equal distance from the shoes on either side.

She felt heavy, as if a great weight had been set on her. Each breath was a struggle. Moving slowly, as if in a trance, she changed out of the black dress into a cashmere jogging set. The softness of the fabric felt like a gentle hug, momentarily alleviating some of the suffocating weight threatening to overtake her.

In the bathroom, she glanced at herself in the

mirror, but once again she didn't recognize the woman staring back. The woman in the mirror looked old and tired, but mostly she looked defeated, like someone about to give up—about to throw in life's towel. And why shouldn't she? She stared at the dark circles under her eyes, made more severe by the way her hair was pulled back. The pain and regret were unbearable, and she made herself turn away.

She walked through Elliot's closet, drawing a hand slowly across the sleeves of his shirts. They were arranged by color, and she moved from light to dark. She smiled, remembering the times Elliot told her she didn't need to organize his closet so meticulously, but she'd kept doing it for him anyway. Her smile faded when she realized she wouldn't need to do it any longer.

Her hand stopped at one of Elliot's favorite shirts—a flannel Ralph Lauren she had gotten him for Christmas the year before. She pulled the sleeve toward her, put it to her nose, and shut her eyes. Then she drew in a slow breath, hoping she could still smell him. But he was gone.

She squeezed her eyes tight, fighting the wave of grief that had been building since the night she'd found him dead. But the wave overtook her.

Pulling the shirt from its hanger, Victoria fell to the floor and finally sobbed.

CHAPTER 40

HAROLD LAMKEN FELT every day of his fifty-two years. Back from the funeral, he sat in his recliner, the television tuned in to a Rockies game that he hardly noticed.

He reached over and pulled a can of Keystone Light from the carton—his sixth in an hour.

Tyler was asleep in his room, still high or hungover from the night before. The kid needed some direction, but mainly Harold just wanted him gone.

Harold popped open the can and drank from it. He stared at the television, but his mind was still reeling. His guilt had reached a crescendo he couldn't control. He had spent the drive home pounding the dash of his truck with a closed fist and cursing God.

He didn't want to quit, but he knew he had to. Doing what he wanted was a luxury he couldn't afford anymore, thanks to Tyler.

He would be at the house on Monday. He would put in a whole day, getting as much done for Victoria as he could, and then he would tell her he was quitting. There was no other way.

He had found the gold pyrite and two bottles of liquor in Tyler's room the day after Elliot's murder and had been waiting for the right time to replace it. It wasn't the first time Tyler had used Harold's key to get into the Bankses' house, and it wasn't the second. He had no idea how many times Tyler had been in, helping himself to the liquor and God knows what else.

Harold remembered what Elliot had said after catching Tyler stealing a couple of bottles of wine. "That boy is going to end up in jail like his mother." At the time Harold had been insulted by Elliot's callous comparison of Tyler to his baby sister, but deep down he knew Elliot was right.

Earlier in the week, when Harold knew that Victoria would be at the funeral home making arrangements, he had snuck into the house. He'd put the pyrite in the same spot on the desk where it had sat since Elliot and Victoria moved in years earlier.

For days Harold was terrified someone would notice the pyrite missing before he could return it. But the police hadn't asked him about it, and Victoria hadn't either. It seemed no one noticed it was gone, and Harold was relieved.

But even with the pyrite back, Harold worried about which night Tyler had stolen it. He had been caught once. Had Elliot caught him again?

Harold didn't like to think his nephew was capable

of murder, that he could intentionally hurt someone, but he wasn't sure. He hadn't confronted Tyler about the pyrite because he wasn't sure if he really wanted to know.

And besides, the more Harold knew, the worse it could be for the boy. At least in his ignorance, Harold could truthfully deny knowing anything about Elliot's murder.

For several minutes, he tried focusing on the baseball game, but it was no use. He drained what was left of the sixth beer, crushed the can in his fist, and hurled it toward the kitchen, where it bounced off the countertop and clattered to the floor.

"Geez. Not good for the hangover, Uncle."

Harold turned to see Tyler standing behind him, pressing his palms to his eyes and rubbing, his greasy hair a mess.

"I don't give a damn about your hangover."

Tyler pulled his hands away and looked at him. "What's got you all sore?"

Harold ignored him, trying to concentrate on the game. He wanted to forget about everything—about everybody. And as much as he hated to admit it, despite his promise to his dying sister, Harold wanted the kid gone—for good.

He leaned over and pulled a seventh beer from the carton.

Tyler whistled. "Dang, Uncle. It's still early." He

plopped down on the couch next to him, not bothering to move the fast-food trash first. "Want some company?"

Harold looked over, saw the stupid grin on the kid's face, and couldn't take it anymore. He jerked forward in the recliner, the footrest slamming shut. "No, Tyler, I don't want any company."

The kid stared at him, shocked by his response.

Harold squinted hard, his face taut. "Let me ask you something. What day did you take that pyrite from Elliot's desk?"

The kid's expression went from shocked to confused. "The what?"

"The pyrite! The rock you stole off Elliot Banks's desk."

Recognition relaxed Tyler's face. "Oh," he said, nodding, "the gold."

"It wasn't yours! What the hell were you thinking?"

Tyler stood up and looked around, then bolted to his room. A few seconds later he was back. "Where is it?"

Harold feigned ignorance. "Where's what?"

"The gold!" Tyler said, agitated.

"I put it back."

"You what?"

"I put it back!"

Tyler looked at him in disbelief. "Do you have any idea how much gold is going for? They don't need that money—but we do! I was going to pawn it. Split the cash with you."

"It's not real gold—it's *fool's* gold, you idiot. And that's just what you are—a fool." Harold stabbed the air with his finger. "I've already told you, but I'll tell you again. Don't ever go near that house—or Victoria Banks—again. Got it?"

There was a long pause. Tyler's face was hard, anger and resentment burning in his eyes. "Got it."

"Good." Harold nodded once, reached over for the wooden handle on the side of the recliner and lifted it, throwing the footrest back out. "Now get out of here. I don't want to look at you right now."

Tyler shook his head, threw open the door to the trailer, but turned back. "Just one thing."

Harold let out a long sigh, grabbed the remote, and turned the television volume up. He had vented, had let the kid have it. Now maybe he could finally relax and watch the game.

But Tyler stood at the door still staring at him.

"What?" Harold replied.

"One question, Uncle."

"What is it?" Harold asked, rolling his eyes and turning the volume back down.

"Why did you ask me what day I took that gold? What difference would it make?"

There was a sly look in the kid's eyes that made

Harold uncomfortable. He didn't know how to answer him. "I was just curious."

"Bullshit."

"No, not bullshit, Tyler. I just wanted to know." The kid's stare was making him nervous. Harold swallowed.

After an awkward silence, the kid finally spoke. "You think I went in there and your boss found me stealing again."

Harold sat silent.

"You think I killed him, don't you?"

Tyler waited for Harold to reply. When he didn't, Tyler let the trailer door slam shut behind him and left.

CHAPTER 41

AFTER THE FUNERAL, Jack went back to the trailer on Shadow Mountain Lake and let Crockett out, then sat in a folding chair and watched him chase birds at the edge of the forest. He checked the sky and hoped the dark clouds didn't mean rain.

There were files to go through, notes to read, but first Jack wanted to process what he had seen and heard that morning. He laced his fingers behind his head and leaned back against the trailer, leaving the files scattered across the card table in front of him closed. He had been in Colorado for more than a year and had found he did some of his best thinking outdoors.

As he watched Crockett play, he mentally went through his list of suspects.

In his gut, Jack knew Charles Stratton was the type of guy capable of doing something illegal and probably was guilty of *something*, but was it murder?

At the funeral, Stratton didn't appear to be upset, but he also didn't act like a man who was guilty of murdering the guy lying in the coffin a few feet in front of him. Jack would have expected Stratton to fidget, sweat, or dart his eyes around the room as if he knew someone would be watching him.

Jack had seen guilty behavior before, knew what to look for, but he also knew appearances could be deceiving. On several occasions, he had come in contact with sociopaths so evil that there was no inkling of any remorse, and he had studied many others. They were men like Ted Bundy, the Son of Sam, and the Hermes Strangler.

They were the type of criminal Jack feared the most—and were the hardest ones to catch. Someone devoid of empathy, filled instead with deadly hatred or rage, someone who could kill a man one day and then go about their business as if nothing had happened the next. Was Charles Stratton one of these monsters?

Then there was Derek Lowe. He was on the top of Jack's list of people to talk to next. But as far as he could tell, Lowe hadn't been a benefactor of Elliot Banks's death like Charles Stratton had. Stratton had been immediately promoted to CEO. Did Derek Lowe also have something to gain from Banks being out of the way? Jack would find out.

Miles Preston. Elliot Banks's oldest and best friend, and now Victoria's attorney. There wasn't any evidence of past animosity between the two men. On the contrary. From what Jack could tell, the two had been close friends—vacationing and working together—up until the day Elliot was murdered. What would Preston stand to gain from Elliot's death? The only thing Jack could come up with was Victoria. Jack had never seen Victoria when Preston wasn't somewhere nearby. Was Victoria the spoils that went to the victor—to the last man standing?

And there was Harold Lamken. A guy who acted nervous but also appeared genuinely distraught at the funeral. What would he have to gain by killing his boss? There would be no promotion, as in the case of Charles Stratton. Could he have murdered Banks in some sort of spontaneous fit of rage? Had there been an argument between the two? When Jack met with him, Lamken didn't seem to be the type. But he had been nervous. What was Lamken hiding?

Jack thought about Boots Hamer. Good ol' boy and longtime friend of the deceased. Outward appearances indicated the old guy was deeply saddened by Elliot's death. But there was the threat of a lawsuit. Just how disgruntled was Hamer? And what was the real reason Hamer wanted Jack to keep him informed about his investigation?

Then Jack's mind went to the one person he didn't want to consider but knew he had to. Victoria. Was the grieving widow really a black widow in disguise? She had been visibly distraught, looking exhausted at the funeral. But was it grief that weighed on her, or guilt? Jack remembered the man who had tried to kiss her but was rebuffed, the tall Brad Pitt look-alike she wasn't glad to see. Who was he? Could he have had something to do with Elliot's murder?

Jack ran through the list of suspects closest to Elliot, the ones Jack knew he would have opened the front door for, and the one who was already in the house. But could there be someone else, someone Jack didn't know about yet? Someone with an axe to grind—literally, into the back of Elliot Banks's skull?

Jack thought of the tomahawk and the bloody fingerprints. His investigation—mulling over the possible suspects—could all be a waste of time if the Vail police had been able to identify the prints.

Although Jack could use the money from continuing the investigation, there was nothing better than seeing a bad guy put behind bars. To hell with the money, Jack thought. He'd love to see the bastard who'd killed Elliot Banks get what was coming to him.

Crockett ambled up and placed his chin on Jack's thigh, his tail drooped but still wagging.

The sun had broken through a spot in the clouds and hovered on the horizon, casting the lake and the mountains in a milky haze. Jack checked the time on his phone and saw that two hours had passed since he'd pulled the chair out and sat down. He hadn't realized it had been that long.

"Getting hungry?" he asked Crockett.

The brown dog lifted his head and cocked it to one side.

"Yeah, me too."

Jack dropped the chair onto all four legs, stood up, and took a few steps toward the door to the trailer. When he heard the sound of tires crunching on gravel in the distance, he turned to look but didn't see where it was coming from, the car still hidden by the forest.

He kept watching the road where it entered the campground, and after a few seconds saw a white Range Rover emerge from behind the trees. It looked out of place among all the trucks and Subarus. He was about to turn back to the trailer when the silhouette of the driver caught his eye. There was something familiar about it. He watched as the driver hesitated at the fork in the road, then slowly turned the Range Rover in his direction.

"Well, I'll be damned," Jack said under his breath as it came closer, finally rolling to a stop next to his truck.

Jack stood with his hands on his hips and watched her get out.

"Hello, Detective." Her voice was like velvet, rich and smooth.

"Hello, Victoria. What are you doing here?"

"I was out for a drive and..." Her voice trailed

off when she noticed the skeptical look on his face. "Okay," she said with an apologetic smile. "Maybe I wasn't really out for a drive, but I didn't want to sit at home and didn't know exactly where to go, so here I am."

Jack was still skeptical and not sure how to respond. When he didn't, she filled the awkward silence.

"I wanted to see where the enigmatic Jack Martin lived," she said, teasing him, her eyes sweeping the campground and landing on the lake. The waning rays of sunlight reflected off the water, making it look as though thousands of diamonds had been scattered across the surface. "It's beautiful," she said.

He agreed.

She looked back at him and stepped closer. "How long have you been here?"

"Since Aspen."

She nodded, her face a mask—a beautiful porcelain mask that betrayed no emotion. Jack had no idea what she was thinking.

"How did you find me?" he asked.

She spoke slowly and deliberately. "The first time we met, you told me you were staying at a campground off Shadow Mountain Lake. I wasn't sure how I would find you, but I saw your truck when I pulled up." She looked shy, mindlessly squaring the stack of folders on the card table between them.

Crockett eased up to her, curious. She bent over

and held out a hand. He sniffed it, then let her scratch him behind the ears.

"Who's this?" she asked, smoothing the dog's coat where she had ruffled it.

"That's Crockett."

"A sidekick."

"I haven't had him that long, but I'm getting used to him."

She stood up and looked at the trailer, and Jack was suddenly self-conscious. He hoped she didn't want to go in. He didn't want people in his trailer, wasn't sure if anyone had ever been in it before. It was his personal space, and for some reason he couldn't explain, he wanted to keep it that way. He needed his privacy like he needed water. They were one and the same, one no different from the other. He didn't know why; that was just the way it was.

But she looked from the trailer toward the lake again and seemed lost in her thoughts. Jack didn't know what she wanted, or why she was there.

"Would you like to walk down there? To the lake?" She didn't answer right away, and he added, "It's a great view this time of night."

She turned to him and nodded. They walked down together, Crockett running ahead of them. The last rays of sunshine retreated and disappeared, the sun having dropped below the horizon.

As it usually did late in the day, the campground

had grown tranquil, but there was a smattering of activity; a handful of people milled about. Jack noticed a young couple sitting near the edge of the water and steered Victoria in the other direction. They walked past a family of four outside their tent grilling, the kids running and playing. Crockett joined in for a minute before returning to Jack's side when he and Victoria reached the edge of the lake.

They stood quiet for a while, both looking out over the water. A lone pontoon boat floated in the distance, its lights like colored fireflies as it glided across the lake. They could hear voices in the distance, the sound reverberating over the surface of the water.

"I saw you at the funeral," she said, finally breaking the silence. "You didn't say hello."

Jack didn't know how to respond and took a moment to answer. "It was crowded, and so many people wanted to talk to you. I didn't think it was a good time."

She studied him, then seemed satisfied with his answer.

Crockett brought Jack a stick and he threw it, the dog loping off after it. He and Victoria were alone again.

"What is that?" She was looking down.

"What's *what?*"

Victoria nodded toward his hand. "The ring?"

Jack hadn't realized he had been twirling the large gold ring with his thumb. Fussing with it was a nervous habit. He mentally chastised himself for doing it in front of her.

"It's my college ring."

"It's beautiful. Where did you go to school?"

"Texas A&M."

She nodded. "I remember now. I saw that in one of the articles I read about you on the internet. You played football there."

Jack could feel himself blush and was grateful for the growing darkness. Dammit, he wasn't used to feeling self-conscious, letting someone get under his skin. He needed to redirect the conversation.

"Who was the tall blond guy who tried to kiss you after the funeral?" he asked, changing the subject as smooth as asphalt. *Damn*, he thought. *Where did that come from?*

Victoria stiffened, obviously as surprised by the question as he was.

She answered slowly. "He…he's an old acquaintance. I haven't seen him in a while and didn't know he was coming."

"You didn't look happy to see him."

She didn't reply right away. "I was surprised to see him."

It wasn't enough. Jack wanted more. "Did he go to school with you at Mines?"

"No. But I did go to school with him…years ago."

It's a start, Jack thought. He filed the information away and let her change the subject.

They talked a while longer, her asking him personal questions he successfully deflected. She talked about Elliot, telling Jack again how they had met and about their life together.

Jack watched her closely as she spoke. At one point she met his gaze briefly, then immediately looked toward the mountains, where the sun had earlier dropped below the horizon. But in that split second, Jack saw the sadness in her eyes. Her quiet pain touched him unexpectedly.

When she looked back at him, she had regained her composure, her voice like velvet again. "You're being evasive. Tell me more about yourself, Detective."

For the first time since the incident in Houston, Jack let himself wonder what it would feel like to tell someone the truth. To trust someone who might be able to help him release the dark memories, free him from his own monsters.

He opened his mouth to answer her, then shut it. In the waning daylight, he looked toward the clouds building to the north, narrowed his gaze, and saw lightning flash. "Storm's coming."

They walked back from the lake in silence. The forest had grown dark, the shadows closing in on the clearing where the trailer sat.

Just before she left, she dropped the bomb.

"I want to tell you something so you don't hear it from someone else first." Jack didn't reply, so she continued. "On the way home from the funeral, Miles Preston—my attorney—told me he got a call from the Vail police."

She stopped talking and watched him, her gray eyes searching his face. The direction of the conversation had Jack alert and intrigued.

She went on. "It seems the fingerprints they found on the tomahawk were mine."

The information hit Jack like a freight train. It wasn't what he'd expected, and it had his mind reeling. She went on to say that she didn't know how they'd gotten there, not remembering much from that night, but suggested she must have touched it sometime after she'd found Elliot but before the police got there.

After a few minutes, as the rain began to fall, Jack watched the taillights of the Range Rover disappear back into the forest.

As uncomfortable as he had been while she was there, and despite the fact she would now be solidified as the main suspect in her husband's death, for some reason Jack didn't understand, he was sad to see her go.

CHAPTER 42

Saturday, June 23

THE NEXT MORNING, Victoria woke from a deep sleep, grateful for not having dreamed of being chased through the forest again. Lying in bed staring up at the ceiling, she tried to remember if she had dreamed at all, but couldn't remember anything and was glad.

She rolled over and reached for her phone on the bedside table. It was six thirty, the latest she had slept since Elliot died.

She lay back on the pillows, images of the funeral replaying in her mind. She still couldn't believe that Elliot was gone. She wished it had all been a bad dream but knew it wasn't.

She took in and released a slow breath, got out of bed and walked to the windows, and pulled open the curtains. The storm from the night before had gone. Although it was early, a hint of sunrise colored the cloudless sky a deep shade of purple, the color of mourning. She turned away, the heaviness of the day before still weighing on her.

In the bathroom, she wrapped herself in a chenille

robe and stood at the door to Elliot's closet, looking in. Her gaze came to rest on the spot on the floor where she had sat and cried and had eventually fallen asleep. She didn't know for how long.

The trip to see Jack Martin had seemed like a good idea at the time. She'd wanted to get away from the memories and from the reality of what her life now was. Now she worried the trip to Shadow Mountain Lake had been a mistake.

She'd wanted to tell Jack about her fingerprints in person, that hers were the ones found on the murder weapon. She'd wanted to tell him before he heard it from someone else. But when she did, she saw a flash of suspicion in his eyes, and it had hurt. She wished she had called instead.

Elliot's shirt was still on the floor. Victoria picked it up, gently put it back on its hanger, and returned it to its spot on the closet rod, smoothing the wrinkles out of the sleeve so that it hung perfectly again. Everything was back in its place, she told herself. Everything except Elliot.

In the kitchen, she made a cup of coffee and took it outside onto the deck overlooking the pool. It was still dark. Standing at the rail, she looked toward the faint silhouette of Vail Mountain. It was cold, and she pulled her robe tighter around her.

A few minutes later, the growing light cast dark shadows near the trees at the far end of the yard and at the corners of the house. A gentle breeze whistled through them, sounding like hushed whispers. Victoria watched the trees sway and couldn't shake the feeling she was being watched. She stepped back inside and closed the door behind her.

Sitting down at the table, she pulled her phone from a pocket of her robe and laid it in front of her. She sat a while longer, drinking her coffee and watching the sun rise on another day.

After a few minutes, she decided there had been enough mourning. She was expected at the police station for questioning again in two days. And although Miles hadn't mentioned it, she knew there was a possibility she would be arrested for Elliot's murder. She was running out of time.

Her thoughts turned again to Jack. He hadn't mentioned anything about his investigation the night before and she had been glad. But now she needed to get things back on track. She would call him, but there was someone else she wanted to talk to first.

Victoria pulled the cell phone toward her and scrolled through her contacts until she found the one she was looking for.

"Victoria, honey. How are you this morning?"

Doris Reed's voice was soft and consoling. She was a friend. Victoria had never appreciated the older woman more than she did at that instant.

They spoke for a while about the funeral and about Elliot, and then Victoria got to the point of her call.

"Doris, I'd like to meet in person."

"Sure, honey. What is it?"

Victoria told her about the fingerprints on the tomahawk, that she had to be back at the police station Monday morning, and that she was worried she might be arrested. If Doris was shocked by anything she was saying, Victoria couldn't tell.

"That's positively ridiculous to think you were the one who killed our sweet Elliot." Her tone was indignant. "That doesn't prove a thing, honey. There has to be a good reason your fingerprints were on the thing. We all know you didn't kill Elliot."

"I know it's short notice, but could you meet me this morning?" Victoria asked. "I want to talk to you about some things I found on Elliot's computer. Maybe you can help me figure out what's going on."

Doris was quiet. Her silence was unsettling. Victoria needed her. "I'm running out of time, Doris. And there's no one else I can turn to. I need your help."

"Sure, honey. I'll come see you."

"No, Vail is too far for you to drive. Is there somewhere we could meet halfway?"

Doris suggested the Sunshine Café in Silverthorne and gave Victoria the address.

"Victoria," Doris began, a hint of concern in her

voice. "You really should call that detective, Jack Martin. Have him meet us at the diner."

"How do you know about Jack Martin?"

"He came to the office to talk to Charles Stratton."

Victoria should have told Doris about Jack, but it hadn't occurred to her. Of course there was a chance he would run into Doris at the office.

"No, I don't want him there," Victoria said. "If Elliot was involved in something illegal, I don't want anyone to know about it."

"But what if it's what got Elliot killed?"

Victoria was silent a moment. "If we find something that makes us think it could be connected, we'll go to Jack then. But only then."

"But he's already working for you—investigating the murder."

"I hired him to help find out who killed Elliot. This isn't about that. Not yet, anyway."

"Honey, I think it's a mistake. I think he could help, but if that's what you want—"

"It's what I want," Victoria said quietly. "It's the way it has to be."

CHAPTER 43

JACK WOKE THE next morning thinking he hadn't slept at all. Victoria's surprise visit to the lake had rattled him. While she was there, neither one of them had brought up his investigation. Jack told himself it was because it was too soon after the funeral, that she needed the day to grieve, but he knew that wasn't the whole truth.

Victoria Banks had muddled his head, and he didn't like it. He didn't like surprises, either, especially ones from women. Victoria was attractive, but she was his client, and he was investigating her husband's murder.

He rolled off the cot, stiff and irritated, pulled on his jeans from the day before, and flung open the door to the trailer. He didn't bother to put on a shirt or shoes, but took the metal step to the ground and stood looking up at the stars. It was cold, but the icy shock to his bare chest felt good. He drew in a deep breath, clearing his head and getting his mind right again.

The campground was quiet. Other than a lone

fisherman casting his line at the lake's edge, Jack seemed to be the only person awake.

He would call her, insist on a better explanation of why her fingerprints were found on the tomahawk in Elliot's blood. He was upset with himself for not asking if there were any additional prints found on it. But her visit had shaken him. He should have pressed her on the Brad Pitt look-alike, but he had let that subject drop as well, accepting her cryptic explanation about who he was. In the clarity of the frigid morning air, he knew he should have pressed for more answers.

After a few more minutes of self-flagellation, Jack vowed to keep his emotions in check in the future, not let sympathy or infatuation—or whatever the hell it was—get in his way.

Victoria Banks was elusive and vague, which made her damned suspicious. He wouldn't let her surprise him again.

Jack stepped back into the trailer and checked the time on his phone. It was early, but he wanted answers.

"Hello." Her voice was alert. Jack was glad he hadn't woken her.

"Victoria, it's Jack."

"I was going to call you." He heard a friendliness in her voice but ignored it.

"We need to talk. There are a few questions I need answered regarding the investigation."

She hesitated. "Okay. We can talk now, but I only have a few minutes."

"Not over the phone."

Another pause. "All right. When?"

"This morning. I'll drive to Vail."

"I can't this morning."

"It's important."

"I can't. Maybe this afternoon."

He wasn't going to wait around all day for her. What could be more important than his investigation to find her husband's murderer? Jack wasn't going to settle for "I can't" without a better explanation. Something was going on, and he didn't trust her.

"Why not this morning, Victoria? It's important."

"I just can't. Call me this afternoon."

Then she hung up.

Jack was furious. When he had first met with her, agreed to take the case, she had assured him there wouldn't be any secrets, that she would be completely honest with him. She had lied.

She was up to something, and Jack was going to find out what it was. He finished getting dressed and grabbed a protein bar from a box in the cabinet.

"Come on, Crockett."

The dog followed him out of the trailer. When

Jack opened the door to the truck, Crockett jumped in.

Welcomed or not, Jack was going to Vail. He would show up unannounced, see what was going on, and let the chips fall where they may. To hell with it all. He needed the money, but he didn't need the headaches that came with the job.

Jack drove west on Interstate 70, headed deeper into the mountains. The sun had come up behind him, bringing with it the sharp clarity of a summer morning following a thunderstorm. Jack wanted clarity as well.

Less than twenty minutes outside Vail, as he crested Vail Pass, Jack saw a white Range Rover headed in the opposite direction. He recognized Victoria instantly.

He took the next exit and made a U-turn, sped up the ramp getting back onto 70 headed east, and floored it.

A few minutes later, with the Range Rover in sight, Jack slowed the truck and slid into the slow lane. He would follow her, see where she was going and what she was up to. It might be the only way he'd get an honest answer.

They were headed east toward Denver. Jack checked the gas gauge and saw he had less than half a tank. It could get him to Denver, but he hoped she wasn't going any farther.

But fifteen minutes later she took an exit ramp at

Silverthorne. Jack followed her at a distance as she turned onto Highway 6, then into the parking lot of the Sunshine Café. He couldn't believe it; he'd met Doris Reed there only three days earlier.

Jack turned into an adjacent parking lot, giving Victoria time to park and walk into the restaurant. He then pulled into the café's lot, chose an empty space off to the side and parked, and scanned the area. There didn't appear to be anyone else around, but that's when he noticed it—a bright red Camaro. Doris Reed. What were the two of them up to?

Jack heard a door shut, then watched as a black Ford Raptor slid out of the space beside the Camaro and turn toward the highway. The bottom half of the truck was covered in a thick layer of caliche-colored soil. For some reason, Jack thought the truck looked familiar. He watched as it pulled onto the highway and sped away.

CHAPTER 44

INSIDE THE DINER, Victoria saw Doris already sitting at a booth tucked in a back corner. She was looking down at a menu and didn't see her. Victoria realized she would be able to sit with her back to the room and was relieved. Hopefully, she would be in and out without anyone noticing her.

They could have talked over the phone, but Victoria wanted to see Doris in person. She told herself it was because she enjoyed Doris's company and didn't get a chance to visit with her after the funeral. But deep down Victoria knew it was because she wanted to watch the expression on her face as they spoke—to make sure Doris wasn't lying.

There were questions Victoria wanted to ask her, and she would watch Doris closely as she answered them. Doris loved Elliot like a son, and Victoria didn't know how far she would go to protect him, even from his own wife.

She walked toward Doris, leaving her sunglasses on until she reached the booth and slid in.

Doris looked over the top of reading glasses

twinkling with crystals and smiled, perking up the plump contours of her cheeks. "Hello, honey." She then frowned. "You look like you haven't been eating."

"I haven't."

"Here," she said, handing Victoria the menu. "Find something. I'm having a big lunch, so I need to be good. Just coffee for me this morning. Well, maybe a pastry."

Victoria took the menu and laid it aside. "Thank you for meeting me." She folded her sunglasses and put them in her purse.

"Of course, honey."

A waitress appeared and took their order, two coffees, and a muffin for Doris. Victoria still couldn't bring herself to eat regularly—because of her grief or nerves, she wasn't sure which.

As soon as the waitress left, Victoria continued. "Have you found out anything about what is going on with the company?"

Doris hesitated. "I have…a little."

"What is it? Please tell me the truth, Doris."

"It's not much, but there was a meeting between Bob Hawkins and the forensic accountant. Bob had another meeting scheduled with him that would have included Elliot. But Bob died the night before."

Victoria was confused, not sure what the connection could be. But she sat listening as Doris told her about the timing of the meetings, the argument between Bob and Elliot. Doris believed the argument had something to do with the accountant, something he'd told Bob.

Victoria was anxious and feeling desperate as the pieces slowly fell into place. "So there *is* something going on at the company," she said quietly, feeling her pulse quicken.

Doris nodded.

Victoria watched her closely. "Could it be what got Elliot killed?"

Doris leveled a weary gaze, then sighed. "Honey, I didn't want to tell you all this, but you insisted."

"I did."

Doris took her time answering, her broad torso rising and falling with a giant sigh before she spoke. "Yes, I think that it's all connected...somehow."

The waitress returned with the coffee and Doris's muffin. Victoria and Doris fell silent until she had left.

"I know there's something going on," Doris continued, "some kind of funny business. But whatever it is, you have to know that Elliot didn't have anything to do with it. He was an innocent victim. The only thing our Elliot was guilty of was being too trusting."

Victoria hoped desperately that Doris was right. The best thing in her life had been ripped from her and left in a bloody heap for her to find on the study floor. She wouldn't be able to bear it if Elliot wasn't the man she thought he was.

And if it was fraud, since Banks Oil & Gas was publicly traded, the SEC—maybe even the FBI—would get involved. Elliot's name would be dragged through the mud.

Victoria took a sip of coffee, then set the cup back onto the saucer, cradling it with both hands and thinking. "Are Boots Hamer and the accountant still looking into it? Or have they let the issue go now that Elliot is…?" Her voice trailed off.

Doris's face looked grim. "They're still at it, honey. That accountant—Poindexter—called the office on Friday asking for an appointment to see Charles Stratton, but Charles was at—"

"The funeral," Victoria finished for her. "Maybe I should call Boots myself and ask him about it."

For some reason, Doris looked nervous and hesitated before she replied. "I don't know, honey. Maybe not just yet. Let me see what I can find out for you. I think it's best if you keep a low profile. Elliot's killer is still out there somewhere, and if you go digging too far into this, I'm afraid you might make yourself the next target."

Victoria sat stunned; the thought hadn't occurred to her. Someone had gotten into her house once. What would keep them from getting in again?

"Maybe you're right. But now *you're* involved, Doris. What about *your* safety?"

Doris laughed, dismissing Victoria's concern with a wave. "Don't worry about me, honey. I'm careful. I know how to handle this kind of stuff."

Although she was nervous, Victoria managed a wan smile, remembering the stories Elliot had told her about Doris's quirky obsession with detectives and television crime shows, laughing that she wore the fact that Tom Selleck was a distant cousin of hers like it was a badge of honor.

"Just promise me you'll be careful," Victoria told her.

Doris reached her plump arm across the table and patted Victoria's wrist. "I promise, honey."

They finished their coffee in silence. The waitress brought the check, and Victoria handed her a credit card.

"No, no," Doris said, digging through a giant bag. "I was going to get this for you."

But the waitress was already gone.

"It's the least I can do," Victoria said. "I owe you so much already."

Doris stopped hunting through her purse. She must have recognized the devastating sadness Victoria was trying to hide. She reached across the table again and took Victoria's hand, kindness and concern etching her soft, cherubic face.

"Honey, I know this is hard, but you've got to figure out a way to keep going. Life doesn't always give us what we want, but we need to make the best of it. That's what our loved ones who've gone on before us would want. 'Bloom where you're planted' is what my mother always used to say." Doris patted Victoria's hand. "And I know right now you're planted in a shit storm—excuse my French. But you're still going to have to find a way to keep going. Elliot would have wanted you to."

Victoria felt tears well in her eyes, but she fought them back. She looked down into the empty coffee cup and nodded. No wonder Elliot loved this sweet woman so much. "Your mother must have been a wonderful woman," Victoria said to her.

"She was, honey. And you want to know something? So are you."

Victoria couldn't hold it back any longer. A tear rolled off her cheek, just missing the cup. She quickly wiped its wet track away with the back of her hand. "The police—"

"I don't care about the police. You didn't kill Elliot. I know that, and sooner or later they'll figure that out." She paused, then added, "And as horrible as it seems now, you'll find a way to move on."

Victoria hoped she was right, but it didn't seem to matter. She had known devastating grief in her life before. She sat there, remembering.

After a while, Doris reached across the table again, touching her hand gently. "Are you all right, honey?"

Startled, Victoria looked up and frowned. "He hadn't been himself the last week. He seemed distant. Not angry or anything—just distant."

"Elliot?"

Victoria nodded.

Doris thought about it. "He wasn't the same at work, either." After a brief silence, she added, "We'll figure it out, honey. You and me."

Victoria nodded in silence, grateful for Doris's friendship.

Doris patted her hand one last time. "Thank you again, honey—for the coffee and the muffin. I hate to eat and run, but I'm supposed to be at my sister's for lunch. Her grandson turns twelve this week, and she's having a big family to-do. I told her I'd help her get everything ready."

Victoria knew Doris had never been married, didn't have any children of her own, but she had a large family that loved her. She felt a sharp pain in her heart—one of envy, not resentment.

Victoria smiled across the table. "You go. The waitress will be back with my card any second."

Doris hesitated, then slid her bulk from the booth and labored to stand up. "Thank you, sweetie." She looked at Victoria a second, considering something.

"Honey, why don't you come with me? To my sister's?"

Victoria didn't know what to say.

"There's always plenty of food, and you eat like a bird anyway. You need to get out and be around people—even crazy people like my family." She laughed. "It would do you some good. It's just down the interstate a ways, outside Empire. Nice little place in the mountains. Come with me."

Victoria now fully understood Elliot's affection for her all these years. Doris was the kindest person Victoria had ever known. "Thank you, but you go. Have a great time."

"Are you sure, honey?"

"I am, but thank you. I still have some of Elliot's papers and accounts to go through and figure out. I'll let you know if I come across anything else."

"Well, all right. But if you change your mind, call me and I'll give you the address."

As soon as Doris walked out, the waitress returned with Victoria's credit card. Victoria signed the check, then gathered her purse and put her sunglasses back on.

Outside, she walked toward her Range Rover, but glanced across the parking lot in the direction of Doris's car, wanting to give her a wave goodbye.

But the instant Victoria's eyes landed on the red Camaro, it exploded.

Fire shot upward and out in a fearsome wave of searing orange. Victoria was knocked off her feet by the shock wave, the heat burning her face. Her ears rang with a muffled silence, and she was disoriented. Then debris rained down in a storm of glass and metal shards that brought her back from the shock.

Victoria struggled to sit, pushing herself up from the rough, hot asphalt. With tears already streaking the smudges of soot on her face, she squinted and looked up at the scorched and burning mound of twisted metal where the red Camaro had been.

She felt nauseated and coughed. When she finally spoke, the name came out in a quiet but fierce cry of disbelief.

"Doris."

CHAPTER 45

HAROLD LAMKEN ARRIVED back at the trailer mid-morning with a truckload of groceries. Tyler's car was parked askew to one side. Harold pulled next to it and honked.

The kid lived in Harold's trailer, wore the clothes Harold bought, and ate his food. The least he could do was help unload the stuff.

Harold looked toward the door, but there was no sign of Tyler. He got out of the truck, leaned over and honked again, then walked around to the passenger side and jerked open the door. He pulled as many bags out as he could carry and started toward the trailer. Still no Tyler.

With his hands full, he struggled with the bags to open the front door, sticking his foot inside and kicking it open. He stepped in, his eyes taking a moment to adjust after coming in from the sunlight.

Tyler was sprawled back in Harold's recliner, digging into an open bag of chips he had rested on his stomach. The television was blaring.

"Just in time," Tyler said, grinning and pointing a Cheeto at the television. "It's your hot boss. She's on the news again."

Leaving the door open, Harold stepped into the room and turned toward the television. A news reporter was talking into the camera. She was in a parking lot with what looked like a burned-out car behind her. There were police and firefighters milling about in the background.

Harold was confused and didn't know what Tyler was talking about. Then the reporter mentioned her name, and Harold's heart lurched.

The camera swung around and there she was— Victoria. She was standing in the distance, but when the camera focused on her, Harold recognized her instantly. But she looked all wrong. Harold let the grocery bags fall to the floor, and he stepped closer.

Victoria's hair was a mess. Strands had come loose and were hanging next to her face. She had on white pants, but they were dirty. And she was holding her hands to her mouth like she was nervous, or crying, and someone was talking to her—a cop.

The camera swung back to the reporter, who finished the segment. *Reporting live from outside the Sunshine Café in Silverthorne…*"

And that was it. Coverage switched back to the Rockies game.

Harold wheeled around. "What happened? What did they say?"

Tyler snickered and stuck a Cheeto in his mouth. "Man, she's all over the news these days," he said with his mouth full. "She looked *bad* though, didn't she? Did you see that hair?" He laughed.

Harold lunged at him, stopping inches from his face. "What happened?" he asked through clenched teeth.

Tyler stopped laughing and frowned, held up his hands in surrender. "Chill. Someone died in an explosion—a car bomb."

Harold's heart felt like it was beating out of his chest. He took a step back from the recliner and drew in a shaky breath, trying to steady himself. "What else did they say?"

Tyler brought the recliner forward and looked at Harold, smiling. "They tried to interview her."

"Who?"

"Your hot boss. But she wouldn't talk to them. Then the reporter talked about her husband being murdered and how strange it was that she was there again when someone else died."

"Who died?"

Tyler shook his head. He leaned forward and tossed the chip bag onto the coffee table. "Some woman," he said, licking his orange fingers. "They said her name, but I don't remember."

"What else did they say?"

Tyler bobbed his head, grinning, bits of Cheeto still stuck in his teeth. "They think your hot boss had something to do with it."

CHAPTER 46

"HAVE YOU SEEN it?" Derek Lowe spoke fast, unable to hide the fear in his voice.

"Seen what?" Charles Stratton sounded perturbed by the phone call.

"The news—the explosion."

There was silence on the other end of the line. "No. What are you talking about?"

Derek pushed his fingers through his oiled hair as he paced the living room of the condo. "It was just on the news. A car exploded in Silverthorne. They think it was Doris Reed."

"Huh."

It wasn't the response Derek was expecting. "That's it? Huh? Charles, Doris Reed is dead. Cars don't just blow up."

"Sure they do. Cars are recalled for safety reasons all the time."

Derek couldn't believe it. There didn't seem to be an ounce of shock in Charles's voice, just curiosity.

"Victoria was there."

"Victoria Banks?" Charles finally sounded genuinely surprised. "Is she okay?"

"She's fine. They tried interviewing her, but she wouldn't talk—thank God. But then the reporter brought up Elliot's murder. Made it sound suspicious Victoria was there today when Doris's car blew up."

"It *is* suspicious," Charles said, his voice controlled again, devoid of any emotion. "Don't you think?"

Derek pulled open the sliding-glass door and walked out onto the balcony. His hand holding the phone was getting sweaty. "I don't know," he said, still pacing. "I don't know what I think."

"Calm down, Derek. Get a hold of yourself."

Calm down. How was he supposed to do that? Derek thought. Everything had been going smoothly, like clockwork. Even with Elliot being killed, the merger was all but done except for jumping through a few last hoops for the SEC. It would be a bigger payday than Derek had ever dreamed of. He'd finally be able to pay off all his debts and have plenty left over to live it up for the rest of his life.

Derek was incensed Charles wasn't more concerned. "Doris worked for Banks Oil & Gas. Elliot was just murdered. Bob committed suicide just a couple of weeks ago. You don't think this chain of events is going to cause us problems?"

"I'll take care of it."

"The media's going to be all over this if they make

the connections. If Victoria talks, the story's going to get more media coverage. It'll be disastrous—ruin everything."

"There isn't a shred of proof that anything is connected," Charles shot back.

He was angry, but Derek didn't care. First Bob. Then Elliot. Now Doris. The merger and Derek's future were about to be history. "I can't believe you're not more upset."

"Upset about what? Doris Reed, a nosy busybody loyal to Elliot isn't around anymore? It's a shame, but no, I'm sorry, Derek, I'm not that upset."

Derek was stunned by what he said. He had witnessed plenty of Charles's aggressive power plays, knew the cold and ruthless tactics he was capable of when it came to business, but this was different. Three people were dead.

"Charles, I signed on to being a part of Energy Marketing, but I didn't sign up for this."

"Sign up for what, Derek? Just what exactly are you implying?" Charles spit at him through the phone.

Derek thought about where the conversation was going and reconsidered. He dropped his head into his free hand and shook it. "I'm not implying anything, Charles."

It was what Derek had been afraid of. He felt that all his hard work, everything he had planned for, dreamed about, was starting to unravel and was going to crash down around them—or worse. He should have never trusted Charles Stratton or agreed to his ill-conceived plan to make a few extra bucks with the marketing company. It put everything at risk.

Back inside, Derek poured whiskey into a crystal highball, his hands shaking, rattling the ice against the side of the glass. He carried it back outside and collapsed in a lounge chair, then closed his eyes and held the glass to his temple, letting the cool crystal soothe his throbbing head.

Derek knew Charles Stratton was capable of lying and cheating, capable of things unethical *and* illegal. But was he capable of murder?

Everything will be all right, Derek tried to reassure himself, taking a long drink of the whiskey, then pressing it against his head again. There was no way the three deaths could be related. It was just a coincidence. Bob committed suicide. Elliot was murdered. And Doris…Doris was the victim of an unfortunate accident.

But the harder Derek tried to convince himself that the deaths weren't related, the more he knew they were.

CHAPTER 47

Sunday, June 24

CLARK POINDEXTER SAT picking at a corner of his desk where the Formica veneer had chipped off. The deli was in the midst of the Sunday lunch rush, but Clark barely noticed the clanging of pots and pans from the floor below or the steady stream of diners coming and going, slamming the front door as they went.

In front of him were stacks of paper with production reports and financial data relating to his investigation. He had printed out everything he could think of. There were documents Boots Hamer had given him, documents filed with the State of Colorado and the SEC, everything he could find regarding Banks Oil & Gas and Energy Marketing, the company set up by Charles Stratton and Derek Lowe.

He had called the offices of both companies, Banks Oil & Gas and Energy Marketing. He'd asked for additional information that would have been helpful to his investigation and wasn't surprised when the only documents he'd received were ones already made public. It was a tactic that rarely yielded results—almost no company he investigated ever willingly handed over useful information—even the innocent ones. But he always asked.

Clark had reached the end of his research, couldn't think of another thing he would be able to find legally. The only thing left to do would be to hire a professional hacker to get into the accounts that weren't made public. But that would be futile—and illegal. Besides probably going to jail himself, Clark knew that whatever he found out through illegal means wouldn't be admissible in a court of law.

He stared at the stacks of paper scattered across the desk, then laid his arms across it all and dropped his head, resting it on the documents in front of him. He had pulled an all-nighter. It had been a day and a half since he'd had any sleep, and he didn't think he could go on much longer.

Clark had gone over all twenty-three leases Hamer had with Banks Oil & Gas. He'd gone over the pricing data, what Hamer was being paid for the oil that came out of his land. So far, everything looked to be in line with what was initially agreed upon in the documents. And the prices Hamer was being paid seemed to be in line with industry norms.

Clark had looked but couldn't find any increases in dubious fees charged to Hamer since Stratton and Lowe's marketing company had taken over for Banks

Oil & Gas. But for some reason, Hamer's royalty payments had been steadily declining.

The answer had to be here, Clark told himself, slapping the papers with both hands, his head still on the desk; he just couldn't find it. If he could just figure out the right data to compare, the right numbers to analyze, he knew he *would* find it.

Clark pushed himself up, leaned back in his chair and took off his glasses, and massaged the bridge of his nose. He took in a deep breath and held it before letting it out in a slow sigh of frustration, then scanned the top of his desk, ticking off in his mind the list of contracts and reports in front of him.

It came to him suddenly. He didn't know where from, but he didn't care. He had an idea.

With renewed vigor, he dug through the mounds of documents, pulling out the ones he wanted. Then he took a pad of paper and began charting a graph.

It took less than an hour, but when he was finished, he leaned back and stared at the graph of numbers and dates. And just like that, after days of digging and analyzing, Clark was almost sure he had figured it out.

He felt the weight lift from his chest. His heart rate quickened and his breathing sped up. It was the familiar sense of exhilaration he felt when he knew he had solved a case.

But to be sure, there was one thing left to check. It

was something he couldn't do himself, but he knew Boots Hamer could. Hamer had hired him, but Clark would need his client's help to solve the case.

With shaky fingers, Clark dialed Hamer's number. The call rang several times before it was finally picked up.

"Talk to me, Poindexter."

Clark sat forward in his chair, pushing his glasses higher on his nose. "I think I know what's going on, Mr. Hamer, and you're not going to like it. But I need your help."

CHAPTER 48

JACK WAS ANGRY. It was early Sunday afternoon, and he was on his way to pay Victoria an unexpected visit. She had been interviewed by the police in Silverthorne and the next morning would be interviewed by the Vail police for the second time. He was sure they would ask her about the car bombing, but he wanted to question her first.

He liked Doris and was determined to get at the truth. He wanted to know who in the hell would want her dead and hoped Victoria could help him figure it out.

He spent the drive to Vail going over both cases, Elliot's murder and now the bombing. There were too many unanswered questions. Too many that Victoria Banks was now at the heart of. And to do the job she hired him for, to find out who murdered her husband, Jack needed answers from her—honest ones.

Jack had spent the morning combing through the facts he knew about the cases, making a list of questions he wanted Victoria to answer. Questions about the tomahawk and about Elliot's business, questions about the blond man at the funeral, and now about Doris. He would find a way to get her to talk. He had spent years questioning suspects and interrogating criminals while working for the FBI.

When Jack finally pulled off the interstate in Vail, he was ready. What he wasn't ready for was how Victoria looked when she answered the front door. It was immediately obvious she had been crying. The weariness on her face was palpable. She didn't have on a stitch of makeup, and her eyes were swollen and ringed with dark circles. She looked like hell.

Her speech was slow and deliberate. "Detective Martin, this is a surprise. Although, I guess it shouldn't be."

"I need to ask you a few questions."

Victoria looked at him wearily, motioned him inside with a glass of water—or was it vodka? "Please follow me."

She led him down the corridor and into the study, then waved her glass at one of the leather chairs in front of the fireplace, indicating for him to sit. She sat in the other, placing the glass in front of her on a small square napkin.

Jack pulled his notebook from the front pocket of his jeans and tossed it onto the small table between them, but the notebook skittered across the marble top and dropped to the floor. Before he could pick it up, Victoria had already retrieved it, placing it back on the table.

Jack was direct. "Tell me about Doris."

Victoria's expression tensed, and there was a momentary flash of anguish in her eyes.

"Doris was my friend." Her voice was brittle, like it was about to break.

"Why did you meet her at the diner?"

"How did you know?"

"I saw you on the news broadcast."

"Of course." Victoria dropped her head, looking defeated. "I wanted to talk to her. I didn't get a chance to…after the funeral."

"What did you talk about?"

She shook her head and shrugged. "We just talked."

As he had feared, Victoria wasn't going to be honest. She was hiding something. He debated telling her the truth about Doris but decided he couldn't. He didn't trust her. They sat in silence.

After a while, she cocked her head to one side, still looking sad. "Do you think this could be my last night here, Detective? In this house?"

"Why would it be?"

"I'm being questioned by the police again tomorrow. Miles won't say it, but I know he's worried I might be arrested."

"There's not enough evidence to arrest you." It

was true, but Jack didn't tell her that lack of sufficient evidence wouldn't stop a rogue cop from arresting her anyway. But even if they did, they wouldn't be able to hold her.

"My fingerprints..." Her voice trailed off.

"That's a problem," Jack admitted. "You don't know how they got on the tomahawk?"

She shook her head slowly, almost ghostlike. She was lost in her thoughts again—or memories—sleepwalking through his questions.

"Victoria." He said her name, trying to bring her back around. When she looked at him, he continued. "There's one thing that's bugged me from the beginning about that night—the night Elliot was murdered."

She stared at him, or through him, Jack couldn't tell.

"Yes, Detective? What is it?"

"You told me that you lock your doors at night."

"That's right," she said slowly. "I do."

"When Elliot was still alive, did you lock them, or did Elliot do it?"

"I did. I've always been the one to do it."

"You're sure you locked them the night Elliot was murdered?"

She frowned but didn't hesitate. "Of course I'm sure. I told you—I always do it."

"Then how did the killer get in?"

She shook her head, looking around the room as if she might be able to find an answer somewhere. "I don't know. Isn't that what you're supposed to help me find out?"

Jack knew there were several possibilities. One, Elliot unlocked the door and let the murderer in. Two, the murderer let himself in with his own key. Three, the killer was already inside the house. Or four, Victoria forgot to lock the door like she said she did.

Or maybe she was lying. Jack didn't trust her.

He looked into Victoria's gray eyes. They were empty, devoid now of emotion and betraying nothing. But if she *had* killed her husband, that didn't explain why the police found the front door unlocked when they got there.

According to the police report, when they entered the residence, they found Elliot Banks deceased and Victoria on the floor beside him. The door was already unlocked.

Jack watched her fidget with her glass, carefully squaring the napkin under it with the corner of the table. On a hunch, Jack reached for his notepad, pretended to fumble with it, and dropped it onto the floor. Victoria immediately scooped it up and put it back in the center of the table.

Everything in its place, he remembered her saying when he first met her. He scanned the room. It was spotless. There wasn't clutter anywhere. No mess of papers on the desk. No stacks of magazines on the floor. Not a jacket or sweater left casually on the back of a chair. The other rooms he'd seen in the house were the same. It was almost as if no one actually lived there.

Jack remembered her trip to the trailer, how she had straightened his files scattered across the card table. He recognized the signs of obsessive-compulsive disorder. OCD. It wasn't much, but it was something. He filed the information away in his head.

Jack went over a few details about his investigation—his interview with Charles Stratton. He told her he planned to interview Derek Lowe next. He wanted to ask her more about Doris but didn't. He knew she wouldn't tell him the truth.

As he spoke, Victoria listened but seemed distant. At one point she leaned forward, mindlessly pushing his notepad to one side, then centering it again on the table before sitting back in her chair.

He told her about talking to Bob Hawkins's wife, and she sat very still. He watched her closely as he told her about Doris's theory that Bob's suicide and Elliot's murder were somehow connected. He saw Victoria stiffen, trying to control what was churning inside her. He had hit a nerve. Fear or panic, Jack couldn't tell which.

He stopped talking, waiting for a response from

her—any response. But there was none. She sat quietly watching him and waiting for him to continue.

Jack cleared his throat. "Now that I've told you how the investigation is going, is there anything you want me to know? Anything that you think might help me find Elliot's killer?"

Her gaze drifted over his shoulder to where Jack knew there was an empty spot on the wall where the tomahawk belonged—the tomahawk used in the murder.

Her lips parted as if she was about to speak, but she pressed them back together and shook her head. "I can't think of anything." Her voice was soft and halting, and she wouldn't look at him.

Jack was frustrated. Getting information out of her was more difficult than he ever would have imagined, but he needed answers.

"Who was the guy at the funeral, Victoria? The one who tried to kiss you?"

"I already told you. He's an acquaintance…from long ago."

"Why did he come to see you?"

"I don't know. Probably to pay his respects to Elliot."

Jack leaned toward her, growing irritated. "Who is he, Victoria?"

Her voice shook. "It doesn't matter."

"What's his name?"

She dropped her gaze to the floor and shook her head. "I can't tell you."

"I don't know why I'm here. If you really want me to find out who killed your husband, you would be honest with me—trust me. Honesty was one of the conditions I insisted on when you hired me."

She looked on the verge of tears, but Jack kept pressing.

"Who was the guy at the funeral, Victoria?"

"I can't tell you," she repeated, still not looking at him.

"I can't work this way. To find out who killed Elliot, I need honest answers. Are you sure you can't tell me the truth?"

Tell me, Jack wanted to beg her. *Please, tell me.*

Victoria slowly turned away from him and shook her head again.

Jack released the breath he had been holding and stood up. "Then I quit."

CHAPTER 49

Monday, June 25

DETECTIVE WAYNE CONNER was in his early forties and had spent his entire law enforcement career in the mountains. First as a patrol officer in Glenwood Springs, then in Breckenridge, before finally being hired as a detective in Vail.

The Vail job had been a nice promotion three years earlier, but he now had his sights set on an even bigger position. The chief of police in Grand Junction was retiring, and Conner knew he was perfect for the job. And the publicity surrounding the Elliot Banks murder case could help him get it.

For over a week, since he first saw her at the house covered in her husband's blood, there was nothing Conner wanted to do more than to arrest Victoria Banks.

It was obvious to Conner that Victoria was guilty of murdering her husband—she had motive and means, there was no one else in the house, and her fingerprints were found in her husband's blood on the murder weapon.

And now there was the information they had uncovered about her past. It wasn't evidence, but it was damned intriguing. He planned on asking her about it.

Victoria was due in his office any minute for further questioning, and Conner wanted to arrest her. But the district attorney's office had pushed back, wanting more evidence. *Get a confession,* the prosecutor had told him, like it was an easy thing to do. What do politicians know?

Conner sat at his desk, frustrated with the progress of the investigation. He had been changing the oil in his truck Saturday when his wife had come running out of the house. *Victoria Banks is on the news,* she'd told him. *And it's not about her husband this time.*

When Conner got inside to the television, he'd sat stunned by the story unfolding that morning in Silverthorne. He watched Victoria refuse to speak to the media, then listened to the reporter's account of what little they knew about what had happened. A car had exploded, and the driver had not been found and was presumed dead.

The car belonged to Doris Reed, Elliot Banks's former personal assistant. Conner didn't think for a minute it was a coincidence that Victoria Banks was there when it happened. She was up to her pretty little neck in something deadly—not once, but now twice.

But that meant she would now be investigated by the Silverthorne police as well, and Conner hoped to hell they wouldn't be able to arrest her first.

Wayne Conner sat at his desk at the Vail Police Department, thumping a pen while he waited for Victoria to arrive. He thought about her—her designer clothes and her mansion. It bugged him that suspects with money and connections were often given sweetheart deals regular schlubs couldn't get. He'd be damned if that was going to happen on his watch.

But unless she confessed, Conner wouldn't be able to arrest her—not yet. He wouldn't tell her that. He would draw the questioning out, make her sweat.

Victoria Banks was a slippery one, but she was guilty of murder, and he wasn't going to let her get away with it.

CHAPTER 50

IT WAS JUST before dawn on Monday. Jack tilted the folding chair back onto two legs and rested his head against the cold skin of the Airstream.

It had been another restless night with little sleep. At four thirty, he'd finally given up and had been sitting outside ever since.

An ink-blue sky was flecked with thousands of twinkling stars, and he could just make out the silhouette of the mountains to the east. The campground was quiet.

He leaned over and looked down at Crockett lying next to the chair. "It's beautiful here, isn't it, boy?"

Jack sat longer, watching the sun slowly break the horizon, spilling morning light across the campground and the lake. He took in a slow deep breath, letting the cold morning air fill his lungs before he released it. As hard as he tried, he couldn't stop thinking about the day before.

He had never quit a job in the middle of an investigation and wasn't sure yet how he felt about doing it. The shock—or hurt—he had seen on Victoria's face when he quit had haunted his sleep.

But how could he be expected to continue investigating the murder of her husband if she wasn't willing to be honest with him? It was like hiring him to paddle her upstream and withholding an oar. It was a futile effort, and although he could use the money, he didn't want to waste his time.

After a while Jack remembered the message on his phone from Boots Hamer. Hamer had called the night before while he was with Victoria. Jack hadn't bothered to call him back; there probably wasn't a reason to. But he decided to call the old guy later, explain he was no longer investigating Elliot's murder. Jack wasn't up to explaining anything just yet.

He dropped his chair down and stood up. "Let's go for a hike," he told Crockett.

The dog began to dance at his feet.

A good workout would help clear his head. He needed to forget about Victoria Banks and figure out where he and Crockett would go next.

As they hiked, Jack thought of the different places he could move the trailer. He decided they would go south before winter—somewhere the snow wouldn't get as deep, lowering the risk of becoming snowbound. They could go to Durango or Trinidad, camp in the Sangre de Cristos.

But maybe it was time to go back to Texas. There

were always jobs in Texas. He could find something temporary, until he found a job in law enforcement. Maybe get on with a construction crew in Houston, or work the oil fields around Midland. And there was Jordan Rose, his former teammate at A&M who now ranched his family's land outside Del Rio. Maybe Jordan could use some temporary help.

After three hours and an elevation climb of over two thousand feet, the exhausted duo returned to the campground—the dog happy and sated, Jack with no answers and still haunted by thoughts of Victoria.

He showered, then turned on the small television in the Airstream and tuned in to a local Denver station. He pulled a canister of oatmeal from a cabinet next to the tiny cooktop and sprinkled some into a pan, and was about to add water but stopped.

On the television, a reporter was talking. Jack heard her say Victoria's name, and he looked up. A red banner that stretched the length of the television screen revealed the location—VAIL POLICE DEPARTMENT.

The young journalist was twentysomething, dressed in a bright red business suit. And she wasn't alone. Clusters of other reporters and cameramen milled around outside the police station. Jack couldn't believe he had forgotten about Victoria's appointment to be questioned again.

Forgetting the oatmeal, he stood inches from

the television mounted almost eye level in an upper cabinet.

The reporter looked directly at the camera and spoke into a microphone. "We're waiting for Victoria Banks to emerge from another round of questioning by the Vail Police Department. Sources have speculated it's possible Banks could be arrested today. Will she, in fact, emerge from the building? Or will the next sighting of Victoria Banks be at a bail hearing?"

Jack watched as the camera suddenly swung from the reporter to the entrance of the building.

"She's coming out," the reporter said, almost breathless.

Strobe lights flashed. Microphones and cameras were jostled for positions around Victoria and Miles Preston as they made their way down the steps of the building to the sidewalk. They were accompanied by two men dressed in expensive suits. Jack immediately recognized the type—defense attorneys.

Victoria ducked her head and tried to shield her face with a purse as Miles Preston held her by the elbow and steered her toward a parking lot, the defense attorneys following closely behind.

The reporters swarmed Victoria and her attorneys, shouting questions. *"How did the interrogation go, Victoria…?" "Are you surprised you weren't arrested today…?" "Did they ask you about the bombing in Silverthorne…?"*

She kept her head ducked and let Miles guide her to his Mercedes. The reporters and photographers still surrounded her, still peppered her with questions. *Vultures,* Jack thought. *They don't want the truth. They want a salacious story.*

The camera caught brief glimpses of Victoria's face, and Jack watched her for clues. Did she look agitated or calm? Was she angry, or did she look guilty?

He studied her closely and saw only fear.

She was pale and thin, her eyes wide like a caged animal's. Despite his better judgment, Jack's heart went out to her.

The reporters continued their assault even after she was seated safely in the front seat of the car. Cameras were pressed against the window only inches from her turned face.

Jack heard one last question shouted at her as Miles Preston slid in behind the wheel. *"Victoria, did you murder your husband?"*

Only when the car sped away did they finally stop their assault.

The young reporter then turned toward the camera, smoothing her hair and clearing her throat. "Victoria Banks refused to answer questions as she left the Vail Police Department this morning following a second round of questioning regarding the recent murder of her husband, Elliot Banks…"

Jack didn't want to watch anymore. He turned

off the television and sat staring at the dark screen. Victoria hadn't been arrested. That was good. Deep down, he didn't think she was guilty. She might be guilty of something, Jack thought, but it wasn't the murder of her husband—or Doris.

Jack dragged both hands down his face. There was more to Victoria's story—more than what she was willing to tell him, and more than what he could find out about her on his own.

He rested one hand on the cabinet above him, leaned against it, and dropped his head, thinking. If only he still had access to the government databases he'd used when he was with the FBI, or even the ones he'd had access to as a detective in Aspen.

He thought about it, searching for options—any option. After several minutes, he could think of only one. There was someone who might be willing to help, someone who Jack knew shared his primal itch for justice.

Jack took his cell phone from the counter in front of him and scrolled through his contacts. He stopped at the name of the one man he knew could help him find out who Victoria Banks really was.

CHAPTER 51

WHEN THEY REACHED the house, Victoria thanked Miles and the two attorneys who were sitting in the back seat. She opened the car door, ready to be home alone. It had been an exhausting morning.

Katie was on her way to spend the afternoon with her, and Victoria wanted to process what all had occurred during the police questioning before she got there.

But it wasn't to be.

"Can we use your dining room, Victoria? I'd like to discuss some things with the guys before they head back to Denver."

"You're staying another night in Vail?" Miles had gone out of his way to be nearby. His concern was endearing, but Victoria was starting to feel suffocated. She just wanted time alone.

"A couple more days," Miles said with a friendly smile. "Then I'll need to be back in Denver."

"You must have tons of work to catch up on in the city. I really don't want to be such a burden."

He dismissed her concern with a hand wave, and they all got out of the car.

Inside, Victoria excused herself, using the explanation she wanted to change clothes, but really wanting to take refuge in the master suite for a few minutes of silence.

Once in the bedroom, she closed the double doors behind her and leaned back on them. It wasn't yet noon, but the day had already taken its toll. The encounter with Detective Wayne Conner had drained her of what little energy she had started the day with. But it wasn't just about being tired. She was now struggling against the urge to give up.

Detective Conner had been brutally blunt, accusing her of Elliot's murder and threatening her with arrest. He also brought up the bombing of Doris's car in Silverthorne and insinuated she might have had something to do with it. Victoria was grateful Miles had warned her that he might act that way and try to bully her into a confession. But she had been ready and had withstood the detective's onslaught of questions and accusations for more than three hours.

But it wasn't only the police. First Elliot, now Doris. Victoria felt the rumble of growing grief threatening to explode like a volcano inside her. She forced it down but was nervous she wouldn't be able to do so much longer.

Victoria was starting to worry that Miles suspected

she was guilty as well. It wasn't anything that he asked or said, but the small sideways glances he would take when he thought she wasn't looking. Victoria knew that if Miles came to the conclusion that she was guilty of murder, he would pull away. She would have nowhere left to turn.

Victoria thought she could actually feel her heart ache. It was tight, like someone was twisting it in knots. Still leaning against the doors, she realized she was holding her breath, and she drew in air. She pulled the stilettos from her feet and carried them to her closet, carefully tucking them into their place on the shelf. After she changed her clothes, she lay down on the bed, not bothering to pull back the covers. *Just a few minutes,* she thought to herself. Just a quick rest before Katie got there.

Sometime later, there was a soft rap at her door. Victoria didn't know how long she had been sleeping, but through the window, she saw the slanted rays of the afternoon sun. She jumped out of bed, turning to smooth the rumpled bedcovers before she opened the bedroom door.

"Victoria, are you all right? We're leaving now." It was Miles.

"I must have fallen asleep," she said, embarrassed, self-consciously smoothing a strand of hair behind her ear.

Miles gave her a sympathetic smile. "I'm glad

you got some rest. I'm sure you needed it after this morning."

His comment brought back the memory of the harrowing hours at the police station. Victoria felt the heavy weight threatening to return, but steeled herself and forced it aside.

"Thank you for everything, Miles," she managed to say.

"It's nothing," he said with an easy head shake. "The ball is in the police's court, but I think we're ready for whatever comes next."

"Ready for an arrest?"

It obviously wasn't the reply he was expecting. He looked at her, his eyes compassionate. "It probably won't come to that, but if it does, we're ready."

She nodded. It was the best she could hope for.

After they left, Victoria freshened her makeup and brushed her hair. Katie had called and was only a few minutes away.

In the kitchen, Victoria prepared a small char-cuterie plate, pulled two wineglasses from the cabinet and a bottle of her best Pinot Noir from the wine cellar. A few minutes later, the doorbell rang.

Katie looked resplendent in her fitted dress, her long blond curls set off by the bright colors in the fabric. Pucci—Victoria recognized the designer instantly, and Katie looked fabulous in it. Victoria was suddenly aware of how plain she must look in her jeans and black T-shirt that she had put on earlier.

"You look beautiful, Katie," Victoria told her. "Thank you for coming."

Katie kissed her on both cheeks. "You look fabulous, too, darling. You always do. A little color wouldn't kill you, though, but it's your style—I get that."

She was teasing, and Victoria knew better than to be offended and was genuinely happy to see her. "Come in. I'm glad you're here."

Katie sailed into the house in a cloud of hair spray and expensive perfume and followed Victoria to the kitchen.

"I'm glad Charles let you come," Victoria said, opening the bottle of wine.

"Why wouldn't he?" Katie popped a cheese cube in her mouth.

"There might be a reporter hanging around—"

"I saw them swarm you on television today. Horrid creatures."

Victoria agreed. "Pinot Noir okay?"

"You know me, darling. It's *all* okay."

Victoria poured them each a glass. They carried everything outside, setting the cheese and wine down on the outdoor dining table. The sky was cloudless. It was a glorious June afternoon in the Rockies.

"God, it's beautiful here," Katie said, looking

toward Vail Mountain and drawing in a breath of air redolent of summer grass and pine.

"I thought maybe Charles wouldn't want you to come. The reporters might snap a picture of you with a notorious husband killer," Victoria said, trying to make it sound like a joke.

Katie had placed a grape between her teeth but pulled it back out. The look on her face made Victoria wish she hadn't said it.

"Why would you say that?" Katie asked.

Victoria waved off the question. "Bad taste in jokes, I guess."

Katie stared at her, then stuck the grape back in her mouth and ate it. "Terrible thing about poor Doris."

Victoria instantly felt a knot form in her stomach. She remembered the fire and the heat, then looking at the scorched car and realizing Doris would have been inside. She looked down into her wineglass and swallowed back her grief. "It was horrible."

Katie leaned across the table and placed a hand on her arm. "I'm sorry you had to be there to see it."

Victoria nodded, still fighting to keep her emotions in check. Her voice shook as she spoke. "Doris was such a nice woman."

Katie watched her a second, then took a sip of wine and grabbed another grape. "She was nice— but a bit looney." When Victoria started to protest,

Katie held up a hand. "I know, I know, don't speak ill of the dead. But you have to admit, she was a little...off. At least now she won't have you on some wild-goose chase, looking for a connection between Elliot's murder and Bob Hawkins's suicide."

As convoluted as it was, it was Katie's way of changing the subject, trying to cheer her up. Victoria knew it, but it didn't work. Watching Doris die was a tragedy Victoria would have to live with and remember forever.

Victoria was now confident there was merit to Doris's theory, especially now that Doris was dead. The Silverthorne police were still investigating the explosion, but even if they ruled it an accident, Victoria was convinced it was murder. And although Doris was no longer here to help her, Victoria wasn't about to give up trying to find out what was going on at Banks Oil & Gas, and whether or not Elliot had been a part of it. Victoria was convinced the murders were somehow connected.

Without Doris, it would be harder to unearth the truth, but Victoria would find a way. As a last resort, she could always ask Miles for help. Miles had been Elliot's best friend, and she knew they had discussed the business from time to time. Being an attorney could prove useful. But most importantly, Miles had loved Elliot like she had. And if they found out Elliot had been involved in something illegal, she could count on Miles to keep the secret.

Katie fidgeted, smoothing invisible wrinkles from the front of her dress. "What about that detective?" she asked. "The one from Aspen?"

Victoria stared at the wine in her glass. "It wasn't working out."

"You fired him?"

"Something like that."

"Just as well. I think the police will figure it out anyway. You can save the money."

Victoria turned in her chair and looked directly at Katie. There was no way of asking it delicately. "Charles thinks I murdered Elliot, doesn't he?"

Katie sat wide-eyed. "Now, why would you say that?"

"Tell me the truth, Katie."

But Katie's worried expression revealed what Victoria already knew. Katie set her wine down, reached over, and took Victoria's hand. "He thinks it's a possibility."

"A possibility that I murdered Elliot?"

She nodded once, an apology in her eyes. "Yes."

It hit Victoria hard. She looked directly at Katie. "You don't think that I'm capable of it, though, do you?"

Katie sat silent for a few seconds, but to Victoria it was an eternity. There was a look in her eyes that

Victoria had never seen before. She didn't know if it was alarm or disbelief, but it bothered her.

Katie shook her head. "Of course I don't think so."

Once again Victoria felt emotion well in her, but again she fought it back. She managed a quiet "Thank you," then changed the subject.

For the next two hours they talked about fashion and politics. Katie gossiped about celebrities and people they both knew. Then she regaled Victoria with the plans she had made for their trip to Capri. After the brief talk of murder, it was as if everything were back to normal. They talked like they had since the first time they'd met years ago. It was a lighthearted, trivial conversation, one Victoria found she needed more than she had realized.

Before Katie left, she made Victoria promise to come stay with her and Charles in Denver after the chaos surrounding the investigations died down. Victoria told her she would, but she didn't mean it. How could she stay in the same house as a man who thought she was capable of murder?

When Katie was gone, Victoria cleaned the kitchen, then sat on the sofa in the family room alone, finishing the last of the second bottle of wine. She thought of the moment of silence after she'd asked Katie if she agreed with Charles, if she thought it was possible Victoria could have killed Elliot. Katie had assured her she didn't, but the sinking feeling in Victoria's heart told her otherwise, and she had never felt more alone.

Her best friend thought it was possible she was guilty of murder.

CHAPTER 52

JACK MARTIN WAS back on the highway headed to
Weld County, northeast of Denver. Boots Hamer
had called and told him that Clark Poindexter had
figured out the scam. Hamer also had information
on Banks Oil & Gas that, although Jack was no longer investigating Elliot Banks's murder, he wanted to
hear.

Jack passed the turnoff for the gravel road he had
taken to the drilling rig the week before. Glancing at
the directions on his GPS, he saw the road he needed
was two miles farther. For some reason, this time
Hamer wanted to meet at one of the wells.

Once off the highway, Jack saw a cluster of large
storage tanks in the distance and assumed that was
where he was headed. The tanks were painted the
same caliche color as their barren surroundings. As
he got closer, he could see them more clearly. There
were three rows of three, nine tanks in total. Attached
to one of them was a set of metal stairs that stretched
to the top and was connected to an elevated walkway.

To one side, Jack could see steel pipe stacked in

piles according to their size. There were parts and equipment clustered together and laid out in rows. Besides being an operating well, the site looked like it was used as some kind of storage yard.

It was a hot June afternoon. The sun blazed, turning a turquoise sky a hazy shade of blue-gray in the heat. A dust devil swirled in the distance.

Jack pulled onto the property. There was only one other vehicle there—an early-model Chevrolet truck, dented and begging for a paint job. It was parked next to a small building with reflective glass that looked like it could house controls for the storage tanks behind it, or was maybe a small office for the storage yard.

Jack got out of his truck, opened the door to the building, stepped inside, and was immediately hit by a blast of frigid air being cranked out by a window unit. The room was lit by a fluorescent light; the window blinds were shut to block out the heat. Except for a single cheap desk scattered with papers and a computer monitor lit up like Christmas, the room was empty.

Jack stepped back outside and caught a glimpse of Hamer on the opposite side of the yard. Poindexter was with him, the two men bent over something mechanical.

Hamer looked up when Jack approached. "Howdy, Detective." The two men shook hands. "Poindexter here found something out I think you should know about."

"So, what's going on?" Jack asked.

"Tell him, Poindexter."

The skinny accountant was wiping sweat from his forehead. He stuck the handkerchief back in his pocket, pulled out a sheet of paper, and unfolded it, his hands shaking slightly.

He spoke fast. "I compared the production numbers of Mr. Hamer's wells before and after Energy Marketing took over selling the oil for Banks Oil & Gas. I then cross-checked the numbers for all of the wells and discovered a consistent drop in production since the very *day* the marketing company took over."

Boots held out a hand. "Slow down, son, so the detective here can follow you."

Jack frowned. "I'm not sure I understand. Banks Oil & Gas is still on the sign. This isn't their well?"

Boots spoke up. "Banks Oil & Gas is just the drilling company now. When those two good-for-nothings Stratton and Lowe set up Energy Marketing, Elliot let them take over the selling of the oil once it was out of the ground. Elliot was a good man, Detective, but he got taken by those two."

Doris had already explained it to him once, but Jack wanted to make sure he understood. "So Banks drills the oil, then Stratton and Lowe sell it."

Hamer nodded. "Exactly. Stratton and Lowe buy

the oil from Banks Oil & Gas once it's drilled. Then they go and sell it to one of the big guys like Conoco, Exxon, whoever."

Poindexter spoke up, visibly excited but trying to calm himself. "I cross-referenced production reports with dates. The production of all of Mr. Hamer's wells have been consistently declining by the *exact* same rate since the day Energy Marketing took over."

Jack looked back at Hamer. "So what does that mean?"

Hamer set his feet wide and stuck his hands on his hips. "It means I'm being screwed, my boy. After Poindexter here called yesterday, I had one of my guys set our own meters on ten of my wells. We checked them all today, and all ten read a fraction higher than the ones controlled by Banks Oil & Gas—the exact same fraction."

Jack thought he was beginning to understand. "So you think the original meters—the ones that set your royalties—are rigged to read low? Deliberately?"

Hamer nodded. "I do."

Poindexter shook his head. "It would be an unprecedented statistical anomaly for all ten of Energy Marketing's meters to be reading low by exactly the same amount."

Jack turned back to Hamer. "So someone is deliberately shortchanging you."

Hamer nodded again. "That's right."

"Who has access to the meters?"

"The production manager."

"And who's that?"

Hamer leaned over and spit, "Luther Byrd."

CHAPTER 53

VICTORIA DIDN'T KNOW it yet, but it was Harold Lamken's last day on the job.

Harold had spent the day outside, first supervising the landscape crew hired to trim back trees blocking views of Vail Mountain, thin and shape a few others in the front of the house. He'd spent the afternoon completing a few odds-and-ends projects he'd put off but wanted to have finished before the end of the day. He would leave with the clear conscience that nothing at the house was left undone.

Harold had reminded himself over and over throughout the day that he didn't have a choice. He had to quit. It was because of Tyler and because of his promise to his baby sister on her deathbed to take care of him.

Harold would protect his nephew, but this would be the last time. He had made up his mind, he would kick Tyler out, force him to find his own way. Then, as much as he hated the thought of it, he'd put the trailer up for sale, move as far away from Vail and Victoria Banks as he could.

He had intended to tell her he was quitting when he got there that morning, but she didn't answer the door when he rang the bell. He had walked around the house, glancing in windows, but all the lights were off and there was no sign of her. He thought about using his key to get in and check, but then decided it wouldn't be a good idea. What if she came home and caught him inside?

When Victoria finally returned, she was with Miles Preston and two guys Harold assumed were also attorneys. They dressed alike and carried themselves in the same self-important way Preston did.

Harold had waited more than an hour for the trio to leave, but almost as soon as Preston and the goons were gone, Katie Stratton showed up. Not that Harold minded a glimpse of the curvaceous Mrs. Stratton, dressed in a colorful snug dress that showed off her tan legs. But he was disappointed he would be delayed again in talking to Victoria. The anticipation of telling her he was quitting had his guts tied up in knots.

When Katie Stratton finally got into her giant Escalade and drove away, Harold gave Victoria a few minutes, then knocked on the door. His mouth suddenly went dry as his pulse started to race.

"Harold?" Victoria smiled at him, and his heart immediately sank. She must have seen it on his face.

Her expression morphed into a look of concern. "What's wrong, Harold?"

He dug into his pocket and pulled out the key. "I need to quit." Harold held out the key, his hand shaking slightly, but she didn't take it.

She stared at him, a tiny frown creasing her forehead between her eyes. "Quit? But why?"

He swallowed. "Uh, I just think it's for the best... now that Elliot's not around."

"Harold, you can keep working if you like. Just because Elliot is gone doesn't mean you can't work here anymore. That doesn't matter." She looked bewildered.

The guilt was eating him alive, and he averted his eyes. "But it does matter."

"It doesn't," she argued. "If it's about money, I can give you a raise."

Harold shook his head. "It's not about money."

"Do you need to work more days? More hours?"

He shook his head again. "No, ma'am, that's not it."

"Then what is it?" She was getting frustrated.

He should have planned it better, thought of what he was going to say. He had gone over and over it in his head the last few days, trying to think of what he was going to tell her, but he hadn't been able to come up with anything. He hoped that when he saw her, it would come naturally, that he would be able to come up with something on the fly. He hadn't.

There was a long silence.

"Harold, do you think I killed Elliot?"

He looked up. The intense expression on her face surprised him. Her mouth was set in a thin, hard line, her eyes boring into him as she waited for an answer.

Harold swallowed. He didn't know what to say. He hadn't thought of it—he could let Victoria think he was quitting because he thought she murdered Elliot. Then she wouldn't suspect anything. He considered it a second, then decided against it. That would be the coward's way out. But he couldn't tell her the truth—that he had to quit because his nephew could be Elliot's killer.

Harold thought about telling her the truth, that it was personal. It was about *him*, not about her. He could make up something that was close to the truth, just distort it a little—say something that wouldn't be lying.

Harold opened his mouth to speak, but too much time had passed.

"I didn't kill Elliot, Harold. But if you think I did, then I don't want you here. I just have one question."

Harold waited and realized he'd rocked back on his heels, not able to think of a single intelligent thing to say but trying to distance himself from the situation.

"What were you doing here Wednesday?" Victoria asked.

"Huh?"

"Last Wednesday. You weren't supposed to work that day. But you came into the house for a few minutes and then left."

She stared accusingly at him, and again, Harold didn't know what to say. He wanted to melt into the shrubbery to the side of the front door.

"You know, Harold. You've been acting really strange lately. And I didn't kill Elliot, but maybe *you* did."

Victoria snatched the key from his outstretched hand, then shut the door, leaving Harold standing on the sidewalk with his mouth still open.

CHAPTER 54

CHARLES STRATTON WAS sitting at the large gilt desk in the mansion's study. Katie had purchased the desk at a Sotheby's auction in New York years earlier. The legs were shaped like winged eagles, the apron carved with elaborate scrollwork of ivy and fruit. Except for the pink marble top, the whole thing was painted gold.

At the time, Charles thought the grandiose desk was a bit over-the-top, but he had grown fond of it. Something about sitting at it made him feel invincible. He imagined King Louis XVI sitting at a similar one in France two hundred and fifty years earlier.

I am *a king,* Charles reminded himself. A king of business. A titan of energy. The merger had cleared the remaining hurdles and was scheduled to close the following week. *Just a few more days,* Charles thought, pounding a celebratory fist on the marble top. Victory was near.

He had already ascended the throne of Banks Oil & Gas, and after the merger with Centennial State Energy, he would reign at the helm of one of

America's largest energy conglomerates. He drew in a deep, satisfied breath and rubbed his palm across the cool marble.

Outside, the late-afternoon sun cast the backyard in a smoky haze. Charles sipped bourbon from a crystal glass and looked out through the large windows and across the manicured lawn to the swimming pool. Facing the house, on the opposite side of the pool, was a marble replica of Antonio Canova's statue of *The Three Graces.*

After he and Katie had purchased the house, Charles had commissioned the sculpture from a contemporary Italian artist. Katie had wanted palm trees, fake rocks, and a waterfall, but Charles had put his foot down. When he showed her the artist's rendering of what their version of *The Three Graces* would look like and told her the original was displayed in the Hermitage Museum in Saint Petersburg, Katie hadn't been impressed. Only when he told her the beauty of the women in the sculpture reminded him of her own classic beauty did Katie finally relent.

Charles got up from the desk and walked to the window for a better look. He raised the crystal glass to his lips and sipped the bourbon, letting the warm liquid slip slowly down his throat as he admired the sculpture.

There was a fluttering movement beyond the statue in the far corner of the yard. Charles squinted for a better look and saw a nest. Two small birds were furiously defending it from a crow. Each time the ugly black crow came close, one of the smaller birds would leave the nest and fight it away.

Charles watched as the crow attacked the nest over and over. Each time, one of the small defenders furiously deflected the assault. It was only a matter of time, Charles thought. The larger, stronger bird would prevail and snatch its prize. He watched, sipping the bourbon, enjoying the late-afternoon drama playing out in his yard. After several minutes, the crow disappeared, the nest still intact. Disappointed, Charles turned away from the window.

"Charles, can you come help me?" Katie called from somewhere in the house.

He found her in the kitchen, setting bags down on the breakfast table.

"There are several more in my car," she said. "I couldn't help myself. After I left Victoria, I drove right by Gorsuch and had to stop. *Look* what was in the window."

She was nearly breathless with glee as she pulled the zebra-striped ski suit from the shopping bag. She dug back into it. "And since I was in there for the suit, I looked around and found this. Isn't it fabulous?" She pulled a full-length shearling coat from the bag and put it on. "There are a few more things in the car. And before you say anything—it was all on sale. Well, almost all of it."

She kept talking, but Charles wasn't listening. He retrieved the remaining bags from her car and was setting them down when his cell phone rang.

Luther Byrd.

Charles left Katie in the kitchen and walked back toward the study. "What is it?" he answered.

Byrd's voice was deep. He sounded worried. "I saw Boots Hamer again today."

"So?"

"They were at the well by the storage yard, looking at the meter. He was with the same two guys he was with before."

"Which two?"

"That skinny accountant was one of them. The other was some guy I saw leaving the drilling rig the other day."

"What did he look like?"

"Tall, with dark hair—kind of long and wavy. Late thirties. Had on cowboy boots and jeans."

Old man Hamer was like a pesky bulldog that had ahold of Charles's pant leg and wouldn't let go. Hamer had called the office after Elliot's funeral, threatening a press conference if he couldn't get any answers. The feisty old man was becoming a real problem.

If it were any other time, Charles could deal with it. He'd have Luther reset the meters, bump up the old guy's royalties for a while, and get him off his back. But there wasn't time for that now. They were too close to the merger.

Charles wondered who it was that Boots Hamer had met with at least twice—and with the forensic accountant. He thought about Luther's description of the man, then narrowed his eyes at the possibility. "Was it Jack Martin?"

"Who?"

"Detective Jack Martin, you idiot. Have you been living under a rock?"

Luther was quiet. Charles knew he had insulted the ogre, but he didn't care. "Let me text a picture. You tell me if it's the guy."

A few seconds later, Charles heard Luther's phone ping with the text.

"Yep, that's him," Luther said. "Who is he?"

Charles sat down at the desk and threw back what was left of his bourbon, then closed his eyes and rolled the cool glass across his forehead. He felt a headache coming on. "Jack Martin is a detective Victoria hired to find out who murdered Elliot."

"Is he a problem for us?" Luther sounded anxious.

At the far end of the yard, Charles could just make out the silhouettes of the two small birds perched peacefully on the edge of the nest. The crow was nowhere in sight, and Charles was frustrated. It was survival of the fittest, and the crow should have won.

Damn bird had given up too soon and let the weak claim his victory.

Charles wasn't going to give up. The merger was his prize. Then there would be a merger after that, and another after that. This was only the beginning.

"Martin could definitely complicate things," Charles finally said, pressing the glass against his temple. "But our immediate problem is Boots Hamer."

CHAPTER 55

LUTHER BYRD SWUNG his truck off the gravel road and onto the highway. His heart raced as he pressed the accelerator, headed home.

He flexed his meaty fingers, then tightened his grip on the steering wheel. Things were coming to a head. Charles Stratton had given him another job, and with the merger only a week away, Luther could almost taste payday.

"Finally." He said it aloud in a low growl, then rolled his tongue around in his mouth and pressed it thick against the back of his uneven teeth.

He thought about the job at hand. There wasn't as much time to prepare as he had for the woman, but it didn't matter. He welcomed the challenge and knew whatever the plan ended up being, he would execute it with precision.

He swung through the McDonald's in Greeley. On the way home, he would eat, drive, and plan the job— killing three birds with one stone. He was nothing if not efficient. Nobody could accuse Luther Byrd of being an amateur.

Back on the road, Luther pulled one of the Big Macs from the bag and took a bite. He wiped mustard from his mouth onto the back of his hand and sifted through the memories of his training as he chewed.

There would be no explosives—no time for that. But the tactical options were numerous. It was just a matter of selecting the right one for the job.

Luther thought about the target—old and weak. But he knew to underestimate an enemy was to risk failure, and he was too smart to do that.

He weighed different options, running through the pros and cons of a frontal assault or guerrilla warfare. Maybe a direct attack on the target's home. He decided against it—too much exposure.

After several minutes, Luther finally settled on one of the oldest and most primitive field tactics still in existence—the ambush. He would rely on concealment and surprise, lure the unsuspecting target in close, then...

"Bam!" Luther slammed his fist against the steering wheel and laughed, spitting bits of lettuce onto the truck's dash and floorboard. He couldn't wait to get to the house and work out the details.

His excitement grew as he thought about it. Tomorrow this time, Boots Hamer would be dead.

CHAPTER 56

AFTER SHE FIRED Harold, Victoria wandered into the study, sank into one of the leather chairs in front of the fireplace, and buried her face in her hands.

She shouldn't have been so short with him. She had accused him of murdering Elliot and now realized how ridiculous that had been.

She remembered Harold's stunned expression. He looked hurt, and Victoria was ashamed. She decided she would make it right; she'd call him later and apologize. She was upset that he had quit, but it wasn't his fault—it was hers.

It had been nearly unbearable when Elliot died, but now things had gotten even worse. Almost everyone thought she was guilty. The police, Charles and Katie, maybe Miles and Jack, and now Harold.

And Doris was gone. Victoria felt a deep, sinking feeling in her chest thinking about Doris. She would miss her desperately.

Victoria's life was again as it had been before—lonely and isolated. The last few years she had lived her very own fairy tale. But she reminded herself that every story comes to an end, and not all of them have happy endings.

Victoria sat for a few minutes, then decided she couldn't stand the wallowing in self-pity any longer. She drew in a deep breath and stood up, smoothed the front of her jeans, and pushed up her shirtsleeves. The stars had been aligned against her before. If they were aligning against her now, she'd deal with it. In the meantime, there was work to do.

She sat down at Elliot's desk and opened his laptop. Doris was no longer around to help dig into the inner workings of Banks Oil & Gas, but Victoria was no stranger to business.

Boots Hamer had hired a forensic accountant to look into what was going on with the company. Victoria realized that if she was going to uncover the truth, she would have to think like an accountant.

She leaned over and switched on the printer, then made sure the tray was full of paper. She then logged into Elliot's account on the company website—thank God he had trusted her with his password, and no one at the company had thought to change it yet.

She started with the corporate documents— service contracts, leases, production reports, SEC reports, lists of the company's investors. She printed all of it, sorting it into neat stacks and refilling the paper tray when it ran out.

She had a plan. She would take it all into the dining

room, organize it, then go through every page. Even with her knowledge of the business, Victoria knew it was a long shot she could figure it out on her own, but she had to try.

If she needed help, she would hire her own forensic accountant, have them sign a confidentiality agreement, ensuring whatever secrets they uncovered about Elliot and the business would never be exposed.

Victoria had to know the last several years of her life hadn't been a lie. She had given Elliot everything, trusted him with her past. Told him things no one else knew; told him about the demons she had buried long ago. Now she was determined to find out if the man she loved so unconditionally had ever really existed at all.

Afternoon turned to night. Victoria had stacks of paper organized across the dining room table, prioritized by what she felt was most relevant. She would start with the financial documents, the income and expense reports, and go from there.

She sat down in a chair near the center of the table, the documents stacked in rows to either side of her. She would work left to right, starting with the row closest to her, then move outward, keeping it all organized. If something looked suspicious or she thought needed further investigation, she would set it aside.

As she pulled the first stack of papers toward her, her cell phone rang.

She considered letting it roll over to voicemail but saw that it was Miles. It could be something about the police investigation. Did they want her in for questioning again? Were they planning on arresting her? Maybe it was about the police in Silverthorne this time.

She answered the call.

"Victoria, I wanted to check to see how you were doing. I worried about you after the guys and I left earlier." Miles's voice was warm and full of concern.

Victoria set the papers aside, frustrated by the distraction when she realized the call wasn't about the police. But Miles had done so much for her, the least she could do was give him a few minutes of her time.

She leaned her back against the chair. "I'm fine, Miles. But thank you for your concern."

They talked for several minutes. He insisted on taking her to dinner the following evening. "You need to get out. It's time."

After initially pushing back, Victoria gave in, knowing he was probably right. She had a lot of work to do, but by the next evening, it would be time to take a break. She was determined not to get buried in it, forgetting to eat and sleep as she had done several times in college. She needed to keep a clear head, not get so deep into the forest that she wouldn't be able to see the trees.

Miles spent several minutes filling her in on the strategy the defense attorneys had formulated should she be called back in for questioning. He said it was probably only a matter of time before the police wanted to talk to her again, but they would be ready. He didn't mention anything about an impending arrest, for which she was relieved.

Victoria listened to him talk, but her mind began to wander. It was all about her—the police investigation, the defense team's strategy. What about Elliot?

It was as if everyone had forgotten about Elliot and was now focused solely on her, and the police were the enemy. She knew that wasn't true. Miles was only trying to protect her, but Victoria still wanted justice. She wondered if the police were any closer to catching Elliot's killer, or if they were focused only on her.

It had been a mistake to let Jack Martin go. She should have stopped him, come up with some explanation for why she wasn't being honest. She wanted Jack back on the case, needed his help to find the killer. She decided she would call him.

Still holding her phone, Victoria walked into the kitchen. She filled a glass of water and drank it, standing at the counter as Miles talked for several more minutes. When they finally hung up, she was relieved.

She slid the phone into her purse, then closed it, wanting to avoid any more distractions. There was too much work to do.

As she placed the glass into the dishwasher, the doorbell rang.

"What now?" she wondered aloud as she walked into the foyer. She glanced through the peephole and immediately pulled back. She couldn't believe he would come.

The doorbell rang again.

She hesitated, then reluctantly unlocked the dead bolt and pulled open the door.

He flashed a handsome but malevolent grin. "Hey, Vicky."

He leaned in to kiss her, but she took a step back. "What are you doing here?"

His grin faded, and he ran his fingers through a mop of dirty-blond hair. "I need more money."

CHAPTER 57

WHEN BOOTS HAMER told Jack that Luther Byrd was the production manager for Banks Oil & Gas and that Byrd had access to the well meters that were shortchanging him, Jack knew Byrd would be at the heart of what was going on with Hamer's royalties.

When Jack mentioned investigating Byrd further, Hamer told him Poindexter was one step ahead of him. The nervous accountant opened his briefcase, pulled out a thin file, and gave it to him.

"I'm not supposed to have this," Poindexter told him. "It's biographical information on Mr. Byrd—school records, military service records, employment records."

Jack looked at Poindexter and raised his eyebrows. "How'd you get this?"

"Let's just say an old friend owed me a favor," Poindexter said, obviously hoping Jack wouldn't press the issue, and he hadn't.

Jack didn't care where the information came from. He needed to know more about Byrd, but he knew the scam wouldn't stop with him. There would be someone higher up in the corporate food chain, someone who was pocketing the extra cash that was supposed to be going to Hamer. And whoever that was, was probably giving Byrd just enough money to keep him in on the scam.

Crockett had settled into the passenger seat of the truck and fallen asleep. Jack spent the drive back to the campground mentally sifting through everything. He thought of Doris. What was she on the verge of discovering that was so threatening that someone wanted her dead?

He thought of her theory that Bob Hawkins hadn't committed suicide, that he had been murdered, and that somehow it was tied into the royalties scam Poindexter was investigating. Had Bob Hawkins figured out what was going on and become a liability?

And what about Elliot?

Jack knew Elliot's murder wasn't random—murders rarely were. Somehow it was tied into the web of deceit surrounding Banks Oil & Gas. But if Elliot was involved in the scam, why was he killed? It didn't make sense.

And then there was Victoria. The beautiful, distant widow who'd been in the house when her husband was murdered and at the diner in Silverthorne when Doris's car blew up. Jack knew she was hiding something. But what was it?

As the interstate wound around the west side of

Denver and started up the foothills, Jack slid over into the fast lane, avoiding the traffic struggling with the elevation climb. He was anxious to get back to the trailer and read the contents of the file Poindexter had given him.

Jack pulled off the interstate in Idaho Springs to put gas in the truck, painfully aware of his dwindling funds as he slid his credit card into the reader at the pump. But he didn't have time to worry about that now. He was nipping at the heels of solving the case. And although there were several pieces to the puzzle still missing, he knew he was getting close.

By the time Jack pulled into the campground, the sun was low on the horizon. Although the sky was growing dark, he stood outside throwing a stick for Crockett. He had to make up for the poor dog being in the truck all day.

But Jack itched to read the file. And when he couldn't stand it any longer, he threw the stick one last time.

"That's it, boy. I've got to get to work."

In the trailer, Jack grabbed a Shiner from the refrigerator and popped off the cap with his ring. He slid onto the bench at the far side of the table, not putting his back to the door, then opened the file and started to read.

Luther Byrd had been born in Chicago to working-class parents, attended local schools, where he'd had a less-than-stellar record. But he'd managed to join the army, spending two years in Afghanistan before being dishonorably discharged for insubordination and spending a year in prison for beating up an officer. Jack raised an eyebrow when he saw Byrd's specialty while in the army—explosives.

"Now we're getting somewhere," he said aloud, then drained the last of the Shiner. He reached around, grabbed another from the refrigerator without having to stand up, and continued reading.

Once out of prison, Byrd had bounced around, working odd jobs for several years before landing one on a drilling rig. First he had worked for a small company out of Texas, then for Banks Oil & Gas. Byrd had been a Banks employee for only a few years when he was promoted to production manager, but there was nothing in his records to indicate he was qualified for the job.

Crockett whined at his feet, and Jack realized he had forgotten to feed him.

"Sorry, boy," he said, getting up from the table and scratching Crockett behind the ears.

A few minutes later, as he was setting the food on the floor, Jack's cell phone buzzed. He looked at the caller ID. Detective Mark Thurmond with the Denver Police Department. Thurmond had been investigating Georgia Glass's stalking case at the same time Jack was looking for the Hermes Strangler in Aspen.

It had been a long day and Jack had almost forgotten he'd called Thurmond that morning asking for his help.

"I have to admit it," Thurmond said. "I was surprised to hear from you earlier. I thought you'd dropped off the map. Where are you?"

"Camped at Shadow Mountain Lake."

"Well, that's on the map, but just barely. But I'm glad you're still in the area."

Jack liked Mark Thurmond. Although he had spoken with him only a couple of times, and only over the phone, Jack knew the odds of getting Thurmond's help were in his favor. Even though Thurmond was a generation older, Jack saw him as a kindred spirit, a fellow peace officer hell-bent on righting the balances for Lady Justice.

"I'd like to buy you a cup of coffee sometime," Jack said, "hear how you solved Georgia Glass's stalking case."

"That's a deal. In return, you can tell me about catching the Hermes Strangler—give me the details your chief left out of his reports to the media."

"Anytime," Jack said, and meant it. "What did you find on Victoria Banks?"

"Are you sitting down?"

Jack felt his pulse quicken. "No. Do I need to?" The tone of Thurmond's voice had him worried.

"Victoria Banks was born Victoria Christina

Harper. Her mother was accused, tried, and convicted of murdering her father when Victoria was just eight. Stabbed him to death. Then her mother committed suicide in prison."

The news hit Jack like a sledgehammer. He processed the information for a moment. Victoria's mother had murdered her husband. "Like mother, like daughter?" Jack wondered aloud.

"Maybe."

But Jack couldn't believe it. "I've arrested a hundred killers, Mark—including women. She just doesn't seem the type."

"You know as well as I do, Jack, there isn't a 'type.'"

But it didn't make sense. "She hasn't exhibited any indications…any behavioral…"

"Jack, we both know there's no standard behavior for a murderer. You told me she was your client, but you need to seriously consider the possibility she murdered her husband."

Jack knew he was right, but he wasn't ready to concede the point yet. "There are usually benchmarks or signposts—something."

Mark Thurmond was silent.

Jack dragged his free hand down his face. "Shit. Of course you're right. It's just not what I expected to hear."

"Are you working with the Vail PD?"

"No. Not yet. But if I find out Victoria Banks murdered her husband, I'll have to turn the information over to them."

"Good," Thurmond said. Jack could hear the approval in the veteran detective's voice. Thurmond continued. "I want you to call me when you get this Banks case wrapped up. You don't have to live in Denver long to have heard of Elliot Banks and to know what a great guy he was. You find out who killed him."

Jack knew what Thurmond was implying. Find out who killed him, *even if it ends up being your client.*

"I will," Jack said. "Thank you, Mark. I really appreciate—"

"There's something else."

The last thing Jack wanted was another surprise. He drew in a long breath. "What is it?"

"She's got a brother."

CHAPTER 58

AFTER STARTING THE morning being interrogated by the Vail police for three hours, Victoria thought the day couldn't get any worse, but it had.

She now knew that almost everyone thought she was capable of murder, even Harold. It was only a matter of time before Miles pulled away. The housekeeper would quit on her next. Victoria knew the mansion was too big for her to manage alone. But without Elliot, she didn't want to stay anyway. There were too many memories—good and bad. She made up her mind to sell it.

She thought about where she would go. The possibilities seemed endless yet nonexistent at the same time. She had the money to go anywhere she wanted, but she had nowhere to go.

There was only Gary. As her brother, Gary was technically family, but they had never been close. And as long as Victoria was around, he would hit her up for money every time his luck ran out—and it ran out regularly.

It had been hard for both of them, growing up

in the foster system, bounced around from family to family after their father died, murdered by their mother. Victoria had lost herself in books and school, erecting a shield by refusing to acknowledge their past. She had fought hard to put it all behind her—and had—but Gary had done the opposite.

Gary had let their past define him, had gotten into trouble with the law and dropped out of school. More than a decade later, he was still the same rebellious kid lashing out at the world for the rotten hand they had been dealt. And as long as Gary was around, Victoria knew she would be shackled to the past she had fought so hard to bury.

At first she had kept her past a secret from Elliot, but as time went on, she knew she couldn't keep it hidden forever. Before they were married, she'd told him the truth about Gary, and about her parents.

Victoria's heart ached when she remembered how kind Elliot had been. There had been no judgment, just understanding. No shock or revulsion, just concern. She told Elliot it was a part of her life she wanted to forget, and he never brought it up again, even looking the other way when Gary would show up on occasion with his hand out—except the last time.

Elliot had had enough. He saw what Gary's visits did to her, each one briefly pulling her back into her shell as she tried shielding herself from the world and its cruelty. The last time Gary came to see her, Elliot had confronted him, told him to stay away and leave her alone. It had upset Victoria and they had argued, but she knew Elliot was right.

Victoria never gave Gary much, a couple hundred dollars here and there, knowing giving him money was like giving a crack addict more drugs. But today had been different. Today Gary wanted more.

"I guess this is all yours now, sis," he had said with an appraising grin, looking over the outside of the house and front lawn.

He gave her a story about being between jobs and needing to get back on his feet. It was the same story he'd given Victoria numerous times before. But this time he wanted more money, $10,000. And for the first time, Victoria refused.

He'd gotten angry, and they'd argued, Victoria imploring him to turn his life around and telling him she wasn't going to enable him anymore. Gary was a dangerous thread to her past that she wanted to finally cut free.

When she asked him to leave, Gary had threatened her, saying he would "let everyone know who the *real* Vicky Harper was."

Her hands shook as she closed the door on him and turned the dead bolt, locking him out of her life for good.

Back in the dining room, Victoria attempted to

forget about the argument with Gary by burying herself in work, sorting through the documents again. But as hard as she tried, she couldn't focus—the numbers blurred together, and nothing made sense. She put her elbows on the table and pressed her fingers to her brows. Then, after another hour of trying to find something—anything—regarding fraud at Banks Oil & Gas, she gave up.

In the bathroom, Victoria filled the large tub with hot water. She wanted to wash away the pain, cleanse herself of all the memories that still haunted her. Slipping down into the water, she leaned back on the cool enamel of the tub and closed her eyes.

An hour later, after bathing and dressing in soft pajamas and her robe, Victoria felt better.

Back in the dining room, she pored through the company documents with a renewed determination. She would find out the truth about what was going on at Banks Oil & Gas. If it turned out Elliot was guilty of fraud, she would once again bury the past. But she had to know before she moved on.

It was nearly midnight when she finally pulled back the covers to her bed and slipped in. She had a nagging feeling that there was something she needed to do before she went to sleep. She thought about it for a while, then gave up. The day had been horrendous and she was exhausted, but she was content that tomorrow would be a new day. She would call

Jack Martin, think of something to say to get him back on the case. He would help her find out who'd killed Elliot.

She leaned over and turned off the lamp, then settled back onto the soft down pillows and almost immediately fell into a deep sleep.

Sometime later, from somewhere in the depths of her slumbering darkness, Victoria heard a familiar chime, and she stirred. It was followed by a loud bang that startled her fully awake.

Victoria groped in the darkness for her phone on the bedside table, but it wasn't there. Then she remembered putting it in her purse. It was still in the kitchen. She didn't know how long she had been asleep and had no way of finding out what time it was.

Bang.

Her heart lurched, and she sat up, her eyes wide open but useless in the dark. What was the sound?

She got out of bed and stood up. Grateful for the bars of moonlight through the windows, she left the lights off.

She stood still, the long stretches of silence between the bangs threatening to swallow her whole. She moved closer to the door, but froze in the threshold, afraid to go any farther. But it continued.

Bang.

Silence. She waited again, holding her breath.

Bang.

She cursed herself under her breath for leaving the phone in her purse. She could picture the Celine bag in the kitchen, its edges neatly squared with the corner of the stone counter, her cell phone tucked safely inside.

Bang.

Silence…

With outstretched hands, she felt her way into Elliot's closet and fumbled with the lock to his safe. Once open, she groped the shelves until she found his revolver. Then, holding her breath, she made her way back through the bedroom and stepped out into the corridor, pressing her back to the wall.

Although fear reached down, causing her legs to go weak, Victoria forced herself farther down the curving hallway. She inched along in the darkness, running one hand along the wall, the revolver in the other.

Moonlight shined through the windows, providing dim pockets of light, but she avoided them, choosing the safety of the shadows. She peered around the bent wall ahead of her, but couldn't see anything. She was hidden in the darkness. Was someone else hidden in it, too?

She forced herself to continue.

Bang. Victoria squeezed her hand tight around the revolver. The sound was coming from the kitchen.

As she got closer, she heard the wind and realized the back door was open, the wind blowing it back and forth against the jamb.

In the kitchen, she flipped on the lights, but they made her feel vulnerable, and she immediately shut them back off. She rubbed the side of the revolver with her index finger, then slowly slid the finger over the trigger as she moved across the kitchen lit only by moonlight.

With the revolver still in one hand, she caught the swinging door with the other and held it still, then looked out across the deck and toward the pool. The full moon cast everything in a milky light. She squinted, her vision sweeping the yard as she tightened her grip on the gun. She didn't see anyone and was relieved.

But beyond the pool there were trees, tall pines that cast deep shadows the moonlight couldn't penetrate. The wind howled, swaying the trees side to side in a ghostly dance. Victoria closed the door and locked it, trying the handle to make sure it was secure.

Then it dawned on her. Someone could already be in the house.

She quietly slipped the phone from her purse and dialed 911, but ended the call before it rang. She had been scrutinized enough by the police. The last thing she wanted was to raise their suspicions by calling in a false alarm. She spent the next twenty minutes stumbling from room to room, upstairs and down, checking closets and behind doors, shaking the revolver in front of her as she went.

But there was no one there.

She sat for several minutes in the dark kitchen, her head in one hand, the revolver hanging at her side in the other. They'd never had a door blow open before. How could it have happened?

Then she remembered being outside with Katie and decided she must have forgotten to lock it when they'd come back inside. Victoria knew it was unlike her not to check and recheck the locks and turn on the security alarm before she went to bed, but it had been such a horrible day. She must have forgotten.

Back in the bedroom, Victoria went into her closet and stood in front of the full-length mirror, the revolver still in her hand. The woman looking back at her was a stranger. She wondered if life had finally dealt Vicky Harper more than she could bear.

She studied the dark circles under her eyes and pulled at the sallowness of her skin with her free hand. She wasn't the same woman as before—before Elliot died. That Victoria no longer existed. Or did she?

Victoria took in a deep breath, squared her shoulders, and stared into the mirror, desperately trying to hold on to the strength she felt slipping away. It was all too much—Elliot's murder, then Doris; Katie,

Charles, and Harold; the police threatening her with arrest. She needed to get away, but there was nowhere to go.

She thought of what her mother had done all those years ago in prison, and felt the pull to release her own burdens, one final dark surrender that would make all her problems go away. That had been her mother's way out. It could be hers, too.

Shaking, Victoria held the revolver at her side, rubbing the cold barrel with her thumb and searching the depths of her steel-gray eyes for the answer. She had a decision to make.

For several minutes, she took in and released slow deep breaths, finally willing the tremors to stop. She stared hard into the mirror and for a moment saw a glimmer of the girl who had defeated the wretchedness of life so many times before. A glimmer was all she needed.

With an immediate sense of relief and the feeling that a massive weight had suddenly lifted from her, Victoria realized that girl was still in there somewhere.

Standing in the warm cocoon of her closet, she closed her eyes and made that young girl a vow similar to the one she had made decades before. Somehow she would find a way, muster the strength to overcome what life had thrown at her. She had done it before, and she would do it again.

Victoria took the revolver back into Elliot's closet,

unlocked the safe, and carefully laid it inside. She pushed the heavy steel door closed and locked it, then leaned her forehead against the cool metal and swore to never consider her mother's way out again.

Back in bed, Victoria set her phone on the nightstand, then leaned over and turned off the lamp. She soon fell into a tortured sleep, dreaming again of the man chasing her through the forest.

CHAPTER 59

Tuesday, June 26

BY EIGHT O'CLOCK Tuesday morning Jack was headed back to Weld County to see Boots Hamer. The long round trips were getting expensive, but at least he was employed again.

Victoria had called him before daybreak, wanting him back on the investigation, and although Jack still had mixed feelings about not being able to trust her, he knew he sure as hell could use the money. He had never stopped investigating the case anyway, so he might as well get paid for it.

Jack drove out of the mountains and through Denver, winding his way around Mile High Stadium and past downtown before heading northeast. It was still early, but the sun already baked the flat, dry landscape. Heat waves danced over the highway in the distance.

Before moving to Aspen, Jack had never been in the mountains, and it never ceased to amaze him how a few thousand feet in elevation could drastically affect the temperature. He had on a light jacket and carefully pulled it off as he drove. It was going to be hot, and he was glad he had asked the nice family of four at the campground to watch Crockett for him.

He had a funny feeling about the text from Boots, telling him it was urgent they meet at the well. Hamer had dropped a location pin on a GPS map and sent it with the text. It was the same well Jack had met him at before.

Jack tried calling Hamer twice as he drove. Both times the call went unanswered, rolling over to an automated voicemail message. Hamer hadn't mentioned Poindexter in the text, but Jack assumed the accountant must have uncovered additional information.

Jack pulled through the gate and saw Hamer's truck parked in front of the small office building. It was the only other vehicle there, and Jack pulled up next to it and parked.

Because of the reflective glass, Jack couldn't see into the building. He scanned the storage yard and tanks, but he didn't see anyone. It was quiet. Too quiet. Something didn't feel right.

Jack kept his eyes lifted but slid his hand to the floorboard and found the 9mm he had brought with him instead of the dog. As he got out of the truck, he slipped the pistol into the back of his jeans and loosened his shirt to hang over it. He regretted having taken off his jacket too soon.

He took a step toward the office, and Hamer stepped out, pulling the door closed behind him.

"Detective, what brings you all the way out here?" Hamer ushered Jack toward an open area closer to the tanks and away from the office.

Jack was confused. "You tell me, Boots. I got your text and here I am."

Hamer stuck his hands on his hips and frowned. "I didn't text you," he said. "You texted *me*. I was checking the progress at the rig this morning and got it on my cell phone. Damned if I didn't misplace the blasted thing right after that." Hamer patted the pocket of his shirt. "Still haven't found it. But you said to be here at eleven, and here I am. So, what's going on?"

Alarm pulsed through Jack's body. He knew immediately it was a setup—someone had lured both of them there. He started to warn Hamer, but a shadow emerged from between two of the storage tanks.

Luther Byrd. And he had a gun.

"Like shooting fish in a barrel," Byrd said, pointing a rifle toward them. "This is gonna be fun."

Jack got his first real look at Byrd, and aside from the rifle, he wasn't impressed. Byrd was a bear of a man with a shag of dark hair and a dull fleshy face with a pockmarked nose that looked like someone had once taken an ice pick to it. He was big, but he looked soft.

Jack slowly reached back for the pistol tucked in his waistband.

"Hands up!" Byrd shouted, thrusting the rifle at him.

Jack complied, several options racing through his mind. If Byrd had had a pistol instead of a rifle, Jack could try a roll move. But with the accuracy of a rifle, the move was a no-go.

Talk to him, Jack thought. *Stall.* But Boots Hamer got to it first.

"What in the holy hell is this all about, Byrd?" Hamer asked, sounding like he was scolding an errant child instead of staring down the barrel of a rifle at a crazy man.

"Shut up, Boots." Byrd raised the rifle at Hamer.

"Hey!" Jack shouted, taking a step forward. "The least you can do is tell us what this is about." It was a lame stall, but Jack had run out of ideas.

Byrd turned the rifle on him. "You should have stayed out of it, Martin." Byrd sighted the rifle on Jack—he was about to shoot.

There was a deafening explosion to Jack's left. A gunshot—he knew it immediately. Jack instantly ducked and crouched close to the ground, his ears ringing. He looked up in time to see Luther Byrd drop to his knees. Boots Hamer staggered and fell forward, rolling to one side.

Jack twisted to his left and saw Clark Poindexter

standing next to the office, quaking violently. He held a smoking shotgun with both hands toward Jack like he wanted to give it away. Every ounce of blood had drained from the skinny man's face.

Jack stood up. Poindexter was still shaking and offering him the gun, his mouth opening and closing uncontrollably until he managed to spit out, "Boots told me to do it."

CHAPTER 60

CHARLES STRATTON SAT at a prominent table in Elway's having an early dinner with Katie. When she had called his office an hour earlier and suggested it, he'd at first refused, but then immediately reconsidered. Everyone had left the office for the day, and with still no word from Luther, Charles realized he might need an alibi.

As he and Katie followed the maître d' to their table at Elway's, Charles had made a point to stop and greet several businessmen he knew.

At their table, Charles had listened intently as Katie told him that Victoria had fired the detective from Aspen. One less thing he would have to worry about.

But then Katie had changed the subject, and Charles had too much on his mind to sit and listen to her chatter about her afternoon shopping spree at Neiman Marcus. When she started prattling on about a Ralph Lauren pantsuit, he tuned her out.

Charles had wasted enough time calming a nervous Derek Lowe earlier, spending nearly twenty minutes talking Lowe back from the proverbial ledge—reassuring him the merger was still on track and that no one was privy to their side hustle.

As Katie talked about her day, Charles's thoughts turned back to Luther Byrd. He should have completed the job hours ago. Why hadn't he called?

Charles pulled up a starched cuff, exposing his gold Rolex to check the time and realized only ten minutes had passed since the time he'd checked before. If he didn't hear from Luther soon, he would know something had gone terribly wrong.

He tried thinking of ways he could distance himself from Byrd but quickly decided it was pointless. There would be no way to cut his losses if Byrd failed—he knew too much. The only option would be to find a way to cover it all up.

The waiter appeared with their order, setting a salad in front of Katie and a steak and baked potato in front of Charles. But Charles didn't have an appetite and sat picking at his food, not listening as Katie mentioned something about a trip to Capri.

A few minutes later, Charles checked his phone again. No call. No text. Damn it, Byrd. Where was he?

Charles sat with his back to the restaurant's entrance but knew the door had opened when the room was momentarily flooded with the sounds of downtown traffic. He heard voices. Several people were talking at once.

Katie had stopped eating and her eyes grew wide. A look of shock or confusion spread across her face as she watched whatever was going on near the entrance.

Before Charles could turn to see what was happening, she looked across the table at him, her voice shaky and panicked. "Charles?"

Charles felt someone behind him and looked up, surprised to see a thin, bald man in a cheap suit standing over him, his hand on the back of Charles's chair. He was accompanied by two uniformed police officers, each with a hand resting on the butt of their revolver still holstered at their hip.

"Charles?" Katie's voice quivered.

Charles felt the muscles in his chest constrict, and he suddenly felt nauseated.

The bald man spoke next. "Charles Stratton, I'm Detective Hastings with the Denver Police Department. You're under arrest for conspiracy to commit murder."

CHAPTER 61

DEREK LOWE STOOD on the balcony of the penthouse with a glass of whiskey in his hand, watching over the rail as two police cars pulled up to the entrance of the condominium building. Four police officers emerged from the vehicles and made their way toward the front doors. Derek knew it was over. The great Charles Stratton had been brought down, and Derek was caught in his undertow.

Derek had called him an hour earlier, needing to clear up a last-minute issue before closing on the merger. After several rings, a nearly incoherent Katie Stratton had answered the call. She told him that Charles had been arrested, and Derek knew immediately that it was only a matter of time before the police came for him. He had poured himself the whiskey, then stood for an hour on the balcony waiting.

He watched as the officers disappeared into the building and knew he had less than five minutes before they would reach the door to the penthouse.

He looked toward the mountains clouded in a gloomy fog as day was quickly turning to night. He sipped on the remaining whiskey and watched as a hazy sun crept closer to the horizon.

When the whiskey was gone, he turned and set the glass next to a half-empty bottle on the patio table, then slowly pulled a chair toward the railing, pushing it against the side of the short glass wall.

He watched an eagle float silently in the distance before it disappeared into the murky sky. He turned his attention back to the dark silhouette of the mountains, his gaze sweeping from left to right—from Mount Evans north to the peaks of Rocky Mountain National Park. Even in their smoky haze, the mountains were beautiful.

The day's heat was gone. The temperature had dropped steadily with the sun. He took in a deep breath, filling his lungs with the cool summer night. It felt good.

With one hand on the railing, Derek carefully climbed onto the chair. How had it come to this? It wasn't supposed to end this way.

He looked toward the mountains once more. His vision blurred as tears slid from his eyes.

There was a knock at the door.

Derek Lowe stood motionless for a moment, then put one foot on the rail and stepped up, swaying slightly.

Still staring at the mountains in the distance, he took in one last cool breath, then stepped off.

CHAPTER 62

AFTER A WEEK and a half of being sequestered at home, Victoria thought it felt good to be out. She had insisted on driving when Miles offered to pick her up. The simple freedom of driving herself was exhilarating.

She and Miles were seated at a table for two next to the famed wall of wine bottles that stretched floor to ceiling in the plush dining room of Sweet Basil. After she'd eaten like a bird for days, just the smell of the gourmet menu items that wafted through the restaurant brought back her appetite. She started with the lobster bisque, surprising herself when she finished it.

When the dishes were cleared away, she and Miles sat waiting for their entrées and making small talk, discussing the weather and mutual friends. Victoria appreciated his attempt at light conversation, but she soon wanted more.

She knew Miles was in regular contact with the Vail police and wanted to ask him about the progress of their investigation. She wanted to know if she was still their primary suspect. But more importantly, she wanted to know if they had any other leads. She would ask Miles about it later, but she wouldn't broach the subject just yet. She could tell he was trying to make it a nice evening for her.

"I got a call from the alumni foundation today," Victoria said. "They told me about the scholarship you're setting up in Elliot's memory. Thank you, Miles."

He looked surprised, maybe even blushed. She wasn't sure in the dim light. "I was going to tell you about it, but I guess they got to it first."

Victoria smiled at him. "I guess they did."

Miles looked down into his glass as he swirled the wine. "Elliot was my best friend. It was the only thing I could think of to honor him. I told the foundation I wanted to set up a scholarship in Elliot's name for first-generation students—students like him who are having to pull themselves up by their own bootstraps, put themselves through school on a shoestring and a prayer."

"It's very generous of you. Elliot would appreciate it. *I* appreciate it."

Miles dismissed her gratitude with a wave of his hand. "I know it's a paltry amount compared to what Elliot gave to the school every year, but it's something I want to do."

"He would have loved it, Miles. Thank you."

This time he didn't dismiss her appreciation, but nodded.

Victoria sipped her wine and glanced around the crowded dining room, grateful she didn't recognize anyone she knew. She wasn't ready to deal with public condolences just yet.

But she noticed several people watching her. A couple at a nearby table was huddled together looking at her over their menus. A man across the room stared at her but looked away when Victoria made eye contact.

She suddenly felt self-conscious, the levity of the evening having instantly disappeared.

"It was a mistake for me to come," she said, looking down at her napkin and ignoring an elderly woman openly gaping at her from an adjacent table. "I shouldn't be out yet."

Miles set his wineglass down. "Now, why would you say that?" There was kindness and concern in his voice. "Victoria, Elliot would want you to get on with life. I know you don't want to hear it, and God knows your pain is still fresh—mine is, too, but you're going to have to find a way to keep going."

If anyone else had said it to her, she might have been offended. But she knew Miles was hurting as much as she was.

A waiter appeared and set their entrées in front of them. When he was gone, they continued their meal in silence. Victoria knew Miles was right. She would have to find her way, and she would—but not yet. She wouldn't rest until she had answers to two questions: Who murdered Elliot? And what was going on at Banks Oil & Gas? Jack Martin would help her with the first, and she would find a way to answer the second.

When she finished her meal, Victoria set her fork down and looked across the table. Miles was still eating, but it was time to change the subject. "Miles, am I going to be arrested?"

He didn't answer her right away, and Victoria could tell by the look on his face that he was considering what to say.

He spoke in a hushed tone. "I honestly don't know if you will be or not," he finally answered. "But if you *are* arrested, we're ready. We've got the best legal defense team in Denver ready to help."

It wasn't the answer Victoria wanted to hear, but she knew it was the best Miles could give her.

"I'm going to Denver in the morning to meet with them," he said. "I'll be back tomorrow night. If it's all right, I'll come over and fill you in on what we're going to do next."

She hesitated, watching him. "Miles, are you sure you still want me as a client?"

He looked stunned by the question. "Of course I do."

Victoria nodded and adjusted the napkin on her lap. "Because of Elliot."

"No…yes." He shook his head, then set his fork down, reached across the table, and laid a hand on hers. "Yes. I *am* doing it for Elliot, but I'm also doing it for *you*."

He was trying to make her feel better, and she was suddenly embarrassed at having come across as being so needy. She asked him about the police's investigation, and he told her there didn't seem to be much progress.

"These things take time, Victoria," he said. "We have to be patient."

But she didn't want to be patient. That was why she had hired Jack Martin. She had talked to Jack on the phone that morning and was relieved he had agreed to continue his investigation. He had pressed her about being honest with him, and she had reluctantly agreed, but she still wasn't sure how much she wanted to share.

"I've been thinking about the night Elliot was murdered," Victoria said. Miles stopped eating again and sat watching her, interested. "I'm sure Elliot let someone into the house that night."

Miles frowned. "But you said you were asleep. How would you know?"

"I *was* asleep," she said. "I can't really explain it, but I know I'm right. And there's something else. I always check that the doors are locked every night before I set the alarm. You know how afraid I am that a bear will get in. But I know I did it the night Elliot died. Do you see what this means?"

"Not really."

"It means that Elliot must have disarmed the security system to let someone in. He let in whoever killed him. The police said the door was unlocked when they got there. And I didn't unlock it."

Victoria's cell phone buzzed, and she pulled it from the seat of her chair where she had placed it. "It's Jack Martin. I'm sorry, Miles. I need to get this."

Victoria listened in stunned silence as Jack filled her in on the shooting at the well site earlier that day. He was on his way to Vail and told her that he would give her more details when he got there.

When she got off the phone, Miles sat waiting, questioning her with his eyes. But Victoria was still processing the information, wondering how Charles Stratton's arrest would affect things.

"What did he say?" Miles finally asked.

Victoria snapped back to the present and looked at him. "The police have just arrested Charles Stratton," she said. "They charged him with conspiracy to commit murder."

Miles's jaw dropped. "Murder?"

She nodded.

"Who was he trying to kill?"

"Boots Hamer. And Jack Martin."

Miles was silent a moment, then suddenly laughed out loud. "This is perfect."

Victoria was confused and frowned at him.

"Don't you see?" Miles asked. "This is great. Now Charles Stratton will be at the top of the suspect list for Elliot's murder."

Victoria was struggling to understand his sudden mood change.

Miles kept talking. "Charles Stratton had motive— he's the new CEO. And he had means. If what you say is right, that Elliot turned off the alarm and let someone in—well, he would have opened the door for Charles, wouldn't he?"

Victoria was still sorting through all the information, trying to connect the dots.

"And Doris Reed," Miles continued. "She would have worked for Stratton after Elliot died, right?"

Victoria nodded slowly.

"He's tied to all of it," Miles said, smiling. He raised his wineglass as if to give a toast. "This is great news, Victoria. Great news. Congratulations." He waited for her.

Victoria hesitated, then slowly lifted her glass.

Miles leaned in, tapping his wineglass to hers. "This changes everything," he said.

But Victoria wasn't sure it did.

CHAPTER 63

AT NINE THIRTY, Jack Martin was parked in front of Victoria's house. No one answered the door when he rang the bell, and there weren't any lights on inside. But he was early and decided to wait in the truck.

He had gotten to Vail quicker than he'd expected, not realizing he was driving faster than normal, hopped up on adrenaline until he had been pulled over for speeding on the interstate outside of Frisco.

When Jack presented the highway patrolman with his driver's license, the officer did a double take, shining a flashlight on him and peering into the cab of his truck.

"Are you *the* Jack Martin? The Aspen detective who caught the Hermes Strangler?"

Jack wasn't going to use his new notoriety to get out of a ticket, even though he knew he probably could. He couldn't stand guys like that and was sure as hell not going to turn into one. He just wanted the damn speeding ticket he deserved so he could get back on the road.

"Yes, sir, that's me," Jack answered, polite but unfazed.

The officer fell all over himself congratulating Jack on the arrest. Then, rather sheepishly, had asked Jack if he would sign the back of his ticket pad so he could show the guys at the station.

Jack sat in the dark, waiting at Victoria's curb, and laughed at the absurdity of his sliver of celebrity. His fifteen minutes of fame might have lasted longer than fifteen minutes, but Jack knew it would fade fast. But before it did, he hoped he might parlay that notoriety into a regular paying job—one in law enforcement. But he'd worry about that later.

First he needed to brief Victoria on what had gone down at the well. Then he needed to get back to the campground and retrieve Crockett from the family of four who had agreed to watch him for the morning, but not for the day. He would find some way to repay them.

When Victoria Banks finally pulled into the driveway, Jack checked the time on his phone. He had been waiting almost fifteen minutes, but she was right on time.

"I hope you haven't been waiting long," she said as she opened the front door for him.

"Just got here."

She ushered him down the corridor toward the kitchen. "I'll make us some coffee."

As they passed the dining room, Jack glanced in. The room was dark, but from the light in the corridor, he could see stacks of paper neatly arranged in equidistant rows on the long table. He hadn't noticed them before and wondered what it was all about.

In the kitchen, Victoria pulled coffee from a cabinet and two mugs from another, straightening things that already looked in place as she went. She was keeping herself busy and acting indifferent, but Jack could tell she was nervous. Her rapid breathing and the quick rise and fall of her shoulders gave her away.

"It sounds like you've had an eventful day, Detective," she said, putting a filter into the coffee machine.

Jack pulled out a barstool from under the counter and sat. "It has been that, yes. I wanted to give you a complete rundown."

"And I'd very much like to hear it. The restaurant was a bit noisy. I want to make sure I heard you right." She poured a scoop of coffee grounds into the machine and turned it on, then sat on a stool next to him. "It must have been terrifying. Charles Stratton tried to kill you?"

"Not Charles, but he hired the man who did—Luther Byrd."

There were tiny creases between her eyebrows.

"He works for Banks Oil & Gas," Jack said.

She looked surprised. "A Banks employee?"

Jack nodded. "He was the on-site production manager."

Victoria brought a hand to her mouth. "But why? Why would he do it?"

"The police are still questioning him, but he's already given them details about a financial scam Stratton and Derek Lowe were running. He told them that Stratton was the mastermind behind everything. Said that Lowe went along with it, but wasn't sure how much he knew."

"But why would they want to kill you and Boots?"

"Hamer was investigating it all."

"Of course," Victoria said. "And a scandal this close to the merger would have ruined everything for them."

Jack agreed. "And it seems Stratton didn't like me snooping around either. He was worried you were causing unneeded attention by hiring me. There was a good chance you might have been next on his list."

Victoria tried to cover it, but she looked stunned at his insinuation. "I can't believe Charles would do it," she said, shaking her head. "They really arrested him?"

"They did. I saw him from a distance at the station when I went in to give my statement. And the last I heard, they were on their way to pick up Lowe. I'll call and confirm that on my way back to the lake."

"What about Katie?" Victoria asked nervously. "Did you see her?"

"I didn't."

"Was she there? When he was arrested? Or at the police station?"

"I'm sorry." Jack shook his head. "I don't have any information on her."

Jack filled her in on the details they knew about the fraud scheme.

Victoria filled two cups of coffee and sat back down on the stool. She looked down into the cup but didn't drink. "I don't know what to think about it all. I really can't believe it."

Jack debated on how much to tell her but decided she should hear it from him and not from some reporter on the news. "I wish that was everything, but it's not."

She looked up at him. "What else?" Her voice was pinched.

"Byrd admitted to pulling off other jobs for Stratton." Jack let that sink for a second. "He admitted to shooting Bob Hawkins…and planting the bomb under Doris's car."

Victoria drew in a sharp breath, bringing her hand to her mouth and turning away. It was the first real emotion Jack had seen.

"That's horrible." She sat motionless, staring down

at the floor, before looking back up. "This means he must have killed Elliot, too, doesn't it?"

Jack shook his head. "Byrd denies any involvement in Elliot's death. And there's no evidence that he *was* involved, despite there being motive."

"What motive?"

"To keep the royalty scam going. Elliot had found out about it from—"

"From Boots Hamer and that forensic accountant." She was putting the pieces together.

Jack nodded. "Byrd is spilling it all—how Stratton and Lowe had him adjust the production meters at the wells so they intentionally read low."

"Shortchanging the landowners their royalties." She took her first sip of coffee. "And it's the marketing company that benefits from shortchanging the landowners. You see, Banks Oil & Gas is responsible for paying the royalties, but they go off the production recorded at the meters. That's the amount of oil they would, theoretically, sell to the marketing company. But the marketing company would then get more oil than they paid for. They would take possession of the actual amount extracted and would then be able to sell the *true* production amount to their customers. Everyone is shortchanged—Banks Oil & Gas *and* the royalty holders. Everyone except the marketing company." Her eyes were hard as she thought about it. "Over time, even altering the production amounts only slightly, they could make out like bandits."

Jack was impressed with how much she understood about the business. "And the marketing company is owned by—"

"Charles Stratton and Derek Lowe." Victoria took another sip of coffee. Slowly, her eyes grew wider, and she reached over and put her hand on his arm. "This is wonderful."

Jack sat silently.

"You see what this means, don't you?"

He had no idea what she was talking about.

Victoria continued. "If they murdered Elliot because he found out about the fraud, then he wasn't a part of it."

"Part of what?"

"The fraud. Cheating the landowners out of their royalties." She thought about it, then turned to him again, her eyes glassy. "Jack, Elliot was innocent. I knew it. I just needed to know for sure. They murdered Elliot because he knew about the scam and was going to turn them in. Even if it meant sacrificing the merger, sacrificing everything he had worked for, Elliot was going to turn them in. He wasn't part of it." She looked back down into her coffee cup. Quietly, she added, "It wasn't all a lie."

Jack understood now, understood her evasiveness

and her secrets. He understood the secret meeting with Doris Reed and probably the stacks of paper on the dining room table. Victoria had been conducting her own investigation, looking into Banks Oil & Gas, wanting to make sure her husband hadn't been involved in a scheme that had gotten Bob Hawkins, the company's controller, murdered.

"The problem is Byrd's denying any involvement in Elliot's murder," Jack reminded her. "And if he didn't do it, there's a good chance Elliot wasn't murdered to cover up the fraud."

Victoria frowned. "But Luther Byrd *had* to be the one who killed him."

She was frustrated and hurting, and Jack decided not to press the issue of another killer too hard. "Byrd probably thinks he can get a plea deal for ratting out Stratton, and he's right. But admitting to Elliot's murder would complicate things. That could be why he hasn't confessed yet—if he did it."

Victoria looked at him skeptically. "But if he wasn't the one who killed Elliot, who did?"

Luther Byrd was guilty of a lot of things, but Jack wasn't convinced he'd murdered Elliot.

Jack shook his head. "I'm still working on it."

He wished he had more to give her. He could see on her face that her hope had melted, and he felt a pang of guilt for having caused it. But the turn of events had him optimistic. Something would shake loose.

She looked at him with sad resignation. "The police still think I killed Elliot, don't they?"

Jack knew, with no confession from Byrd and Victoria's fingerprints on the murder weapon, she would still be at the top of their suspect list. But he couldn't bring himself to tell her. "Maybe, maybe not."

She walked to the sink and rinsed her cup, then opened the dishwasher and set it on the top rack, turning it so the handle faced the same direction as several other cups already there. Jack had never seen such a neatly arranged group of dirty dishes. He looked around the kitchen. Somewhere around here, there had to be a mess. People just don't live like this. Or do they?

He couldn't remember for sure, but thought it was Churchill who had called something "a riddle, wrapped in a mystery, inside an enigma." That was Victoria Banks. He still didn't understand her completely, but he was going to try.

"I need to ask you some personal questions," he said.

Victoria took her seat back on the stool, regarding him skeptically. "What do you want to know?"

Jack finished his coffee before answering, studying her. "Your background. Your family."

She first appeared surprised by the question, then settled back onto the stool with a sort of acceptance. She was hesitant to talk about it but finally did, telling Jack about the night her mother had murdered her father and child protective services had taken her away. She told him how her mother had committed suicide in prison and what it was like growing up under the specter of it all, being shuffled from one foster family to the next.

"I haven't talked to anyone about this since I told Elliot years ago." She smoothed a strand of hair behind her ear. "When it happened, it wasn't easy, but I put it all behind me. Or so I thought. I lost myself in school, kept busy, kept to myself. But I was young. I think that made it easier."

Jack watched her talk, telling the horrific stories of a broken childhood. Underneath the cool reserve, he detected a sadness, but she was also resolute and proud. Life had done its best to break her, but she had withstood it all—so far.

He understood her better now. As hard as she had tried—and succeeded—in putting it all behind her, she found she still needed to keep her past a secret. What had happened with her parents was too similar to what happened to Elliot. It would be easy for people to point fingers, saying history had repeated itself. Jack finally understood.

He saw glimpses of the real Victoria Banks, the

one behind the chilly, polished veneer. She opened up more than he'd expected, but he knew there was still something she was holding back.

When Jack asked the question, he watched her closely for a response. "And the man at the funeral?"

Victoria studied him, then drew in and released a slow breath. "He's my brother."

CHAPTER 64

Wednesday, June 27

AT ELEVEN THIRTY on Wednesday morning, Jack pulled into the parking lot of Denver General Hospital. He was there to see Boots Hamer, who had taken a few stray buckshot to the torso when Clark Poindexter shot Luther Byrd the day before.

Jack pulled the paper sack from the seat of the truck and got out. As he walked through the sliding-glass doors into the hospital lobby, he saw Poindexter getting off the elevator.

"How's the old man?" Jack asked when Poindexter approached him.

The accountant switched his briefcase to his left hand and held out his right for Jack to shake. "He's doing good. Better than I expected." Poindexter pushed his glasses higher on his nose. "But I guess *anything* is better than I expected since I thought I'd killed him."

Jack raised his brows. "Yeah, it all went down pretty fast, didn't it? It took me a second to realize what had happened. But thank God you were there.

There's a good chance Boots and I wouldn't be alive today if you weren't."

"It was Boots's idea I go along. We were supposed to have lunch in Greeley yesterday to go over the details of the fraud case—Boots was trying to decide what to do next. I was at the drill site with him when he got your text—or what he thought was your text. But something about it didn't sit right with him, and he asked me to go along.

"When we got there, Boots pulled up next to the office and let me in, gave me the shotgun and said it was ready to shoot, and that I'd better damned well shoot if something happened and it looked like I needed to."

Jack laughed. "That's sounds like Boots."

"Then you showed up, and I thought everything was fine. But then a few seconds later Luther Byrd appeared out of nowhere."

"The police found his truck parked around the other side of the tanks. He must have gotten there early and was waiting for Boots and me to show up. A classic ambush."

Poindexter nodded nervously. "I was in the office and just about to put the gun down, thinking everything was okay, when Byrd showed up and I saw *he* had a gun."

Jack watched Poindexter swallow, then shift his weight from foot to foot. Poor guy was still reeling from the day before. But Jack knew from experience that shooting a man was a traumatizing experience, even when that man needed shooting. It would take Poindexter weeks, maybe months, before he would come to terms with it. The memory of it would last forever. But Jack was glad to see he was holding up well under the circumstances.

Jack clapped him on the shoulder. "You did good, Poindexter. And for what it's worth, thank you. You probably saved my life, and I'll never forget that."

Poindexter blushed from the compliment and nodded his acknowledgment. The two men then said goodbye.

Jack found Boots Hamer in a suite on the hospital's top floor. The room had a small sitting area near a window that overlooked the mountains. Hamer was propped up in a hospital bed at the far end of the room.

Jack knocked on the open door to get his attention, and Hamer looked up.

"Come in," he said, waving, his smile visible from across the room.

Hamer was dressed in a light-blue hospital gown and looked tiny in the spacious room, but somehow his toothy white grin and larger-than-life personality filled every inch of it. Jack was suddenly aware of how glad he was that the old guy wasn't dead. He'd grown to like Boots Hamer.

"Boots, you look healthy as a horse. How long are they going to keep you here?" Jack took a seat in a leather chair next to the bed.

Boots shook his head. "I can tell you right now, I'm not stayin' as long as they want me to. They say I'll be here maybe a week, but I guarantee you, I'm busting out in a day or two." He rolled over to one side and pulled up the gown, revealing a gauze patch the size of a sheet of paper. "This ain't nothin'," Hamer continued. "I've had plenty worse in my lifetime."

Jack laughed. "I'm sure you have. And I'd like to hear all about it sometime." Jack took the paper bag from under his arm and held it out.

Boots frowned, taking the bag. "What's this?" he asked, then broke out in a grin, sliding the bottle of Jack Daniel's out. "You remembered."

"I did."

Boots waved the bottle at him before putting it back in the bag. "I told you those ol' boys would be behind my drop in royalties." He settled back onto the bed and nodded. "You're all right, Martin. When I'm out of here, you come over to the house. We'll have us a proper visit. Maybe I'll take you fishing on the Poudre."

"I'd like that."

Boots then turned his attention to the small rolling table pushed over his lap. "Would you look at what this blasted hospital saw fit to bring me for lunch?" he said, pointing to the tray of food in front of him. "A bunch of vegetables and a piece of rubber chicken I wouldn't throw to that dog of yours. They must think I'm some kind of damned rabbit to feed me like this."

Jack laughed. "It's supposed to be healthy."

"I don't care if it'll add another year on to my life." He shook his head in disgust. "Bless her heart, the missus promised to smuggle in a juicy rib eye tonight. You just missed her, Jack. You could have met her."

"I'd like to meet her sometime."

"You will," Boots said. "Poindexter was here, too."

"I saw Clark on my way in."

Boots took a carrot stick from the tray, then pushed the rolling table aside. "Should have sent this food with Poindexter. The boy could use a few more pounds."

Jack thought the statement was ironic since Boots Hamer probably didn't weigh a hundred and thirty pounds soaking wet.

Boots was still talking. "But he did a damned fine job uncovering that scam for me, didn't he?"

Jack agreed.

They were silent a moment, and then Boots shook his head. "And he did a damned fine job of saving our hides from being blown to smithereens by that

SOB Byrd. I heard he's now spilling his sorry guts about everything."

"He is."

"He admit to killing Elliot yet?"

Without any evidence to back up his suspicions, Jack didn't mention he thought Byrd could be innocent of Elliot's murder. "Not yet," Jack said, "but they're still getting information out of him."

"Well, good. When he finally admits to it, I hope they throw him in the slammer and throw away the damned key," Boots said, stabbing the air with the carrot stick.

Jack assured him that if Byrd were convicted, he would never see the light of day. He told him that Byrd had been working at the direction of Charles Stratton, then filled him in on the other crimes Byrd had committed—including shooting Bob Hawkins and planting the bomb under Doris Reed's car, both in an attempt to cover up the royalty scheme.

"It started out as simple financial fraud," Jack told him. "Then it escalated to covering up the fraud for the sake of the merger. Charles Stratton and Derek Lowe were set to become very wealthy men following that merger."

"Well, I can tell you one thing," Boots said, pointing the carrot stick at Jack. "Now that it's been exposed, this royalty scam is gonna kill that merger. And the stock price of Banks Oil & Gas is gonna plummet.

Take my word for it, if Luther Byrd hadn't already killed Elliot, a disgruntled investor would have."

Hamer popped the carrot stick in his mouth and shook his head as he chewed.

CHAPTER 65

WHEN JACK MARTIN left her house the night before, Victoria had cleaned up the kitchen and gone straight to bed. It had been another long day.

After several minutes of restless dozing, she had dropped into a deep sleep. Hours later, a familiar dream broke through the void. The man was chasing her again, but something was different this time. As she ran through the forest, the branches that clawed at her retreated. It was then she heard the man behind her calling her name. The wind died down, and his voice grew louder.

"Victoria."

The voice was familiar. She stopped running and heard his footsteps slow as well. Curiosity melted her fear, and she turned back to look.

She squinted. It had been so long, but she recognized him instantly. Her voice caught in her throat. "Daddy?"

With a gentle smile and a nod, he stepped toward her. "I've been trying to catch you." His voice was kind.

Victoria was confused. "Why were you chasing me?"

He took another step closer. "To tell you that everything is all right…I'm all right. You don't have to run anymore."

Victoria tried to answer him, but she couldn't speak. He reached out a hand, but when she went to take it, he faded away, and she fell back again into a deep sleep.

The next morning, Victoria stirred awake and lay in bed, trying to remember the dream. Something inside her had changed. Somewhere, a door had been opened for her grief and shame to escape. It was still there, and she knew it wouldn't go all at once, but she was hopeful.

After lingering a few minutes, she got out of bed. There was so much left to do. Since Luther Byrd hadn't yet confessed to killing Elliot, Jack Martin was back on the case. She would keep closer tabs on his investigation now that she didn't have anything to hide from him. Jack knew all her secrets. Well…most of them.

Now that she knew Elliot wasn't involved in fraud, she wouldn't have to hire an accountant. But she wanted to talk to the one who worked for Boots Hamer, find out exactly what was going on and if there was anything she could do to remedy the situation.

Banks Oil & Gas had been Elliot's company, but now it was hers. And she was determined not to let what Charles Stratton and Derek Lowe had done destroy what Elliot had spent a lifetime to build. In the kitchen, she poured coffee grounds into the filter and turned on the coffee maker, then walked to the window and looked toward Vail Mountain. She thought about the dream again and felt that something inside her had changed. The sun had broken the horizon and colored everything various shades of orange and pink. It was a new day, and it surprised her when she realized she was looking forward to it.

When her cell phone buzzed, she pulled it from the pocket of her robe, but she didn't recognize the number and debated on whether or not to answer the call. But there were still too many moving parts in the investigation. It could be someone from the defense team Miles had hired for her, or maybe it was Boots Hamer or his accountant, or someone from Banks Oil & Gas, which was now, with Charles's arrest and the death of Derek Lowe, a rudderless ship. If only Doris were here, Victoria thought, letting out a deep sigh.

She answered the call.

"Is this Victoria Banks?" It was a woman's voice she didn't recognize.

Victoria hesitated. "Yes, it is."

The woman spoke in short staccato bursts. "My

name is Liz Kelly. I'm with *The National Tattler*. I'd like to ask you a few questions."

The name didn't ring a bell, but Victoria had heard of *The National Tattler* and knew it was a tabloid. She wished she hadn't answered the call.

The woman didn't wait for Victoria's consent before she launched into a series of questions. At first they were innocuous queries about Elliot—his life and his charity work. Victoria danced around the few personal questions she didn't want to answer, giving the reporter just enough information to satisfy her. She knew that saying "no comment" and hanging up would make her seem guilty.

But then the conversation turned.

"I'd like to ask you about yourself now," the reporter said.

Victoria remained silent.

"About your background."

The reporter recited a list of accomplishments and dates, things Victoria knew anyone could google and find online. It was uncomfortable talking about herself, but the questions didn't seem threatening. Victoria confirmed the year she graduated from Colorado School of Mines and the company she worked for before joining Banks Oil & Gas.

"Now tell me about your childhood," the reporter said.

Victoria felt her throat constrict.

"I understand your mother murdered your father when you were…" There was rustling of paper on the other end of the line. "When you were eight. Is that correct?"

"Uh—"

"And that your mother then committed suicide when she was in prison. Isn't that right?"

"Listen, Ms.…."

"Kelly. Liz Kelly."

"Ms. Kelly. I don't think I want to answer any more questions right now."

"You were bounced around in the foster system, weren't you? With your brother? And, like your mother, he's had his fair share of run-ins with law enforcement, hasn't he?" There was more rustling of paper. "Gary, isn't it?"

Victoria's fingers shook as she punched the phone to end the call. With her hand still trembling, she set the phone down on the kitchen counter, pressing it into the cool granite with her palm, trying to settle her nerves. She took in a few steady, deep breaths, letting each one out slowly.

She pulled a cup from the cabinet and poured herself coffee, but didn't drink it. Her hands were still shaking, and she didn't want to spill it. It would make a mess, and she couldn't take any more messes right now.

Leaving the coffee cup on the counter, she walked

out onto the back deck. She stood at the railing, looking toward the mountains. It was a beautiful June morning—the sun now up and shining, a crisp breeze swaying the trees at the edge of the yard.

For the moment, Victoria couldn't appreciate any of it. The new day now promised a set of new problems.

She squeezed the railing with both hands and closed her eyes tight. Who would give the reporter her phone number? And how did she find out about her past? About her parents? And Gary?

Then Victoria remembered the conversation she'd had the night before. She opened her eyes and felt her blood pressure rise.

Jack Martin.

CHAPTER 66

AFTER THE VISIT with Boots Hamer, Jack was winding his way around downtown on the interstate, headed from the hospital back to Shadow Mountain Lake, when his cell phone rang.

It was Victoria.

The call took less than a minute, and he wasn't sure if he got a single word in after he answered the call. She was angry. She said something about a tabloid reporter calling and asking about her past. She accused Jack of divulging the information about her background that she had told him in confidence the night before. Before Jack could protest, she had fired him and hung up.

Fired twice in the same week. Jack scoffed at the absurdity of it all as he swung the truck around the last turn and started the climb into the foothills. He was beat. He would think about it later. It was still early, but he wanted a cold beer and his dog.

Back at the trailer, Jack let Crockett out, threw a stick to him a few times, and promised him a hike. Instead, he sat down on the bed, pulled off his boots, and fell asleep. He woke nearly two hours later to Crockett licking his face.

Jack rolled over and sat up, feeling like he'd been hit by a Mack truck. He had only gotten a few hours of sleep the night before. It was becoming a habit—a bad habit, one he was determined to change. And now being unemployed again, he didn't have an excuse not to. He would have plenty of time to sleep in the near future.

But having to sleep on a four-inch foam mattress shoved next to the metal skin of the trailer didn't help, he thought, as he rolled off the bunk and stood up, rubbing his lower back. A new ache for a new day, and he wasn't getting any younger.

Outside, the sun was already on its descent toward the horizon; daylight would fade fast.

"Sorry, boy," Jack said patting the dog's head. "There's no time for a hike. But let's go find you a stick."

Crockett danced around him as he sat back down to pull on his boots. When Jack opened the door, Crockett raced out, circling the trailer several times before finding a small branch and bringing it back.

Jack took the stick from the excited dog's mouth and threw it toward the trees.

As the dog fetched tirelessly over and over, Jack ran through the facts in the case—cases, plural—he reminded himself. There was the fraud, the murders, the attempted murders.

It would all be over soon. There was still a chance Luther Byrd would confess to killing Elliot Banks. Then everything would be wrapped up in a neat bow. Charles Stratton and Luther Byrd were both going to prison, and Derek Lowe had already paid the ultimate price.

Jack took the stick from Crockett and rubbed the rough bark with his thumb, thinking. If Byrd confessed, Victoria would no longer be a suspect, and that was good. Jack was out of a job again, though, and that wasn't. But the bad guys had been caught. At least, he hoped so.

Crockett danced impatiently at his feet, and Jack threw the stick again, watching as the dog ran toward it, then abruptly changed course midstride. A rabbit had appeared from out of the shadow of the trees, and Crockett was headed straight for it.

Jack remembered the image of Byrd emerging from the shadows between the oil tanks. It should be clear as day that Byrd—along with Charles Stratton and Derek Lowe—was guilty of Banks's murder. All three had motive and opportunity. Elliot would probably have opened the door for any one of them. As far as the police were concerned, it was a foregone conclusion that Byrd, at the direction of Charles Stratton, had killed Elliot.

Yet something about it didn't sit right.

Byrd was spilling his guts—about the royalty scam, the hits on Bob Hawkins and Doris Reed, yet he was still denying any involvement in killing Elliot. And Charles Stratton was still trying to deny *everything.*

Could there be someone else? Who else could have killed Elliot? Who else would have wanted to?

Jack remembered something Boots had said at the hospital: *If Luther Byrd hadn't already killed Elliot, a disgruntled investor would have.*

It gave Jack an idea.

He left Crockett circling the trees looking for the rabbit and raced back into the trailer to find his cell phone.

He called Victoria. After several rings she answered, and by the tone of her voice, Jack knew she wasn't happy to hear from him. He tried to ask her a question, getting out only half of it before she cut him off, telling him she would transfer payment for the last week to his account but he should not call her again. She then mentioned Miles would be over later to discuss whether she was still a suspect. If she was, she said she was sure Miles would help her find another investigator. Without saying goodbye, she hung up.

Jack tried calling back, but she didn't answer. When he tried a third time, he could tell his number had been blocked. He threw his cell phone at the bed in the front of the trailer. She was going to drive him crazy.

Thinking of another way to find the information he wanted, Jack grabbed his laptop and booted it up. After logging onto the internet, he went to the website of the Securities and Exchange Commission and searched for the public information on Banks Oil & Gas.

Jack scrolled through the available documents until he found the one he was looking for—a list of the company's largest shareholders.

CHAPTER 67

HOW DARE HE. Victoria was fuming after she hung up the phone on Jack Martin. When he tried to call back, she blocked his number.

Less than twenty-four hours after she had trusted him with her most personal secrets—information she had worked years to hide and overcome—he had sold them to the tabloids.

Earlier, when Liz Kelly had tried to call her back, Victoria had blocked her number as well.

It was past eight o'clock, and with everything that had happened, Victoria had forgotten to eat dinner. She felt her stomach grumble, but she was now too busy to stop. She wanted to get the house straightened up before Miles got there. He was on his way back from Denver and said he would come by and update her on the progress in the investigations. He would be there any minute.

Victoria was in the dining room, stacking the company documents into two cardboard filing boxes. She had debated on throwing the documents out but had decided to keep them, thinking they could be useful in trying to straighten out what remained of the company when the investigation and inevitable lawsuits were over.

When it was all said and done, maybe there would be enough of the company left to salvage, or maybe she could hire a business broker to try to sell it for her. But the idea of selling Elliot's company broke Victoria's heart, and she pushed the thought aside. She knew she was running out of options, but decided to think about it later.

Right now she needed to finish packing it all up. She would store the papers in an empty closet in one of the upstairs bedrooms. And if she hurried, she might be able to have everything put away and cleaned up before Miles got there.

As Victoria lifted the last stack off the table, she remembered Jack Martin had been trying to ask her something. She had been upset and didn't want to talk to him, cutting him off and then hanging up the phone. But she remembered now what he had wanted—a list of the company's largest shareholders.

On the top of the stack she was holding was the list he had asked for, and Victoria couldn't shake her curiosity about why he wanted it.

She sat down at the table, pulled the sheet from the top of the stack, and pushed the other documents aside. Why would Jack want this? she wondered. What was he looking for?

Victoria read through the list of names. Most of the largest shareholders of Banks Oil & Gas were sizable institutional owners—mutual funds, a university endowment—but there were others. There were private equity companies and what looked like small partnerships, and there were a handful of individual stockholders.

Victoria thought about what would happen to their investments now that the merger with Centennial had been called off and that Banks Oil & Gas would be fighting for its very survival. The stock price was already starting to plummet. It would be one thing for the institutional investors that had investments diversified in markets and companies across the world. They would be able to weather the storm. But it would be different for the smaller companies and the individual investors, including herself.

Victoria stared at Elliot's name on the page. His portion of Banks Oil & Gas was now hers, but she realized it could be worthless. She would be okay. She could sell the house, take the money, and start over again. She had reinvented her life once before and knew she could do it again. But for other stockholders, it could be devastating.

Victoria set the page back on the stack, then lifted

it off the table to put it into the box. But as she did, one name on the list caught her eye.

She heard a car door shut. Miles was there.

Victoria quickly put the documents into the box, then placed the lid on the top, hiding it all.

CHAPTER 68

JACK SPED THROUGH a thick fog, headed to Vail. It was an overcast night, no moon or stars to help light his way. He switched the truck's lights from low beam to high, but the fog reflected the light back at him and he switched them back again.

In the darkness, the specter of pine trees cloaked in fog appeared and disappeared as he sped by. At any second, he knew an elk or bear could step out in front of him before he could stop. But he pressed on. He had to get to Vail.

Victoria had blocked his number, but he fumbled in the darkness and tried calling her again. No luck. She was a piece of work, that one. Beautiful but withdrawn and completely unreadable. He thought of her compulsively straightening things, putting things back where she thought they belonged. Even among the chaos of life, she was righting what she could in her world.

Jack thought back to how she had squared his folders on the table outside the trailer. He remembered the notebook he'd purposefully dropped onto the floor of the study and how she had immediately scooped it up and put it back, confirming his suspicions about obsessive-compulsive disorder. He thought of the rigid orderliness of dishes in her dishwasher, the neatly stacked rows of papers on her dining table, each the same distance from the next. He remembered the funeral, and the flower she had righted on Elliot's casket.

Then it dawned on him—the tomahawk, Victoria's fingerprints in Elliot's blood.

Jack squeezed the steering wheel as he thought about it, satisfied he had solved one of the last missing pieces to the puzzle. In the shock of finding her husband dead, Victoria had instinctively picked the tomahawk up off the floor and placed it gently on the desk.

Victoria Banks might be obsessive-compulsive, he thought, but she wasn't a murderer. Jack knew she couldn't have killed Elliot, but he was now almost positive he knew who had.

As he drove, his concern grew. He remembered the few things Victoria had said before she hung up. She would hire another detective. Miles would help her; he would be over later that night. It gave Jack an idea.

The back end of a slow-moving truck came into view. As it struggled up the mountain, Jack swerved to keep from hitting it. When he was clear, he scrolled through the contacts on his phone until he found Miles Preston's number. He listened to the call ring twice on the other end before it was sent to voicemail. Miles had rejected it.

Jack grew angrier at himself as he drove. He should have suspected it sooner. But the list of the largest shareholders in Banks Oil & Gas had finally triggered his suspicion. And thank God Mark Thurmond was again willing to help.

After Jack jumped in the truck and headed to Vail, he had called Thurmond to have him check phone records for the cell towers around Vail the night Elliot Banks was murdered. Twenty minutes later, Thurmond called back and confirmed what Jack already knew.

Thurmond told him that Miles Preston had *not* tried calling Elliot Banks late on the night he was murdered, as he had told police. In fact, phone records indicated Miles hadn't talked to Elliot since hours earlier that day.

But around midnight, when he had called Victoria—a call that *was* detailed in the records— Miles Preston was already in Vail.

CHAPTER 69

IN THE FOYER, Victoria heard the familiar chime from the security system as she swung open the large bronze door. It triggered a fragment of memory, something from the night Elliot was murdered, but she couldn't put her finger on it.

"I brought us a bottle of Château Pontet to celebrate," Miles said, holding up a bottle of red wine.

Victoria didn't understand his exuberance. Yes, Luther Byrd and Charles Stratton were behind bars for fraud, and for killing Bob Hawkins and Doris, but both were denying any involvement in Elliot's murder. Miles must have other good news, she thought.

She gave him a reluctant smile. "Come in. I'll fix us a cheese plate. I haven't eaten a thing all night."

"Perfect." Miles followed her into the kitchen. "You get the food ready. I'll take care of the wine."

"The corkscrew is in the far drawer, under the glasses," Victoria told him, pulling an antique French cutting board from the cabinet of platters and trays.

As she took an assortment of cheese and fruit from the refrigerator, she heard Miles rummaging around in the drawer, then opening the bottle of wine.

As they worked, they made small talk, nothing of significance. Miles brought up the fog that had rolled in, remarking how harrowing it had made the drive from Denver. He talked about the wine festival the coming weekend.

"We should make it a day," he said. When she didn't answer right away, he added, "If you feel up to it."

Victoria's answer was noncommittal. *Maybe I'm being paranoid*, she thought to herself, but the last thing she wanted was to be around groups of strangers pointing and talking about her.

It took her a few minutes, but when she was finished, Victoria turned to Miles, holding the platter of food meticulously arranged on the antique board. "Shall we take it into the study?"

It took him a moment to answer, but then he nodded. With the two glasses of wine and the bottle tucked under his arm, he followed her into Elliot's study.

They settled onto the sofa near the window, and Victoria placed the tray of food on the coffee table in front of them. She used her phone to turn on the music system, selecting an acoustical guitar playlist and lowering the volume.

She noticed how dark it was outside. Foggy, with

no stars or moon to help light the yard. There was a chill radiating from the window behind her. The temperature must have dropped, she thought. Victoria shivered.

"To the future," Miles said, holding up his glass, a smile spread across his face.

They clinked their crystal glasses together, then watched each other over the rims as they each took a sip.

There was something different about him, Victoria thought. Something in his eyes that she didn't quite understand, or maybe she did.

Victoria took another sip of wine, steeling herself. "Miles, I'm anxious to hear about the investigations, but I have a few questions to ask you first."

"Sure." There was a curious expression on his face. "What do you want to know?"

"I was going through some of the company paperwork, and I didn't realize you were such a large shareholder."

He didn't respond, but sat still, listening to her.

"You must be upset that the merger isn't going to happen. You'll lose a lot of money."

Something flickered in his eyes before he spoke. "It doesn't matter now," he said, looking away and gesturing like he was waving off her concern. "Elliot gave me the stock years ago—when I helped him file the first set of corporate documents. He didn't have any money at the time, and I offered him a trade. It was a way for him to save face—legal work for stock. At the time, neither one of us expected it to amount to much. Well, *I* didn't expect it, anyway."

Victoria nodded, then took another sip of wine. "You never mentioned it."

"Neither did Elliot."

"I guess not." For some reason, Victoria found it hard to keep her thoughts straight. She took in a deep breath, trying to clear her head. "You know, Elliot found out about Charles Stratton and Derek Lowe's fraud scheme before he died."

"What makes you think so?"

"He was going to confront Charles and Derek, despite it devastating the company." Victoria thought she heard her speech slur, but she kept talking. "Even with what it was going to cost him financially, Elliot was going to do the right thing."

"I'm sure he was."

For several minutes they sat in silence while the music played softly in the background. Miles took the bottle from the table and refilled Victoria's glass.

During the pause between songs, Victoria started the conversation again. "I think I remember some-thing…something the night Elliot was murdered." Miles didn't reply, so she continued. "Last night when we were having dinner, do you remember when I mentioned I had a feeling Elliot let someone in the house that night?"

"Yes, but you also said you were asleep."

"I *was* asleep, but I heard something."

"Heard what?"

"The chime…from the alarm. I was sleeping, but I know I heard it—twice." She turned to look at Miles and noticed his wineglass was full. She remembered him pouring her a second glass, but he hadn't poured himself another. Why wasn't he drinking? She shook her head, trying to clear it, and continued. "Don't you see, Miles? It must have been someone he knew. He let them in the house. He wouldn't have let in someone he didn't know. Not that late. Someone he knew murdered him."

"Relax, Victoria. You're getting all worked up."

"It was someone he knew. But who?" Victoria felt so sleepy, but she took another drink. "Not Charles. Not Derek. They were in Denver. Not that Luther Byrd person who's now in custody. Elliot wouldn't have let him in, not that late."

Suddenly Victoria's eyes were wide open. She knew who Elliot had let in the night he was murdered. She knew who killed him. Her head felt as foggy as the weather outside, but her mind was suddenly clear. It was Miles.

She couldn't move and sat paralyzed. Her head was throbbing, and her thoughts came in short clips.

The merger. Money. The chime. Elliot would have let him in. Even through her fog, it all suddenly made sense.

Victoria sat forward and set her glass down, spilling some of the wine. Then it dawned on her. Miles had put something in it. She reached for her phone on the coffee table, but Miles grabbed it first and tossed it across the room.

She looked at him in horror, but she saw that he looked sad.

"I could have defended you, Victoria, shown the police you had nothing to do with Elliot's murder—at least poked holes in their theory enough to get them to drop their case against you. But you couldn't leave it alone. You had to go and hire that detective from Aspen. I didn't want to kill you. But now I have to."

Through the fog, Victoria felt her panic rise. She slurred her words. "You won't get away with it."

"I have once. Why wouldn't I be able to again?"

"Elliot?" Her head hurt, and she fell back, sinking into the velvety softness of the couch.

"I didn't want to do it, but I had to kill him. He was going to expose the fraud. He came to me when he figured it out. I told him not to report it. It would have cost me everything. But he wouldn't listen."

"Boy Scout." Victoria's eyes were now closed, but she was listening. He sounded frustrated.

"Yeah, had to go be a damn Boy Scout," Miles said. "Always doing the right thing. But I had everything to lose. And I've lost everything once. I wasn't going to do it again—not even for Elliot."

"No merger now." Victoria wondered why it mattered. It was too late. "Nothing left."

"You're right. There probably won't be much left of the company, but there's the house and the cars and the plane. I'll sell it all. I drew up your wills, Victoria, remember?"

She was almost gone but was vaguely aware of Miles's arm around her, lifting her head. She felt the cool crystal of the glass on her lips.

"It'll be easy, Victoria. It's sleeping pills. You won't feel any pain. Everyone will think the grieving widow committed suicide…just like her mother."

She tried to push the glass away, but he held her arm down.

"Take a drink, Victoria," Miles whispered. "Take another drink."

CHAPTER 70

As HE SWUNG off the interstate, Jack tried calling Victoria again, but his number was still blocked. He then tried Miles for a second time. When he didn't get an answer, Jack tossed his cell phone down on the seat of the truck. He knew now that the phone call Miles had made to Victoria the night Elliot was murdered was to establish an alibi. Miles wanted her to find the body. And by waiting a couple of hours before arriving at the scene, he had ensured everyone—including the police—thought he had driven in from Denver.

When Jack left the campground, he had considered calling the Vail police but decided against it. He was almost sure Miles Preston was the one who had killed Elliot, but what if he was wrong? His instincts were now screaming he was right. And if he had called the police, they would already be there.

On the access road, he caught a red light but looked both ways and then ran it. He groped on the seat for his phone and dialed 911, gave the operator Victoria's address and told her to get an officer there immediately. He should have made the call earlier. Dammit, another mistake.

He sped through the center of town, through the commercial areas, then past condos and houses. He flew over the bridge at Gore Creek and at Forest Road, turned right and raced down the street. He was almost there.

After a few seconds, in the hazy glow the streetlamps cast through the fog, he saw Miles's car parked in her driveway.

Jack jumped out of the truck, leaving the door open, and hoped to hell he wasn't too late.

CHAPTER 71

IN HER FOG, Victoria thought she heard the door chime. It was like a dream, a flashback to the night Elliot died. But then she sensed someone had come into the room.

Victoria's head dropped back onto the couch. Miles had been sitting next to her, but she felt him stand up, letting her head fall.

"Get away from her, Miles."

It was Jack Martin's voice. He sounded angry. Thank God he'd come.

"Victoria, are you all right?"

She tried to speak but couldn't.

"It's over, Miles. The police are on their way."

Miles moved away from her quickly. She heard them fighting, rolling on the floor. They kicked something over but kept struggling.

Victoria tried to stand but couldn't. Her phone was only a few feet away. If only she could get to it, she could call 911 and make sure the police were really on their way.

She rolled off the couch onto her hands and

knees. Her vision was blurred, but she slowly made her way toward where she thought the phone would be, groping at the rug with outstretched hands.

They were still fighting, rolling around on the floor behind her.

Victoria kept crawling, clawing at the rug with her fingernails and pulling herself forward.

Something flew past her. Then she realized someone else was now in the room.

There were still the sounds of a struggle, and someone grunted.

Victoria thought she smelled flowers. She groped the floor in front of her, searching for her phone.

Then something heavy fell to the floor behind her. Victoria twisted around and nearly fell over. She squinted. It was the chunk of pyrite that sat on the corner of Elliot's desk. And there was blood on it.

The fighting had stopped, and someone was standing over her.

Victoria looked up, squinting through the blur again, and thought she saw an angel. "Doris?"

Then everything went black.

CHAPTER 72

Sunday, July 1

JACK HAD THE maps out again and sat at the small table bolted to the trailer floor, studying them.

"Where should we go, Crockett?"

He knew he should go back to Texas, look for a real job, but he still wasn't ready—not yet. If he was careful, he could live a little longer on his savings, and now on the money he had made investigating Elliot Banks's murder. He could move back to Texas when his funds started to run low. But maybe he'd figure out a way to earn more, find a way to stay in Colorado a little longer.

It wasn't the best plan, but it was the best he had.

He folded the maps and stuck them back in the drawer. *Everything in its place.* He thought of Victoria and smiled.

It was Sunday, four days after Miles Preston had been arrested for murdering Elliot Banks and attempting to kill Victoria.

Jack had checked that morning and confirmed Miles was still handcuffed to a hospital bed, still recovering from being clocked in the head with a chunk of pyrite by Doris Reed.

Thinking of Doris, Jack laughed and shook his head. Who would have guessed she had it in her?

Doris had been in hiding at her sister's, lying low and letting everyone except the Silverthorne police think she was dead, to keep her safe. It took some fast talking, but Jack had convinced the police not to confirm or deny Doris's demise in the bombing.

When Jack saw the familiar black truck pull out of the parking lot of the diner that day, he'd suspected something was up. He had waited around the corner while Victoria and Doris met inside.

When Doris came out, Jack had called her over and had her start the Camaro remotely. When the car blew up, he'd had to lift a violently quaking Doris into his truck. In the chaos after the bomb, after seeing that Victoria was all right, and without anyone noticing, he had whisked Doris away.

As he was leaving the campground that evening on his way to Vail, Jack had called Doris at her sister's and asked her questions about Miles Preston without revealing his suspicions—or so he had thought. Doris must have known.

Wednesday night, after knocking out Miles and being questioned by the Vail police, Doris had told Jack that, after his call, her suspicions about Miles grew. She wanted to see Victoria for herself—to check on her—but she also wanted to let her know that she hadn't died in the bomb, that she was still alive. The guilt at keeping it a secret from Victoria had grown too hard for Doris to bear. That was why she had come to Vail, and Jack was glad she had.

That night, after she passed out, Victoria was taken to the hospital in Vail, where paramedics told the police she would have died if they hadn't gotten to her when they did. They pumped a large quantity of sleeping medication from her stomach. If Miles Preston's plan had worked, they would have all assumed Victoria had taken her own life. Why wouldn't they? The grieving widow, the main suspect in her husband's murder and whose past life was about to be splashed across the front pages of tabloids.

But Miles's plan hadn't worked. Thank God.

Jack was outside, throwing a stick to Crockett, when his cell phone rang.

An hour later he and Crockett rode the gondola to the top of Vail Mountain. It was a beautiful July day. The sun was shining, and the cloudless sky was a deep shade of turquoise, setting off the still-snow-capped mountains in the distance.

Jack looked among the summer tourist crowd at the top of the mountain but didn't see her. He walked Crockett to one side and let him off the leash to run in the wildflowers. Jack drew in and released a long breath, taking in his surroundings. He couldn't believe he had never ridden a gondola before. The view from atop the mountain was breathtaking.

He heard her voice in the distance, calling him, and he turned around.

Victoria was walking toward him, wearing shorts, a lightweight jacket, and hiking boots. Jack thought she had never looked more beautiful.

She was smiling. "If I knew you were going to be early, I would have come sooner. You should have called me." Jack brushed the apology aside. She took in the view as she talked. "I wanted you to see it. It's beautiful up here, isn't it?"

"It is."

She took a few moments, then turned to him. "I wanted to talk to you again...to thank you. And to say that I'm sorry I fired you."

"Which time?"

She smiled at him. "Both times, I guess."

Jack nodded once, returning her smile.

"But especially the second time," she said. "I thought you had sold the story of my past to the tabloids. I got a call from *The National Tattler*. But I know now that it wasn't you who called them. It was my brother, Gary."

She looked down, and Jack could tell she had been deeply hurt by her brother again. There was an awkward silence.

Victoria was the first one to speak. "I was released from the hospital yesterday."

"I know." Jack saw the surprised look on her face. "The last time I called to check on you, they said you had been discharged."

She blushed. "Thank you. For checking on me." She took a moment, then continued. "Harold Lamken came to see me. He told me how he worried for a while that his nephew, Tyler, had killed Elliot. He said they'd had a run-in before, when Elliot caught him stealing. I never knew. He apologized for not telling me sooner, but I'm sure he was torn. He said you questioned him and that he was nervous you thought *he* had killed Elliot. Poor Harold. I didn't tell him, but for a while I suspected he might have killed Elliot, too—as crazy as that seems now."

It didn't seem crazy at all. Jack had known Harold was hiding something and was glad to finally know what it was.

"Will he continue working for you?"

Victoria shook her head. "No. But I'm going to sell the house anyway. It's way too big for one person."

They fell silent again, and Jack wondered what she was thinking. He couldn't imagine how hard it would be for her to walk away from it all, start over again. Then he realized he *could* imagine it. He had done the same thing.

"I talked to Katie Stratton," Victoria said. "She

didn't come to see me, but she called." Jack thought Victoria sounded disappointed. "She's already filed for divorce. I'm glad. I know a lot of people probably don't think so, but Katie is a good person. She said she wanted to remain friends, but I could feel her already start to pull away. I'll miss her."

"I'm sorry." It was all Jack could think of to say. He thought about Miles Preston. "I'm sorry it was Miles. I was honestly surprised."

She looked at him. "I was at first, but then it made sense. Miles grew up wealthy. His father was a successful oilman in Denver but lost his fortune years ago. Miles must have felt his inheritance was stolen from him. Then Elliot—the kid from the wrong side of the tracks—succeeded beyond what either of them could have ever imagined. I think Miles must have resented it in some ways. If Elliot had exposed the fraud, it would have killed the merger. Miles would have lost everything, so he killed Elliot."

Jack watched her. She had come to terms with it, accepted the revelation that another friend wasn't really a friend at all. He marveled at her strength.

Crockett ran up to them with a stick. Jack looked around and didn't see a tree anywhere around them on the mountaintop. "Now, where in the world did you find this?" He laughed, taking the stick from the dog and throwing it.

Victoria watched Crockett run after it. "I've never

had a dog," she said. "I don't know why. It just didn't fit into my plans, I guess."

"And your plans now?"

She turned her attention back to him as they walked to a nearby bench and sat down. "I've got the company—Banks Oil & Gas. I know the business, and I miss working. It was Elliot's company. He loved it. I don't want it to die with him. And he wouldn't have wanted that, either."

Jack remained silent, letting her talk.

"Elliot was fiercely devoted to his employees— not just the ones in the office, but the guys in the field. It's funny, but he sort of felt they were kindred spirits. I don't think he ever got used to being an executive."

Jack watched her stare into the distance, remembering.

"So you're going back to work?"

The question brought her back. "I am. It's ambitious, but I've put together a proposal to present to the board, to step into Elliot's place and try to hold the merger together."

"That *is* ambitious."

"I've hired Clark Poindexter to help me."

Jack nodded, retrieving the stick from Crockett's mouth and throwing it again. "Poindexter definitely knows the business."

"And Doris said she would help."

Jack turned to look at her.

Victoria had a mischievous look in her eyes. "I told you Doris was Elliot's first employee," she said. "What I didn't tell you was that he gave her five percent of the company stock on her one-year anniversary years ago. After me, Doris holds the largest block of voting shares in Banks Oil & Gas."

Jack was shocked. He thought of the soda can–colored hair, the polyester clothes, and the cheap flowery perfume. Then he remembered the list of the company's investors. One of the largest, one with a sizable chunk of stock not much smaller than Elliot's, had had a funny name—Red Reed Investments. Doris, he thought, and smiled.

Victoria was watching him and laughed at his reaction. "Doris is not only shrewd, Detective, but she's a *very* wealthy woman." Then her voice softened as she added, "And she's my friend."

Jack explained how Luther Byrd had admitted going to Doris's house early that morning, intent on planting the bomb in her car. But when he got there, Doris was pulling out of the driveway. Byrd followed her to the café in Silverthorne, and while she was inside, had planted the bomb under her car.

"If Doris hadn't left the house to meet you, Byrd probably would have succeeded," Jack said. "You saved her life that morning."

"And she saved mine." Victoria took a moment,

then asked him, "So, what's next for you, Detective? What are you going to do now?"

Jack thought about it. "I'm not sure."

"Well, whatever it is, I wish you the best." She held out her hand for him to shake. "Thank you again, Jack—for everything. I hope we can stay in touch."

She leaned over and gave the dog a quick rub. "See you around, Crockett."

Jack watched as she stood up and started across the mountain toward the horizon, toward hope and new beginnings. She was still hurting, but she was putting the pieces of her life back together. Victoria Banks was going to be all right.

Crockett rested his chin on Jack's thigh, and Jack scratched him behind an ear. "We're going to be all right, too, Crockett."

The dog pulled back and looked at him, cocking his head to one side.

"I don't know where we're going or what's coming next, but we're going to be okay," Jack told the dog, and meant it.

ACKNOWLEDGMENT

Everything To Lose depicts several real locations in Vail, Silverthorne, and Denver, but all events and characters are entirely fictional. Anything negatively portrayed is done so purely for literary purposes. The house on Forest Road is also fictional but inspired by several beautiful, modern homes I've seen throughout Colorado.

To Keri Cauthorn, my friend and part-time Vail resident, thank you for providing scene location suggestions and for being there to answer all my questions regarding your beautiful second hometown.

Thank you to my fabulous editor, Kristen Weber, who once again helped me write a better book than I am capable of writing on my own. Your edits are always spot on and exactly what I need. Thank you for your invaluable tutelage!

To my husband, Chris, whose input into the workings of oil and gas companies was crucial. The information you offered help significantly in shaping the story. Thank you also for tirelessly (and patiently) answering dozens of questions all hours of the day and night while I was writing. You're my hero!

And to my brother, RE Hopkins, for his help in understanding the workings of drilling rigs and wells, and for answering questions like: *"What could you steal and pawn off a rig?"* and *"How could you kill someone at a well site?"* Thank you for consulting your colleagues for their input. I'm sorry for any government watchlists you might now be on.

Regarding the oil and gas aspects of the story, anything I got wrong is all on me. Any negative light shed on the industry by characters in the book is purely for fictional drama. Living in Houston, I know scores of men and women who work directly or indirectly in the energy industry. All are honest, upstanding citizens, and none have ever been involved in committing a murder (that I know of).

Finally, to my three fabulous children: Jordan, Abby, and Patrick. Your continued enthusiasm and encouragement means more than you know. You are my greatest blessings.

AUTHOR NOTE

Dear Reader,

Thank you from the bottom of my heart for continuing on this journey with me.

It's not easy creating something and putting it out into the world to be read and judged. I sincerely appreciate all the personal messages, comments on social media, and positive reviews you offered after reading *Now I See You*. Your encouragement keeps me writing.

I really hope that you enjoyed *Everything To Lose* and that you will keep reading the series. Jack Martin finds himself in Telluride next!

With deepest gratitude,
Shannon Work